Broken Bridge

Book Two of the Glass Bottles Series

J Dark

Cover design © 2017 by Niki Lenhart
nikilen-designs.com

Published by Paper Angel Press
paperangelpress.com

ISBN 978-1-944412-31-9 (Trade Paperback)

10 9 8 7 6 5 4 3 2 1

FIRST EDITION

Dedication

This book is for
Tom, Dale, Dennis, James, Jason, Mark, Jerry, John, Hannah, Cody,
Richard, Dorothy, Heather, Charles, Joanna, Rebecca, Timothy,
@IK Reborn, @Kill Favored, @Electroidium,
and all the City of Heroes friends who started all this.

To those who've gone onto another adventure,
Damon, Bill, and David.

And, to anyone who's ever picked up a book,
this is for you.

Thank you.

Acknowledgements

Paper Angel Press for taking the chance on a novice writer.

Kimberley Wall, Laureen Hudson,
Beth Thomsett-Scott, and Steven Radecki
for all their work in editing stories so that the true story can emerge.

Most importantly, the reader.
Without your imagination and support in reading these books,
there be no chance to tell stories.

Thank you so very much.

1

I SHOULD HAVE KNOWN I WAS BEING PLAYED.

"Let me repeat what you've said, to make certain I heard you accurately. You're hiring me to find a white rabbit."

It took nearly all my willpower to not ask if it was two meters tall, or wore a Victorian coat and carried a large pocket watch. I also snidely thought that it was too long after Spring for him to be wanting me to hunt down the Easter Bunny because he hadn't gotten his favorite chocolate eggs.

"Mr. Cobb," I repeated, with what I hoped was sympathetic patience, "I'm not really able to handle this kind of job very easily. Now if you'd take this problem to Larry Potter, he may well be able to find your rabbit without the huge charge you'd get from me."

"You're the one I need, not some wannabe finder. I gotta find my rabbit, and I gotta have you find her." The petulant note in his voice was really getting irritating.

I am not the most patient person in the world, and he'd hit my limit. I gritted my teeth, and tried very hard to be polite. Like you'd expect, I didn't quite try all that hard.

"Mr. Cobb, I don't find lost animals. I don't like using magick. You need magick to find a lost rabbit as fast as you're wanting to. There's no way I'd even know where to look and, to be honest, I'm not interested in looking. This kind of job is for a real private detective, or a magicker, not a finder. So tell you what: you get your lazy butt up out of my guest chair, go out the door, and go hire someone else. She or he can whip up a spell to find your little white bunny pretty quickly. Problem solved. Good day."

Mr. Norman Cobb got up very slowly from the chair, and tried to go for intimidating. He stepped over to the edge of the desk, placed both hands on it and leaned forward, trying to get into my face and force me to back up. This action, and the invasion of my personal space, really started to piss me off.

"Ms. Fatelli," Mr. Cobb said in a tense, frustrated voice. "I told you already. I don't want no fuckin' magicker. I want *you* to find my rabbit! Now either you start trying to locate my rabbit, or …"

I respond even less well to threats, and grabbed the paperweight. He saw the motion and came around the side of the desk to stop me from throwing it, and probably to try and intimidate me further. I spun my chair to face him and, as he cleared the edge of the table, I planted my stiletto heel in between his legs, making contact with those soft and extremely tender testicles. He gasped and screamed at the same time, sounding more like a duck than a man. He fell to his knees, then toppled onto his side, moaning. He curled about his injured area like a fetus.

I stood up out of the chair, all one-point-six meters of me. "Mr. Cobb," I said to him. "I don't find lost animals, I don't like threats, and I don't like your attitude. When you can walk, get out. Oh, and if you want to file an assault charge, I have a camera that records all my talks in here, just in case someone tries to pull stunts like yours." I sat back down in my chair and waited until "Mr. Norman Cobb" got back up off the ground.

He groaned again, staggered towards the door, then stopped. I saw his shoulders tighten. I stood up quickly; when someone does that they're usually getting a good mad up just before they try to take your head off. Then his whole body started shuddering, and I heard him whine like a wounded animal. *What the hell?*

He turned around slowly, tears leaking down his cheeks. He stood there, halfway to the door, gazing at me with the most intense anguish radiating from him.

"Please, Ms. Fatelli, I'm … sorry. I need you, not Mr. Potter. The rabbit, that's my daughter. She's been changed. Somehow, something changed her. She was playing in the yard, and I heard her scream, and I got to the door and saw her shrink into a rabbit and run off. Now she's missing. Halloween is tomorrow. I'm afraid someone's going to catch her, and keep her, or kill her. I know a magicker could do it easier, and cheaper, but I can't go that way, Ms. Fatelli, I … just can't."

I sat back down and looked, really looked, Norman Cobb over. He gave every semblance of a man broken by a need so desperate that he'd do anything to fill it. Hardcore crack addicts look less strung out. This made no sense. It bothers me when things make no sense. Why would a person come to me to find a magickly-changed girl, and then refuse to go to the people who could help him most? I decided to take a chance and look at him with my mage sight.

Everyone has mage sight — theoretically, at least. It's that, even in a world where magick has been shown to exist, most people will run from it in a heartbeat. And, of the other ten percent who don't, maybe one in ten of those will actually sit down to study it, and, of those, only about one in fifty actually have the perseverance to become really good. What this means is that magickers — people who *really* know magick — are few and far between.

When I looked at him, I just about went blind as the bright essence of him assaulted my eyes. Looking at a fae can do that to you, especially if the fae in question is strong. All fae are strong in magick, much more so than humans, generally. So they tend to glow when viewed with the sight. "Mr. Cobb" glowed like a blast furnace. The recoil stabbed through my eyes like a knife. I jammed my hands against my eyes to lessen the pain.

Mr. Cobb straightened and threw off the glamour that shrouded him. His whole image changed. Instead of a rumpled grey business suit, he wore a deep violet shirt that looked like silk, tights of deep green, and a deep rich brown leather vest. A short, nasty-looking sword, about as long as my forearm, hung off of his left hip. He gained in height as well, standing just a shade under two and a half meters tall, and rail thin.

"Ms. Fatelli, now do you understand why it is so important to find my daughter?" He rasped out.

"Well, for starters," I said, deadpan. "Because she's your daughter?" That's me, life of the party.

I swear he growled slightly at that, and then took a deep breath. "My daughter has been turned into a rabbit. I need to find her before something irrevocable happens. There are other things involved ... other magick. I am also certain that you have experience with this other kind of magick. That is why I have come to you."

"Mr. Cobb, or whoever you are," I replied. "I have no idea what you're talking about. What kind of magick do you mean, exactly?"

The Elf lord straightened and extended one arm. Just out from the tip of the arm, an object coalesced into view, hanging suspended in the air. When I saw what it was, my stomach flipped over, and I almost started whimpering. He was showing me a glass bottle. The same glass bottle that I had seen destroyed sixteen months ago during the biggest living nightmare of my life. I wanted to curl up and hide in a corner, but that really wasn't an option right now. Zhirk would have told me to get after it; he'd have my back. Only he wasn't here anymore. He'd died when the Fallen Angel, Ahiah, had killed him in the front office.

I stared at the bottle like a bird hypnotized by a snake. Cobb stared at me like a starving wolf watches a crippled sheep.

"Ms. Fatelli, you have seen this before, haven't you? The human who changed my daughter was attempting to use this on her."

"How the hell did the guy get that thing, and why are you sure he's human? If he was, why didn't your daughter just change back after she got away?" My voice was high-pitched, as I was nearly screaming at him. I was angry and scared at the same time. I think that's a standard reaction when you have the absolute life scared out of you like I just had.

He didn't bat an eye, nor show any reaction to my outburst. He just waited, absolutely, completely, nerve-wrackingly still. He watched me a moment more, then replied with a maddeningly neutral voice.

"I believe that he had made a mistake in the spell, that the rabbit was not what he wanted. My daughter may have shifted before he could complete the spell, and he bound her to that form since his spell was tailored for a human, not a rabbit." He shuddered slightly and, if he had not been so still prior to that, I would not have noticed.

Cobb continued in that strange, neutral voice. "He used cold iron in the spell."

Cold iron. Anathema to the fae. I'm not sure why, but cold iron is about the worst thing that a fae would face, and most of them would bolt away if given a chance. It's their poison. A single nail made of cold iron is enough to seriously weaken the most powerful of fae spells, and any typical one is blown away like dust. I wasn't sure what that did in this case, but it probably had something to do with why this child was still a rabbit. Maybe it locked spells like shape-shifting. Who knows? I sure didn't. But the bottle — the fucking bottle — terrified me. I'd never thought to see it again after the huge implosion at the cabin. But god, or, in this case, magick, has got a real warped sense of humor.

I had to admit one thing: I did have more experience with that damned bottle than the rest of the world. I wish I didn't. That bottle sucks your whole self, soul and all, out of you. It converts your soul, and anything that you were or might have been, into magickal energy. You're gone; nothing's left. No soul to reincarnate, or go to heaven, or hell, or wherever you believe souls go. It's a complete destruction of you. The holder can get one huge boost of power, but to keep at high levels, the user has to keep putting more people in the bottle.

I looked back again at Mr. Cobb. I wanted to turn and run. I couldn't though. It wasn't a rabbit anymore; it was a little girl.

"All right, I'll help you find your daughter, but I'm going to get full discretion on who or what's used to do the job, or we can part ways right now."

Cobb smiled and said, "Done."

Like I said earlier: I should have known I was being played.

2

T HE FIRST THING I DID was pack up and head over to see Larry so that I could get a locator spell. I was guessing that the kidnapper was doing the same thing, now that I had more understanding of what was going on. I also packed a few items in a "possibilities" bag. I had a pistol, but didn't trust it. Pistols don't always stop things coming after you, and they give ignorant people a misguided sense of confidence that gets them killed when running — or a little thought — would have saved their lives.

My bag included Kevlar chicken-plate armor for my torso, cold-iron nails, a silver-plated machete, various pieces of rope, glass, and aluminum; a couple of small dolls, sprigs of oak and mistletoe, some charged pebbles, wooden stakes, and an ash baseball bat. Don't laugh. A wooden bat will hurt almost anything magickal, and I had training in its use as a defensive weapon from my sister Fawn, which is where the Kevlar came from too. I added a bottle of water consecrated at a local Lutheran church, and some protein bars and chips in case I didn't get a chance to eat for some reason.

"Mr. Cobb" watched all of this in imperturbable silence, reacting only slightly to the iron nails. His lack of reaction let me know again that he was a powerful fae, and not to let my guard down just because his daughter was in danger. Fae are not human, and don't react to things like humans do. I would do well to remember that.

I called ahead to Larry and Fawn. Larry picked the telephone up on the second ring. "Potter Emporium," he said cheerfully.

"Hi Larry. How are you two?"

"Pretty good, Ferny. You wanting a locater spell?"

I just sighed and shook my head. Larry was extremely astute and, at times, talking with him is like chatting with Sherlock Holmes; you're always a step behind, even though it's your conversation.

"Yeah, a locater spell, but it's going to be a different sort. I want it to track down a rabbit."

There was a long silence Then Larry chuckled. "So it's going to have to be pretty specific then. Only about 90 gazillion rabbits around Halifax, let alone the whole of Nova Scotia. This a person changed into a rabbit is why you want it." It wasn't a question.

"That's the reason, and, no, I don't have any personal items for you to use, but her father is here with me and should be willing to help."

"So he's fae. Christ, Ferny, they know how to pick you."

Like I said: a step behind, even when it's your conversation. I didn't even bother to ask how he knew; I'd just feel sillier after he explained everything to me.

3

T HE TRIP OVER TO LARRY'S PLACE OF BUSINESS WAS QUIET. Literally. My new friend — I'd decided to just call him Cobb — just sat in my old Saturn Vue. As we rumbled over the city streets, he stared rigidly straight ahead: a statue, except for the slight rise and fall of his chest. He didn't offer any conversation and, after two tries to talk with him, I gave up and stewed in silence. I hate silence.

We pulled into the small parking lot in front of Larry's "new" place. About six months ago, someone had firebombed his old one. A police investigation never caught the perpetrator, nor could anyone find a reason why. Larry, being Larry, just shrugged and found a new place in a few days, then re-opened for business.

Larry Potter came out of the Emporium as we drove up. He had his smock on over his robes, which probably meant he'd been laying down a magick circle, or some such thing, as we were driving over. I rubbed the stump of my little finger. Seeing Larry brought back the glade, and the glass bottle I'd destroyed. We'd gotten lucky, and survived. Ahiah had gone back to wherever things like him are kept.

Larry smiled at me as we got out of the car.

"Hey, Shorty. You gotta come over more." He eyed Cobb. "You bring interesting company." He performed a slight bow, hand to forehead, and eyes downcast. "Please be welcome and freely enter."

Cobb cracked a slight smile and returned the bow, bending slightly at the waist.

We all went inside. Larry's new place was narrower than the old one, but longer and had more floor space. Directly across from the door was the small, semi-circular counter. It was an island of brown atop the grey linoleum floor. A door painted a startling green was just to the left of the counter. The walls had been painted with a light blue and patches of white, like looking at a cloudy sky. The books were at the far end to our right. A pair of small tables were near the picture window, where one could read or have a cup of coffee while Larry put their order together. Pale yellowish light shone from glowing rocks held in netting that hung from the white ceiling. Larry led us to the green door and into his "work" room.

This room was a late addition to the front. The walls, constructed from cinder blocks, were wallpapered to look like an old log house. It was a square eight meters by eight, with a silver four-pointed star and circle, two meters in diameter, inlaid to the cement floor at the exact center of the room. Outside of the circle, and at each point of the star, a series of runes or sigils was etched in the cement and inlaid with silver. Along the left wall were two long tables, with shelves hung over them. Jars, tools, pieces of metal, wire, and other items covered each table, seemingly at random. Larry closed the door, then walked to the nearest table. He rummaged through the clutter and pulled up a clear plastic rod. He rummaged a moment more, this time pulling out a long bit of twine. He moved to the western point of the star, and laid the plastic and twine in the small circle.

He looked towards Cobb. "Sir, would you stand at the eastern point of the circle?"

The Fae nodded politely, and moved to stand where Larry had indicated. Larry moved to the north point, and asked me to stand at the south.

Once we were in position, he began a chant that I remembered hearing Rynun, the *Geowludmosiseg*, utter before. Rynun used to live under — or behind, or in — the dumpster between the building I have my office in and the liquor store. He used to live out around my parents cabin, but "moved" into the city about the time they died. He'd used a song, as he liked to call it, as a way of asking his brethren to loan him their essence to do something like light a fire. In Larry's chant, wind sprang up in the closed room, flowing clockwise around the circle. A pale yellowish mist arose from the fae's skin and wafted to the plastic rod. It began to glow like a light stick — a faint greenish yellow, slowly brightening to the strength of a candle flame. The light pulsed once as Larry chanted, and then collapsed into the rod, reducing to a tiny pinpoint of light as the wind died. I found myself thinking back to Zhirk's place, when we hid the general's family there. I'd looked out his kitchen window at sundown and watched the fireflies gather by the back fence, near the graves of his dad and sister. I shook myself from the reverie when Larry left the north circle and picked up the plastic rod.

He walked across the circle and handed the rod to Cobb. "Hold it and turn it slowly. When it is pointing in your daughter's direction, the light will move to the end of the rod. The closer you get, the brighter it will glow. Once you're done with it, break the stick and the spell will break." He held up a hand before either of us could speak. "This has an effective range of about a half-kilometer, so you'll have to do a lot of moving around. There is no price; just think well of me and mine. That will be enough."

I glanced over at him. Larry was a good guy and all, but I've never seen him do a spell for free.

Cobb said "I always remember my friends, and my friends will never stand alone."

Ah. That made sense. Larry just got a favor from the fae, and that probably is worth more than money. I smiled. Larry could have been a con-man — and a good one. He ushered us out and began to clean up the room so no residual magick could remain to cause problems.

Cobb and I went back to my Saturn Vue, got in, and took off into the Dayning suburb of Halifax. While I drove, he held the wand out the passenger window, away from the metal body of the car, and swept it in a one hundred eighty-degree arc front to back, hoping to capture a glimmer that told us in which direction she might be.

We had been driving for an hour when we finally got movement from the mote of light in the rod. Cobb extended the rod past my face in the direction it had flickered.

"That way! She's that way!" he practically screamed in my ear.

His face was transformed by hope; the change was amazing. I had to tear my eyes away from him to make the turn and head more or less in the direction we wanted to go. We followed in the general direction the wand indicated, which took us deep into Dayning, leading us into an area populated by *Hamref*.

Hamref are about five feet tall, and so emaciated-looking they look like a stiff breeze would break them in two. They are put together pretty much like an average humanoid biped — two legs, two arms, one head — but the differences are eerie. For starters, their nostrils are at the edge of each cheek, just about an inch below their eyes. Their eyes are huge, which you might expect to belong to a night-loving species. You'd be wrong. Their eyesight is just fine, day or night. In fact, they're supposed to have the equivalent of six-power binocular vision. Their bodies were hard-skinned; Fawn had seen pistol rounds ricochet off them. Their hands were four-fingered claws. The one thing, though, that bothered me most was that every joint of theirs has almost three hundred and sixty degrees of movement. They were incredibly flexible, and able to contort though openings that an escape-artist could only envy. They were predators, but weak ones. Any human could beat one. Trouble was, they attacked in groups. I may have felt nervous about being out amongst all the *Hamref*, but that was my own human prejudice about so odd-looking a creature. *Hamref* were scrupulously honest.

I drove us up to an old post office building and parked the Saturn. The street was empty, except for a few cars that drove by as we exited mine. The building stood at the corner: a white-washed bygone of earlier times. Its windows were boarded over and painted with the same whitewash. A narrow alley on our left as we faced the building separated the post office and adjoining building. We walked up to the front door. A typical double door with top to bottom glass. Its glass had been painted over, and the doors chained and padlocked. The chain and lock were both old and rusted, but still strong, as a quick tug on them told me.

Cobb stayed a good ten feet away as I tested the chains; fae and iron don't play well together. Failing to open the door, we walked down the alley to the back side of the building to see if there might be another way in. As we moved, Cobb checked the wand, and it indicated that his daughter was inside. I spotted another door in the back, and moved towards it. As I did, Cobb hissed, suddenly grabbed me, and then dragged me back a few feet.

I knocked his hand away and turned on him angrily. "What was that for?" I demanded.

He walked over to a point about ten feet from the door and pointed at the ground. I looked closely, but didn't see anything.

Like a school teacher lecturing an especially dense student, he sighed, "Use your sight, Ms. Fatelli."

Asshole. I gritted my teeth and focused, willing myself to see. A shimmering half-bubble coalesced into view around the door.

"An alarm. Break the shell, and they know you are here," he said in that irritating lecture-voice.

I looked the door over, and saw a largish nail driven into the door, with mistletoe wrapped around it. It wasn't a faerie spell then, but that left a lot of other possibilities. I abandoned the idea of a back entrance, and held my sight up as we walked around the outside of the building. All the first-floor windows were covered in the same way: painted opaque with whitewash, and with the yellowish hemispheres around the mistletoe-wrapped iron nails. The only location not covered was the glass front door.

Most likely, it wasn't warded the same way, as there was no wood to drive a nail into. Cobb stayed back from the door, like before.

"This seems the only way in. What you want to bet there's something nasty inside?" I was nervous and impatient.

Cobb shrugged elaborately and waited to see what I would do. I waited for a moment and looked around.

"I don't like waiting and, if we're going in, we might as well announce it."

I went back to my Saturn and retrieved the emergency duffel. I got my pistol out and put it on, then put on the chicken plate. I strapped the machete to my hip, picked up the baseball bat, and stalked back to the door.

Cobb lost his composure and snarled viciously at me. "My daughter is in there, human!"

"So go get her," I snarled back as I used the baseball bat to hammer at the glass. Two quick swings opened up a jagged hole that I could slip through.

I didn't wait for Cobb; speed was more important to me now. I looked down the short, narrow hallway with my sight to spot any traps. Greenish glowing fog hovered near the center of the hallway about three meters ahead of me. I threw the bat at it, and flattened myself against the wall, anticipating some kind of effect. The bat flew through the cloud, there was a blistering pulse of heat, and the bat landed on the other side of the cloud, badly charred.

The cloud had dissipated to almost nothing, so I charged through it, and got singed as it pulsed with heat, but nowhere near what the bat had suffered. I heard someone crying further in: Cobb's daughter, most likely. I scanned my surroundings. The hallway ended eight meters further on at an interior door. Bathroom doors were on the left side of the hall, just before the end door. I left the smoking baseball bat behind, and charged the door, hoping I had enough momentum to pop it open … and just about dislocated my shoulder when I hit it. It was metal with a wood veneer.

Glass shattered behind me as Cobb used magick to blow a hole in the glass big enough for him to get through. He rocketed past me almost faster than I could follow, and hit the door like a runaway freight train. The door crumpled, the lintel tearing loose from the sheet rock it was anchored to. The wood veneer all but exploded off the door with the impact. Cobb screamed in agony as his body came in contact with the steel. He collapsed on the ground just inside the doorway.

I ran through the door, skipping past Cobb's prone form. Dodging to the right, I dropped into a clumsy baseball slide, skidding almost to the wall. I quickly scanned the room as I stopped moving. The crumpled door was a good three meters into the room, looking like a steel banana. Cobb lay just inside the door, his flesh and clothing smoking from contact with the steel. He moaned in pain, but was starting to get up.

The interior room was large, probably at least twelve meters to a side. Inside the room was a square cage, about two meters on each side. In the cage, on a hammock anchored a meter above the metal floor, sat a small girl, crying and unmoving. Something slithered out of the floor and solidified. It turned its tubular body towards me quickly on its six legs and aimed itself, scrunching up like a coiled spring, and opening its lamprey-like mouth wide.

Oh Gods, a *wurmling!* Two others slipped up through the floor as I watched the first one, and these oriented on Cobb.

I thought about the pistol, but wurmlings are small — and very fast. I'm not that good a shot. I pulled out the silver machete as the *wurmling* readied itself to attack. Then it was on me. I swung the blade desperately, and got lucky, hitting it solidly, and slicing it in half length-wise. The pieces fell to the ground and started dissolving away. My follow-through rang the blade off the cement floor and, unfortunately, got the attention of the other two *wurmlings*. They hissed and began scuttling into launching range. Cobb was still dazed and in pain, so I was on my own. The *wurmlings* recognized the silver blade and moved apart, deliberately working to flank me. I backed up quickly into the corner, and slashed with the machete as the creatures tried to sidle closer before launching themselves at me again. My back hit the corner. Now they were restricted to a ninety-degree arc that was a lot easier to protect.

16

The two *wurmlings* scuttled within launching range, and scrunched up. There was a pulse of heat as a small fireball slammed into the *wurmling* to my left. The other executed a startled leap towards me, but there was no power behind it, and it landed a meter short. I took a quick step forward, and cut it down with the machete before it had a chance to recover.

Cobb looked at me from the ground, and put his hand down to help push himself off the floor. I approached the cage and returned the machete to its sheath. The cage had a lock on the front. I pulled my pistol.

"Sweetie, get as far back as you can, okay?"

The girl nodded, and moved to perch precariously on the far edge of the hammock from me. I aimed the pistol at the hasp of the lock and pulled the trigger. The nine-millimeter slug hit dead on and cracked the hasp; a second shot parted it. I knocked the lock away and pulled the door open. The girl leapt off the hammock and darted through the open door past me to clutch her father in a tight hug.

Cobb spoke gently to the child and rested his hands on her shoulders as she shuddered and only partially stifled her sobs of relief.

"We should be leaving, Ms. Fatelli. Whoever did this knows we are here." Cobb stopped speaking and tilted his head towards me. Then he gave me a disquieting almost-smile and said, "Unless, of course, you want to stay and fight the person who can draw upon the power already stored in that bottle."

I shuddered involuntarily. No way I wanted to stick around for that.

"All right," I said briskly, trying to cover my unease. "Let's get out of here."

We exited the way we came in, jumped into my Saturn Vue, and pulled away. I noticed a couple of *Hamref* watching us leave. They probably had a good look at all of us, and there was no reason for them not to offer the information up. Which meant, if someone talked to them, I might get some guests later. Paranoia, yes, I know, but if that guy did make himself a soul bottle like the other one, odds are that he knew about my experience with one of the gods-be-damned things — that and my sister's experience with it. Oh yeah, a lot of paranoia running around.

All told, this was one of the fastest jobs I'd ever pulled. I was feeling pretty happy with myself for some good planning. Cobb and his daughter were jabbering away in some language that I couldn't identify as we drove back to my office. This is where you'd expect the other shoe to drop.

It did, just not where I could hear it right away. What I was thinking about was the fee I'd get, and how the hell anyone would — or could — make another soul bottle. That part bothered me. A lot.

After seeing to my fee, Cobb and his daughter left, leaving me free to do a little rearranging of all the stuff I have in the office. I couldn't shake the feeling that something was waiting for just the right moment to spring itself into my life. Magick does things like that. It's hard to believe in coincidence with magick around; coincidence can get pretty unbelievable. Kind of like having-an-anvil-solidify-over-your-house-and-drop-on-you -suddenly coincidental.

I had been trying hard to divert myself from thoughts of the bottle with the office cleaning when the lights in the building went out. The air-conditioning fans also stopped. The building became very still. Unnaturally still. My windows let in enough of the noontime light to allow me to easily gather up my emergency bag, put on my pistol, machete, and chicken plate.

After arming myself, I went into the secretary's office just as a low roaring sound began back in the main office. Turning around with machete in hand, I saw an inky sliver haze appear in mid-air. It thickened and lengthened, growing into a floor-to-ceiling gash in mere seconds. Then two clawed hands thrust their way through the slit and began to widen it.

I didn't wait. I dropped the machete, pulled the pistol, and fired four rounds right into the enlarging hole with no visible effect. Bullets didn't work, and I had serious doubts about my machete being any more effective. Discretion instead of valor. I ran out of the small secretary office into the hallway, slamming the door shut behind me.

The hall didn't have any windows to the outside, so it was dark, except for the slight glow of light coming through the frosted glass of my front door. The window still had the rebuilding spell on it, and no one had tried throwing someone through it, or jumping through it, since Rynun did that to me. I ran towards the fire stairs at the west end, figuring, if the power was out, the elevators just west of my office wouldn't be working either.

There was a sound like fingernails being scraped on a slate chalkboard, only a lot louder. It spiked my ears with a sharp pain as I pulled the stairwell door open. Call me stupid, but I reversed course and ran for the bathroom. My thoughts were that, if it followed me into the stairwell, I was trapped in a large tube with no way out until I reached the bottom floor. We were four floors up and I think in a foot race to the bottom, I'd probably lose. I could, however, change the terrain. The building had a hanging ceiling to cover up the unsightly ventilation tubing and electrical conduits, and many a time the repairmen would have to go up into the ceiling to fix a problem. Being a small woman gave me an advantage against a larger creature. Plus, if it was heavy, the ceiling wouldn't support it if it tried to follow me.

I ran to the bathroom and groped around for a few precious seconds in the dark before I bumped into the sink. I quickly clambered up on it and was able to reach the ceiling and push a panel out of its cradle. A small jump up allowed me to lever myself into the ceiling and, working by feel, I replaced the tile. My office door shattered, the sound muffled by the closed bathroom door.

I felt carefully along the support frame as I moved away from my entry point. I wasn't sure what all the creature could do, but scent would be a likely way for it to follow me, assuming the place it came from was as dark as the slit was when it started to come through. Sound was the other way that it might use to locate me. I held my breath as there was a muffled thud of the fire door opening and closing. That made me think scent more than hearing since I had gone there first. Amazing how analytical your brain can get when it's trying hard not to be terrified.

The ceiling was another trap. There were limits to where I could go. Which meant, that if the creature decided to tear the ceiling apart, it would find me. I needed to be someplace else when it figured that out. The load-bearing walls had access holes for the wiring, plumbing, and ventilation to get between rooms and floors. If I could slip through there, it would be even harder for the creature to find me. I realized right after that I had a bigger problem. I'm not the only one in the building, I'm on the fourth floor, which I share with six other businesses, and there are three floors below me with more people and businesses in them. If the creature ran into any one of them, they'd be slaughtered, and I'd have been the one to let them get killed. The creature was sent after me. I had to get near a window; my cell-phone wouldn't work this deep in the building.

I didn't know exactly where I was in relation to any of the rooms here. I'd gone here to hide, and done a good job of moving in the dark away from the bathroom, but in the dark, it's hard to tell distance. Direction I did know, as I was on the hanging frame, and that's oriented square to the halls and rooms. I had gone east away from the bathroom, which put offices to my left.

All I had to do was turn left and go until I hit a wall, then drop through the ceiling and call the police. Fawn — my sister, cop, and a blonde Wonder Woman look-alike — was the new head of the Magickal Response Squad (MaRS). She and her group were very good at what they did: which was taking down supernatural threats. Having them here would do a lot towards getting me and the others out alive.

Crawling slowly along the bracing, groping in front of me for the next wire or the wall, and desperately trying to be as quiet as a terrified *Imrit,* I moved forward until my fingertips brushed cement. I shifted the panel slowly. Dim light in the room below showed a large desk. I started to shift the panel further to make room to drop down, when I lost my balance.

The panel slipped from my grasp, falling down to land on the edge of the desk with a heavy thump. It broke in three pieces and fell onto the carpeted floor with a trio of dull thuds. I stayed in place for a moment, listening again. I looked down at the large, ornate wooden desk. An antique laptop was on the corner, while a modern flat-touch was recessed into the surface — both on and operating. A replica green-shaded banker's lamp had been knocked over by the falling panel, and lay on its back. Light streamed in the opening, allowing me to see the conduit I was holding onto for balance. I listened again and, when I heard no loud or odd noises, I dropped lightly onto the desk. A chair was pushed against the wall to my left. To the right was a pair of chairs facing the desk, with a couch and coffee table just beyond them. Looking behind me, the door into the room was cracked open.

Faint footsteps from the hall caught my attention. I quietly stepped off the desk and crouched behind it. As I peeked at the door from the side of the desk, I saw Art Uhlan push the door fully open. He stepped in the room, vending machine coffee cup in hand, and then froze, staring at the broken pieces of overhead panel. Art was short, overweight, balding with a small black pencil mustache. He's one of the few people I can literally see eye to eye with.

"What the fuck?" he exclaimed. Art half-turned, then saw me as I slowly straightened up, and his gaze turned to confusion. "Fern? Are you okay? What's are you doing in here?" He glanced around the room again, and returned to looking at me, and the broken panel on the floor by the desk.

I stood up, brushing at the dust and cobwebs that clung to me after my time in the ceiling.

Art looked up at the ceiling, then back to his desk, and finally back to me. An angry smile quirked his lips. "Fern, if you wanted to come see me, you could have used the door. Now would you tell me what the hell is going on?"

I looked at him and brought my mage sight up. Art remained Art.

"Umm, Art, did you notice anything weird like lights going out and loud noises from my room?"

Art got an alarmed look on his face and his eyes darted towards the door. "Should I have heard something?" he asked nervously.

"Yeah, I fired four rounds at something in my office! You darn well should have heard something." I said tersely. "That, and the lights went out all over."

"Lights went out?" he said to me as he put his coffee cup down on his desk. Maybe you blew a local breaker, Fern, 'cause I haven't lost any lights."

It took a moment to sink in, and then I returned quickly to my office. Art followed me.

"Fern, what are you doing?" he asked me.

"I'm going to find out what kind of magick was used on me." I was certain that some kind of magick was involved; I just didn't understand why yet.

"Can I watch if I don't get in the way?" Art asked, as he walked with me to my office. He seemed surprised at its dingy condition and the clutter. He looked at me again. "When was that last time you cleaned up?" he asked curiously.

Everyone's a critic. I swallowed my retort, a lump forming in my throat. That was the same thing Zhirk would have teased me about. I flipped the wall switch … and the lights came on with no problem at all. I flipped them off and on twice more to make sure I wasn't just imagining it. Finally, I went back over to my emergency bag and pulled out an iron nail. I put the nail in my pocket, and pulled out a bag of salt and a second bag of iron filings.

I made a salt circle, then an iron circle inside the salt. I tossed the remnants back next to the emergency bag. Grabbing the machete, I laid the blade edge-on in my palm, wrapped my fingers around the blade, and tugged it sharply, cutting a thin slice along the palm of my hand. I dropped blood inside both circles: south, east, north, west. Dragging the tip of the machete clockwise through the blood drops, I made a third circle.

Art watched all the preparations with fascination. I sheathed the machete, stepped carefully over the circles, and got some toilet paper from the bathroom to cover the cut on my hand.

"This is where it gets tricky," I told him. "The creature I'm going to call up will be outside the circle, and won't be happy. You sure you want to stay?"

"Uh, thanks, but I'm not that curious," Art told me and hurried out. I heard a door slam.

Heh. I wasn't going to call up a creature, but I did want Art somewhere safe in case I angered whoever set the illusion here. The circles were made, and I was ready. I pulled out the iron nail, and focused my will. I turned in place, chanting, "Truth in salt, truth in iron, truth in blood."

4

ONCE I FINISHED A COMPLETE ROTATION, I dropped the nail to my feet. It sped to the ground like a released arrow, burying itself halfway into the old wooden floor. My office remained the same: dingy authentic 1930's-style gumshoe office. That ruled out external glamour. The room did not have the illusion on it; I had it on me. I could deal with that, too. Then again, I might have already. The magick I'd most likely been around was fae, since Cobb had been my client today, and he was most definitely fae. The iron nail and the filings should have inadvertently clobbered any fae spell on me, but would leave some kind of trace that could be spotted by a good (meaning: expert) wizard. There were other ways, too — one that a simpleton could magickally use, but they were liable to hurt the caster.

I picked up some of the salt, and a pinch of the iron filings, and placed them under my tongue. Although contact with iron will dissipate a spell, residual traces of magick remain, and will still react to cold iron. A human's finger is not sensitive enough to feel the reaction, so one's lips and tongue are used. There was a scalding *zing* that made me yelp, and I spit the iron filings out. Fae magick.

I looked around. Everything in the room had been pushed up against the wall for the most open space possible. Scuffs on the floor and chops in the wood; it looked like someone had attacked it. My emergency bag peeked out from under the secretary's desk, along with any other steel and iron object I owned. All I had on were my clothes; even my belt and shoes had been removed.

As the last residual effects of the glamour faded, I realized I had never actually left my office. Everything had happened here, under a full-on fae glamour. Cobb had to have done it. I did a very quick burn from puzzled to royally upset. The only thing I could think was to find him and get an explanation why. A more rational part of me, however, smothered the anger after a few moments, and I sat down to puzzle a few things out.

The big question was why he took the time to do this. An even bigger question was where and how did that damn bottle fit in all this? The bottle was something I never wanted to see again. It had been the cause of my parents' deaths — and almost mine and Fawn's as well. It was the kind of magick that only crazed, powerful, and/or really stupid people got close to. For the life of me, I couldn't see any connection, other than the one Cobb had pointed out. Someone wanted to use it to increase their personal power. Pardon. Some fucking lunatic was power-mad, and had somehow figured out how to remake — or find — another soul bottle.

Making something as horrific as the bottle had to be dark, dangerous magick. No one I could imagine would want to make that kind of bottle for no reason at all. It was a huge magick battery — which meant huge powerful spells, and likely some horrific materials.

I rubbed the nub of my little finger where it had been torn off by Ahiah, the Nephelim. That monster had bitten my finger off as an attempt to intimidate me into not resisting as he re-cast the spell my parents had started, but who then died before they could complete it. The spell was supposed to kill Fawn and I. Then Ahiah would have taken our bodies as puppets for something. What the something was, I really didn't have a clue — or care. The glass bottle he drew people's essence into it, and then turned that into magickal power. I still had the last finger joint, but just the thought of that bottle being around made it ache badly.

Our folks had been just a touch crazy, and had made Fawn and me huge storage batteries of magick. We couldn't touch it, but it stayed with us. I don't know how much was there, but Larry said it was a *lot* of magick. No one that I knew really wanted to touch it either. Magick like that draws other magick, like a magnet draws iron filings. We are magnets for weird coincidence.

All of that brought up the question: who knew about the bottle? I went through and tried to remember each person that had contact with — or knowledge of — that bottle: Fawn, her team, me, Larry, Rynun, Uncle Todd, and Ahiah. I couldn't think of any others, but for that bottle to be around, someone must know of it — and potentially of me and Fawn.

The bottle showing up was just another one of those coincidences that really weren't. Right now, the bottle was my biggest concern, along with who was casting spells on me. Both seemed very connected, and the only person who had connections to both was the elf, Cobb. So the question became: why did he ask me to help him and warn me about the bottle?

I'd have to ask him when I found him. But with something like this, I needed backup — good, reliable, backup. It was time for a short trip out to Dayning.

Dayning is that part of Halifax that grew up after the magick came back with a huge bang, almost forty years ago now. It is mostly the non-human section. Almost all of them have enclaves here in one or more places. I came down here because I preferred a non-human partner for this. Humans like myself are good at almost anything; we're nature's great generalists. But if you want a specialist species, Dayning is the place you'd come to find one.

What I wanted was smart and tough. There were a lot of races like that. Trolls were the biggest example. But I hadn't felt right about hiring trolls since Zhirk died. Call it stupid, maudlin, prejudiced, or superstitious, but I just never wanted to hire a troll again. There were other races beyond them. What I wanted was one who stood a chance against fae magick, and there was only one that had any kind of resistance that I knew of: the Troykin.

Troykin are bad news. They have outsider blood in their veins. Outsiders are creatures, or things, that are "outside" of what we call reality. An *Imrit* is an outsider, as is a *Wyrmling*. They're not a True Outsider, more like a kissing cousin. Both *Imrits* and *Wyrmlings* supposedly live in the "overlap" of our reality and the Outside. It's kind of like a creature that can only live in brackish marshes, rather than on land or in the ocean.

True Outsiders are not something you ever want to cross paths with. Most spells will just blow apart unless you prepare the spell carefully, or are hideously powerful. The other side of things is that they are affected by silver, and the merest touch of it causes gaping wounds as their skin dissolves. Salt hurts them, and repels them.

Troykins have been known to resist being repelled by salt, to the unhappy consequence of the object of their displeasure. Troykins are also short-tempered, which may be due to the

Outsider blood. They are not quite hair-trigger tempered, but the next closest thing to it. It generally makes them a poor choice as backup. But, considering the opposition, I was willing to have one with me for their magickal resistance. That would make Cobb at least have to work at doing us in. I was guessing he wanted something from me. Otherwise, why the elaborate illusion?

Too much speculation would start to hurt, so I backed off "what if?", and concentrated on the problem at hand. I planned on negotiating with one of the local Troykin gangs to get my helper. The edge of the Troykin 'hood was obvious. A large green eye had been painted on the side of a dilapidated diner. It was easily three meters tall, and about four wide. I parked the Saturn and stepped out, all one-point-five meters of me, ready to negotiate with two-meter-plus tall Troykin.

The wind blew into my face, and brought with it smells of hamburger and burned vegetable oil. Zhirk and I used to find places like that to go eat and shoot the breeze. I had the advantage that I was human, and a human seen this far into Dayning was generally considered crazy and dangerous. I figured that worked in my favor.

The way to negotiate with Troykin was to get them stirred up some, and then you could get them to agree to almost anything. Plus, losing face was a big thing to Troykin, so what they agreed to they'd stick with, no matter how they agreed to it. I had asked Fawn about the Troykin up here, and she had told me that they were generally willing to work with humans.

Larry Potter was a name known up here, as his shop catered to all races. Considering a lot of the wild racist xenophobia practiced by humans and the non-human on each other, Larry was considered a good man to know, and helping his sister-in-law might mean getting a big discount on something. All told, it was a good thing to be Larry's sister-in-law.

Convincing the Troykins that I was said sister-in-law wasn't so easy; they didn't believe it for a moment. It rankled, but considering that it was five on one, compromise seemed a good option.

"Okay, what will prove who I am?" I asked the supposed leader of the bunch.

"We know of the name of the Nephilim you fought. What was the name you called that creature?"

"That piece of filth was called Ahiah, but I called him 'Baldy'."

It was the right answer. What did I tell you about magick and coincidences? How likely do you think it is that the bottle, and the name of the Nephilim, would come up on the same day, and linked to each other? Really? You're a bigger believer in coincidence than I am, that's for certain.

"Now you are free to ask one of us to help you, but I recommend Zik'k. His family owes Mr. Larry Potter very much for his kindnesses, and he has the largest honor-debt."

A lean, scarred-up Troykin stepped forward, then put his hand over his face and bowed. He held the bow for a long time, his hand remaining over his face.

Hmm. Some kind of ritual greeting? "No need to be formal, Zik'k. We'll work better if you just call me Fern," I told him.

Zik'k stepped back, still holding his hand over his face. "Peeee-eew, human, whab kide ob mabick hab bou beeb rollib ib? Gah, deb sbmell's awbful!"

I blinked in surprise. "You can *smell* magick?" I blurted out.

All five Troykin heads nodded.

The leader who'd suggested Zik'k said, "That we can, but it's not something we advertise much. You have to be a pretty powerful wizard to have a smell on you, and yours is …" I watched his face screw up in concentration as he hunted for a suitably diplomatic word. "… pungent."

"Are you going to get all huffy about it?" I asked, getting huffy about it myself. Hey, it's a girl's privilege to be huffy when called "pungent".

Slightly panicked looks appeared on the Troykins' faces. They assured me hurriedly that there would be no problem at all for Larry's mate-sister.

"Yah, talk all yah wanbt aboub it, ah'b tbde onbe hasta gobe wib her," Zik'k said to the others bad-temperedly.

"Look, I'm sorry. I didn't want to impose so if you don't want …"

"No no no no! Nob abt abll, Magick madeb mah nobse clug up." He took a deep breath through his mouth. "I'db beh fine inna libble bit."

I looked Zik'k over and then at the others. "You all have this problem too?" I asked, half-amused and half-frustrated with the whole situation.

The other Troykin had watched our conversation, and the leader nodded. He rubbed the side of his face, then smiled sheepishly, stepping further back to join the other three on the sidewalk under the green eye. "We all do. The more magick, the more we react to it." He'd backed up about to where the other three were standing. He and the others bowed, this time with hands at their sides. "Well, good day, and say hello to Larry for us."

They whirled, and all but ran away, before I could ask any more questions.

I turned to the red-faced Zik'k, who'd backed up out of range.

"Gah, girl, that is the worst feeling." He looked at my Saturn, and his face fell to around his knees. He looked at me and jerked a thumb at it. "I gotta ride with you all the way back now, don't I?"

"Yep," I said brightly, just to dig it in a little. "Just you and me for twenty minutes, all the way back, and then we get to talk to another wizard." I'd never seen a face drag along the ground before, but his tried very hard as we got in.

Along the way back to my office, Zik'k alternated between holding his nose while breathing though his mouth, and rolling down the window to stick his face out of the passenger window like a dog, nose into the wind, presumably to clear his head of my magickal odor. But he never made one noise of complaint; just a whole lot of body language. Once there, I packed up my emergency bag, filled two extra hand-sized sacks with iron filings, and added them to it.

As I threw the bag in the back seat, Zik'k asked me, "So why dib yuh azk for ubs?"

"Because you guys are tough against magick, and you have a good reputation as being trustworthy."

I started the Saturn, and we drove to a location I knew of where the fae had a presence. I wanted to talk with Cobb, and that would be the most likely place to find him.

5

W<small>E DROVE THROUGH</small> H<small>ALIFAX TO THE NORTHWEST</small> and, just outside of Lower Sackville, I pulled the Saturn over and parked. Just off the road was a hard-used trail that led to the edge of a small pond near a low hill. The place was one of the more beautiful places I'd seen in a while. Peace, and a sense of wonder, permeated the area. Now before you go wondering how I knew about this place, it wasn't exactly a secret. Many merchants have used the location to trade with the fae for a number of years. It was, however, the off-season for trading, so we were the only ones here.

Zik'k trailed me by about six meters, as that allowed him to watch my back and not have an attack of magickal sneezes. His sneezing made me wonder if all that talk about Outsider resistance against magick was all it was cracked up to be.

Regardless, it was a little late to have second thoughts. I didn't expect any real trouble yet, although I was wary of what might happen when I accused Cobb of casting a glamour or three at — and on — me. The path ended between the pond and the hill. Showtime.

"All right!" I shouted to the empty space. "I have a grievance with the fae and demand justice!"

I really didn't like this whole thing much at all, I don't mind telling you. Things had piled up fast, and I was feeling somewhat frazzled with a job, a glamour, hiring backup, and now bracing to face a fae about magick. It felt like something was being overlooked. I just wasn't able to think of what it was. Zhirk would have known. He always seemed to know the right thing to do.

A few moments after I had shouted to the world that I was pissed, the fae showed. Cobb was there. So was his daughter, and six other fae I didn't know by sight. The oldest looking one wore brilliant sapphire blue robes that resembled a monk's habit. He was the Judge and, in this instance, once we got started, his decision would be binding on us all. You call for fae justice; you accept the ruling. Period.

"Why have you called for justice, human? Surely you know the penalty for false accusation," he said with a very serious touch to his voice. He clearly didn't like this. Like I'd said earlier, neither did I. Things started feeling like a slippery slope. I'd asked for the Judge. I had already committed to seeing this through. In for a penny, and all that.

"I'm here because one of the fae cast a glamour on me without my knowledge or consent, that caused near grievous bodily harm to me, and to others I may have contacted while under the glamour."

Doesn't sound like much? It is. Long ago, when fae had the upper hand with magick, such a thing was considered their right, as long as they weren't caught doing it. Power with no consequence. That changed when humans learned how to work with the revived magick. We're on an equal footing now, and the fae found that difficult and hazardous to their well-being. So, forty or so years ago, this form of legalese was concocted to address the problems between fae and human.

If you win, the fae in question owes you service; if you lose, same for you. The penalty keeps most humans and fae from trying to call for it. Plus, the court is always on the homeland of the defendant, so you have to have moxie, or a real grievance, to get yourself to go into the opposition's home to accuse them.

The others settled when the Judge bade everyone be still. Dour-faced, he inclined his head towards me.

"Present your case."

As unhappy as he sounded, the thought that maybe I had interrupted his nap before bedtime flitted through my mind.

Focusing on my grievance, I outlined my association with Cobb, what I was contracted for, and the results of the activity. Then I described the situation when I got back to my office: what happened, my actions, the results of my actions, the possible repercussions. That I had never left my office building in all of these actions. That I could easily have done something unexpected, and hurt myself or others while under the glamour.

I laid it all out. The only thing I didn't do was accuse Cobb of doing it. I wanted the drama of pointing him out when the Judge asked me who was responsible. Let this be a lesson to all of you: don't get pissed to get even; think it through, and really get even.

I didn't think things through. If I had, I might have understood the Judge's reluctance for this trial. He smelled trouble from the get-go, and had tried to let me know without saying so. I was so focused on presenting my case, I wasn't listening to anyone but my own little internal dialogue. The result of which you might see coming now.

The Judge had a very sour face when he asked me, "Do you accuse someone of this manipulation?"

"Yes, sir, I accuse …" and I paused for effect, which shows how stupid and overly dramatic we humans can get, and pointed at Cobb. "… him."

"Are you certain of this, that you accuse him?" the Judge asked, his countenance becoming more sour-looking.

"I am certain that it was him, Cobb, as he presented himself to me."

See the dramatic wording? I still wince when I think about how full of myself I was at that moment. I was so certain that he'd done it. Which only proves that anything — and I mean *anything* — involving the fae: Make absolutely certain you know what happened. Never trust that what you see is absolutely what you're getting.

"I ask, for the third time, is this," and he indicated Cobb, "the one you accuse of this crime?"

"For the third and final time, yes. I accuse the one I know as Cobb," I replied, so unsuspecting of what was coming.

"Then I am unjustly accused and demand redress!" said Cobb, a triumphant smile on his face that belied the angry words.

The fact that I might have been snookered started to seep in.

The Judge turned to Cobb. Oh, yeah, he knew a setup when it fell in his lap. My stomach sank.

"How are you falsely accused then?"

"I had no part in the casting of the glamour. That was the work of another!" he intoned dramatically, sweeping his arm in front of him in a calculated fashion. Humans aren't the only ones that go for drama.

"Can you prove this?" the Judge asked Cobb sourly.

He didn't like how I had been tricked, but laws, being what they are, are notoriously unbending. If you fall in the black and white, no matter how you get there, you are considered responsible under the law, circumstances be damned. No grey wiggle room. No misunderstanding. You're either guilty, or innocent.

Cobb's daughter stepped forward. "I confess, sir, that it was I who cast the glamour on this human, of my own free will, and through no coercion from anyone."

Oh, crap.

"She's lying!" I practically screamed at the Judge.

But fae can't really lie; it's something to do with how they use their magick, Larry told me. They just can't lie. I was well and truly caught by the legal definitions of the agreement between fae and humans. I had accused the wrong fae. Whether I had been hit with a glamour or not didn't make any difference. I made a false accusation, and I was guilty in the court's eye of trying to illegally coerce another being into servitude. The punishment was to perform a service for the one I unjustly accused.

I looked over at Zik'k, to find that he was staring at me as if I was a rabid escaped loony. He stood there gaping at me like all his brains had just leaked out both ears. He stared at me for a good five seconds, then shook his head and looked over at the Judge.

"Sir? I don't mean to be rude, but she hired me a short while ago."

The Judge straightened and looked at the Troykin with irritation. Zik'k continued, his voice quavering under the Judge's stare.

"With her being guilty and all, do I have to serve with her? I mean, I didn't know anything about this, I swear to you, sir ..."

The Judge looked over at me. "Was this being in your hire before these events took place?" He questioned curtly.

"No, sir, I hired him just before I came here as a second if things came to a duel."

The Judge waved his hand at Zik'k and said, "No, you are not bound by the judgment here. But don't ask me to adjudicate your arrangement. I have had quite enough manipulations for one day."

Zik'k sagged in relief and then stared guiltily over at me. I knew he didn't want any part of what I would have to do for the fae and, knowing the fae, I wouldn't quite be certain what kind of trouble I would be in until I was hip-deep in it. With fae, nothing is ever as it looks. I know I said that before, but it really, really bears repeating. They are on their own side. They might act as one of the good guys, but even good guys can have an agenda.

I waved at Zik'k and motioned him to come over. He trundled warily to me.

"Sooooo, what's next?" he asked with a nervous innocence.

"I get to work for the fae, and you get to go home. You finished the job, Zik'k. You were here if I needed help, and, thank gods and grandfathers, we didn't have to do anything."

I was in a funk and, being the drama-queen I am at times, I didn't care who knew it. I owed a fae. I wished I'd listened to my nagging little conscience telling me this was a bad idea.

"Uh, yeah. So how do I get back home then?" He looked at the road. "Walk?"

I shrugged "Walk. That's a good idea, Zik'k. See you later."

"Ms. Fatelli, come over here, please. We need to go to Underhill to prepare you for your service to me," Cobb said with a smarmy satisfaction that really set my teeth on edge.

I noticed that he was about the only one that was happy about the situation. I wondered why. I gave a mental shrug, told my idiot self to shut up, and looked back towards the road. Zik'k had wasted no time at all, and was already jogging back towards town. I turned reluctantly back to Cobb, and walked over next to him. He looked down at me from his towering two-meter height. Sometimes I resented being short.

"Leave anything of iron or steel here, Ms. Fatelli. I promise to bring you back here and, until then, I will have my daughter watch over your vehicle and things until we return."

I glared back at him, then slid my stare over to his daughter. "Fine. Let's get this charade over with, okay?" I growled at him.

I shucked my shoes, my belt, earrings, and pendant. He quirked an eye at me. Oh yeah, I thought sourly, the jeans have steel buttons. I slid out of my jeans and he handed me a dress to wear. I batted it away and stalked over to my SUV.

"No, I am not accepting gifts! I'm not being fooled again!" I dug in the back, pulled out a pair of sweat pants, and put them on. I then reached behind me and took off my bra; its wires were steel, so a no-no. I checked myself over. No steel or iron anywhere.

I walked back to Cobb. He gestured and opened the way into Underhill.

6

T HE SWIRLING MAGICKAL POWER AND BUFFETS OF WIND disoriented me completely. It felt like it continued for hours. I had just started to get used to the sensation when it stopped suddenly. The loss of the constant pressure had me on my hands and knees with vertigo from the instantaneous change. When the dizziness cleared, the first thing I noticed was the clean, earthy smell of the ground. The sky, the colors of the grass and trees, were brighter and more exuberant. The earth exuded a sense of contentment. There was a sadness, too. It was strange, smelling emotions, and not feeling them.

There was no sun. The light seemed to come from the very air. As I pushed myself upright, I noticed that no one cast a shadow here.

"Come this way," said Cobb. "We will see to your comfort, and then we will discuss your service."

He led me along a footpath that led into a gully. As we entered it, another disorienting surge of magick passed through me, and then I gazed into a tremendous foyer. A large circular stand to my left held wraps and cloaks of many different sizes and bright colors. Just behind the rack stood a large wooden box set on its short end and bolted to the wall. Grooves in the box held swords, a mace, and a brass hand-cannon of some kind.

To my immediate right was a huge clay statue that held a gleaming silver sword in one hand, and a weapon that looked like a Maltese cross made out of silver in the other one. Curiosity would have to wait though, as Cobb removed his trench coat and negligently threw it at the circular rack, which extended a hanger and neatly caught the coat in mid-flight, setting it on the rack in an open slot. I kept my sweatshirt; it was much cooler in here than it had been in the open air outside.

In front of us was a huge wooden stairway, which looked to be six meters across, curled clockwise around a wide-latticed pillar. As I got closer, the lattice revealed itself to be a plant — or plants — grown together; the steps were molded from its branches. We mounted the stairs, and he led me to a second floor that was like a ballroom. The room seemed about forty meters across, and was bare of any furniture, except for three rows of, and I kid you not, red British phone booths.

I decided to keep quiet and see what Cobb would do. He had stopped, as if waiting for a question. When I didn't ask, he walked over to the fourth booth in from the end of the second row, and entered it. I followed him in and found myself in a large study.

Directly opposite the doorway was a fireplace with a cheery, crackling fire; a large white polar bear rug lying on the floor in front of it. To the right of the polar bear rug was a large desk with a glass top. On the desk was a flat panel computer.

"I thought you said steel and iron couldn't be here," I said to Cobb.

He smiled and said, "Special order. All the wiring is gold and any screws are plastic. Not as durable, but it doesn't have to be."

He gestured over to the other side of the room, where I saw a sofa facing a wall with a one by one-and one-half meter black rectangle mounted on it.

"That's a television? What's *that* doing here? On second thought, let me guess: custom–built, no-steel, just gold, and plastic along with the circuitry," I said sarcastically.

You think you'd see nice natural things, like grown wood statues or beautiful carvings, but this was a real surprise to me. Another example of "don't assume anything." Cobb gestured, and a silver service tray with two cups of hot cocoa rose up out of the desk and settled on it. He picked one up and handed it to me.

"I claim visitor rights," I told him coldly.

Fae were notorious for offering things without explanation, and that some of those things offered were not declared as being a gift. Some of the things offered were items requiring recompense if you took it, or indicated you accepted it. That's how some humans get trapped in Underhill. You accept something; you are obligated to pay for it — one way or another. I wasn't going to have another debt placed on me.

"Visitor rights" mean that you are a visitor for one night, and cannot be coerced into staying with tricks. It's weird, but the fae are like that: weird, nasty laws that bite you if you don't know about them. Fae cannot lie — but that doesn't mean they have to tell you all of the truth.

Cobb sighed. "You are perceptive. I didn't think that it would work, but we do have to play the game, Ms. Fatelli."

"Play it without me, and let's get this service done with, Cobb — or whatever your name is. I don't like being here."

"Fair enough, but first let's sit and relax a moment." He smiled; a real, genuine, smile that almost melted my knees. This guy could turn on the charm!

I shook my head to clear the charm. "Quit that! You already have a service. Stop trying to get more out of me!"

He smiled and gestured once more, and a chair with a beautiful pantsuit and silk shirt appeared from the polar bear. "Please take them. They look better than your sweat suit."

"No, dammit! Don't you understand what 'no' means!?"

He smiled and gestured, and I felt something shift. "That was three refusals. I no longer have to try to catch you, Ms. Fatelli. This little game is over. I tell you that all here now are gifts freely given, and that you may take without any payment." He relaxed visibly. "And thank you for refusing. I do not like some of our games, but the king has decreed them, and so we all must obey." He took a drink of his chocolate and continued. "Now that you and I have done our duties, would you like to know the extent of your service?"

"Yeah, I want to know, and I hope it's a quick one. I want to get out of here and, honestly, I don't want to see you ever again after this is done."

I was tired, irritable, and still smarting from being trapped so easily by legal machinations. I was deliberately starting to push his buttons. All in all, not very smart, I admit it, but that's life. You're never perfect, and seldom good, and obnoxious is easy compared to the other two.

To his credit, Cobb didn't bat an eye, nor did I see a tensing of any muscle. He just stared at me like he was sad about something. Sad like a general is sad about sending men to die. That got me. Emotions here in Underhill manifest as smell along with visual cues. It makes it real hard to fool people. Maybe it's one of the reasons the fae don't try to lie.

"If you're done trying to irritate me, we'll get started. I'll ask you a question then." He leaned forward as he spoke, and suddenly I was the center of all his attention. "What do you know of The Anolyn Way?"

The answer I gave was what Zhirk had told me. "The Anolyn Way was a way through the barrier around Prince Edward Island that Anolyn the Dragon had set to stop emigrants. There were, supposedly, a series of safe houses on the island. Escapees traveled from house to house to avoid Anolyn's periodic fly-bys. The final stop was a cave on the island shore, near where the barrier came closest. The way through the barrier was by boat." I took time to sip some cocoa. "One wizard got the wild idea to make a giant clamshell boat made of native rock. You might think a rock boat would sink, but as long as the object displaces water equal to its weight, anything can float. Steel oil tankers and freighters are just a couple examples. Anyway, once the wizard got the boat completed, he rowed out to the barrier and closed the clamshell. He drifted through the magickal alarms and the barrier without incident.

Anolyn was enraged by the rock boats, but couldn't alter his barrier spell. It had taken weeks of preparation on Anolyn's part to cast the barrier the first time, and he didn't dare take it down, as the enemies he had made would be certain to attack before he could get the new barrier up. So he did the next best thing and patrolled the water himself, sinking any boat he found. One boat survived Anolyn's attacks, and was found by some of the emigrants who took shelter in the cave where the boat was hidden. Among them was a wizard who was able to spell the clamshell submarine to get through the barrier. It worked, but the wizard was killed before he could teach others how he had modified the spell. This single clamshell boat became The Anolyn Way. It ran in secret for years, until the patrols apparently found it and destroyed it," I told him.

He looked at me in surprise. "I'm impressed, Ms. Fatelli. Very few humans would have recounted the story with that kind of accuracy. Whoever taught it to you is someone I would like to meet."

I went cold inside. My heart clenched at remembering Zhirk as he told that story to me. "You can't; he's dead. His soul was devoured by that damn bottle you showed me when you hired me to help you." I spat the words at him like venom.

Zhirk was the best friend I had ever known. That his soul had gone to feed that monster Ahiah — and now to find that the bottle had been re-created — really had me angry.

"You tell me how you know about that bottle, and who the miserable piece of garbage is that made it. When this is all over, I want to use that bottle on the damned idiot that made that abomination!"

He actually dared smile at that, and my anger went incandescent. "What the fuck are you smiling about, you miserable waste? Tell me who made that damn bottle!"

"There is no bottle. I had a chat with your brother-in-law, Larry Potter, and got the story from him. I used that to get you to agree to take the job I wanted you for."

I sat down on the rug in shock and relief.

No bottle.

But I went ballistic again and tore into Cobb verbally for five minutes while he sat there and waited for me to run down. When I finally pulled myself back together, he told me what I was going to do.

"I want you to re-open The Anolyn Way."

I blinked. Surely he was joking.

"You want me to re-open The Anolyn Way? What the hell for? You got a long-lost love in there or something?"

"Yes," was what he said.

7

"YOU ALREADY KNOW THE STORY, so I don't have to outline that for you. But yes, there are — or were — fae on the island when Anolyn erected the barrier. He did such a thorough job that Underhill was cut off as well. My family is on the other side of that barrier — and has been for the last fifty years. I want them free. You have the power to open the barrier. "

"Listen, you pompous idiot, I owe a service. What if I refuse it? I don't see you have any way of stopping me from leaving."

He straightened and finally looked triumphant. He smelled gleeful, like he wanted me to refuse. "Kaddus! Judge Kaddus! I have need of you!" He roared the name, and a blue nimbus appeared by the fireplace, enlarging and solidifying in moments into the Judge that had overseen the trial.

"What now?" he questioned grumpily. "I have a dinner waiting for me. Why are you calling me here?" He saw me, and understanding wafted from him like wind across a desert. "She is refusing the service? Smarter than you, then." He turned and faced me full-on. "Ms. Fatelli, I understand and sympathize completely with your situation and wanting to refuse the service Cobb wants you to perform."

He smelled of regret and of resignation. Then suddenly he smelled angry. He straightened and spoke sharply to Cobb. "I have had enough of these manipulations! She is going to hear the truth, and *you* will not interfere!"

Cobb's triumphant smell smoldered quickly to a burnt wood angry aroma. I still couldn't get used to smelling emotions.

Judge Kaddus faced me and said, "If you refuse the service, someone else will have to take your place. The laws of Underhill state that it would be immediate family that would have to fulfill the service. Cobb wants you to refuse so that he could entrap your sister and brother-in-law to perform this service."

I was confused suddenly. Mad, mind you, but confused as to why the Judge would be so up front about Cobb's manipulations.

"Why tell me all this?" I asked him.

"For two reasons, Ms. Fatelli. One: Larry Potter has been a voice of reason the last five years, and many of the fae respect what he has done, myself included. I believe, like Mr. Potter, that honest dealings with other races make for better neighbors and allies, should necessity arise." He stopped and smiled ferally, and I caught a smell of malice from him. "The second reason is I do not like Mr … Cobb. He wants fae to not be so accommodating to humans. We have crossed our purposes in the past. Now I find I have an opportunity to ruin a plan of his. Your knowing changes the situation beyond his ability to control, and," the Judge began to look positively gleeful, and smelled it too, "he hates losing control of anything."

Cobb ground his teeth. I could smell hate rolling off of him like a suffocating fog.

I smiled, too. Beyond screwing the manipulative Cobb over, family is very big with me, considering the only family I have left is Fawn and Larry. I knew too, from talking with Fawn a while ago, that she was pregnant. Which meant if Fawn had to take the service, Larry would jump all over it to protect her and the baby. What it meant was still a very difficult situation. I most certainly did *not* want to do the service. Dragon magick is powerful — very powerful from all the stories that have been told. But if I didn't take the service, Cobb was free to force Fawn, which would then have Larry volunteering to do it. A classic rock-and-hard-place situation.

"I'll take the service, and I'll perform it, but I want to know what options I have. Can I hire help, or do I have to go this alone?"

"You have the service; you have to perform it," stated Cobb pompously.

Judge Kaddus spoke up and said, "There are no stipulations in the laws on how the service is handled, only that you perform it. It doesn't say alone, or how swiftly the service needs be done."

He looked over at Cobb, who was acting as if the Judge did not exist. Petty, but I found I enjoyed his attitude. It made it easier to dislike him. The Judge caught my attention with a slight wave of his hand in front of my face. I blinked in surprise, and turned to face him as he spoke to me.

"You do have to work at the service. Delaying can be seen as avoiding. And that interpretation is up to the holder of the service. But, you must have some time to properly prepare for the service. Mr., er, Cobb cannot just accuse you of refusing it for taking a few days to prepare. So before I leave to go back to my dinner, how long do you consider necessary to prepare before you start this service?"

The Judge had given me a breathing space and I took it. "I should need about a day to prepare. Then, I don't know, a couple months to find and read all I can on Anolyn. This may take a long while to finish. Research on The Anolyn Way, research on magick, on the barrier, and on any extra information that might help me decide how best to proceed."

The Judge nodded. "So you will begin your research in one day's time, and you will present an overview of your research at weekly intervals to Mr. ... Cobb. Once you have exhausted your resources for all pertinent information, you will attempt to get The Way operating."

He smiled again, and I could smell the satisfaction flowing off of him like honeysuckle.

"I believe that covers the situation quite nicely. Please call upon me, Ms. Fatelli, if you should have need. I must say I am interested in this. Good day, Ms. Fatelli." He bowed and turned to Cobb. "Good day." A perfunctory bow and he was gone the same way he came in.

I turned to Cobb. "I want to rest at my home. I'll drop by the library tomorrow and see what books there are on Anolyn and The Anolyn Way." That raised a thought. "Do you have any reference materials on Anolyn or The Way? Anything that you have, I want access to." I smiled and smelled my own satisfaction with tweaking this manipulative jerk. "After all, you wanted service. How can I perform the service if I can't learn about the problem?"

8

AFTER COBB MAGICKED ME IN FRONT OF THE BUILDING that housed my office, he said a curt good-bye and vanished. I didn't go inside immediately, but dialed up Larry and Fawn on my cell phone.

"Hey, Short Stuff, how's the private entrapment business going?" Fawn answered jauntily.

"I love you too, sis. How's being preggers feel?"

"Beyond the morning sickness, and nausea near new tires, I'm stoked! Now enough jabbering and let's go celebrate!" I could feel her grin through the phone. It felt really good to smile and laugh after the last two days I'd had.

Larry and Fawn had me meet them at the Calcutta Wharf, a wonderful restaurant that, in spite of the name, served Asian food. I'd asked about the name once. The story came back that the owner had bought the place from the original owner, and had been too cheap to change the sign. After a while, he just left it up because people associated the sign with the restaurant.

As we ate our dinner, Larry asked, "So, Fernie, did that spell work properly?"

I put my utensils down, and took a deep breath. "About that. Larry, it worked fine. It was the other stuff afterwards that was really miserable." I outlined everything that went on after I got back from "'finding and rescuing" Cobb's daughter, including the trial that morning, the discussion I had with Cobb, and what I was supposed to do.

The mood went right down the drain, and I felt bad, really bad, about the kind of stuff we were discussing. This should have been a celebration and, instead, we're talking about how poor little Fernie got screwed over by the big bad fae. Larry sat and just picked at the food as I wound the story down. Fawn looked pale and angry: part at me, part at Larry — because she knew he'd try to help — and a *big* part at Cobb, the author of the whole mess.

"So, what do you think we should do?" Fawn surprised us both by being the one to hint that working together would be a good idea. She looked at our faces and chuckled. "I know that's what it's going to take, Short Stuff. I have to make decisions I don't like all the time as a cop. How's this one any different?"

Got me there.

We decided that I'd check in with Cobb the next morning, getting to work on the fae records, if they had any, and Larry and Fawn could work without letting Cobb know they were helping. I got the feeling that, if he knew, there'd be something he'd try to pull that would lock Larry and Fawn into the service. So I sat down with Larry and Fawn, and wrote out a simple contract saying that they were simply assisting me locating books and reference materials, and that it was the only thing they were doing. I also stated that I was paying him to do so. I wanted to make sure that Cobb couldn't get them with some kind of "volunteer" clause, meaning "volunteer-to-do-the-service".

Once I'd finished the contract, I went back home and packed a few items in a backpack, making sure that I had no iron or steel when I went to see Cobb the next morning. I went with sweat pants and canvas sneakers, half because they were comfortable, and half because I knew Cobb didn't like me looking "tacky" on his time. Petty, but what do you expect? I'm not a saint, and I sure as hell don't like being tricked into being a pawn for some grandiose asshole.

Cobb was waiting when I drove up. He gave my wardrobe a sour look as I got out. I went to the back of the SUV, opened it, and pulled the backpack out. That caught his attention.

"No iron, you know that."

I smiled sweetly. "I know that, Cobb. I just brought along a few other things to help me out." I set the backpack down. "You want to check it over?"

He didn't say anything, but picked up the pack and rummaged through it. I had a bottle of salt, some blessed water from a Lutheran church, four notebooks, ten pencils with the metal eraser holder removed, three pink erasers, my mother's ceramic paring knife to sharpen the pencils with, a silver letter opener, five candles, a box of beads, another box of modeling clay, and two changes of clothes, including one pair of sweats, and a black tube dress, just in case some kind of social event were to happen. Sounds like *deus ex machina* there? Remember, Cobb is an asshole with an ego, and fae like social events to practice their politicking. Plus, although I wanted to piss Cobb off, I didn't want to do so to other fae and, if being polite and playing dress-up helped get information, then I'd play dress-up and trot out my best social manners. The tube dress was just a tad slinky, and a little "slink" might be useful.

He finished looking through the bag, placed everything back in it, handed it back to me, and then took me on that disorienting trip to Underhill. Time to start hitting the books.

"Where to first? You have a library or something?" I tried to sound flippant, but all I got was snappish.

He took me back up to phone booth central and pointed out three booths that had been tinted a metallic green.

"Those are archives that I keep here. The two booths on the end that are white will take you to others that also have references to Anolyn, and are willing to allow you to peruse them. I do not know if they are duplicates of what is here; you'll just have to look through their archives yourself."

He didn't wait for an acknowledgment, but turned away quickly, stepped into one of the phone booths, and disappeared. Oh, yeah, a classy way to make a girl feel welcome: run off and leave her. I shrugged and walked to the white booth on the left to start. I tightened my grip on my backpack, took a deep breath, and stepped into the booth.

There was a disorienting feeling as I stepped over the threshold and entered a large, dimly lit room that looked like any number of clichéd dungeon studies. Dark red and brown bricks made up its walls, with oil lights set on brass poles just above my eye level. In the center of the room was a circular, dark-colored rug, with a reading desk and chair on it. Along the floor, just off the edge of the rug, was a double circle with a series of unfamiliar designs resting between the inner and outer circle.

Book cases started on the left side of the entrance, and went all the way around the walls to the right side of the entrance. Two three-step ladders were visible, apparently for reaching their upper shelves. The bookshelves weren't totally packed, but there were a lot of books. There was a stack by the desk that someone had left out, possibly for me. Knowing Cobb, the books would be on Anolyn.

I didn't dive immediately into the stack, but went around the room looking at the titles. Most of the books were in languages that I didn't recognize. I took one off a shelf at random and leafed through it. The writing was done by someone with a very spidery hand; the characters were tall and thin, and, to me, completely illegible.

Frustrated, I went back to the desk and picked up the top book on the stack and opened it. It was in perfectly legible English. I went through the book, and all the others in the stack, over the next two days. All of them had some account about dragons, and something specific about Anolyn, but none of that was fact. All were presented as stories and, the few that had facts, were about dragons approximately one thousand seven hundred years ago — the height of the previous magickal period.

What I gleaned from all of this was what you probably know yourself from playing those tabletop games: dragons are big, bad, extremely magickal, highly intelligent, and utterly ruthless. Not much for two days? Well, I also learned that dragons have weaknesses. Any silver weapon will cut their hide; for that matter, any weapon will. You just have to survive to get close enough to do it. Bullets will penetrate; bullets will kill a dragon if you hit them in the right place.

But, the "right place" is different for each dragon. Remember magick? Dragons are, according to the few ancient texts, born with the ability to focus their whole life force into one or more places in their body. The adults help the young practice this ability. What it means is that, if you have the world's greatest sniper with the biggest, baddest rifle around, he may blow the dragon's head half-off with a shot into the eye, but everything will just grow back in mere seconds, if you don't hit their particular life-force location, and you will have one very pissed off dragon coming for you.

That is one thing I never want to have happen to me. Dragons are also apparently very creatively vindictive to people that upset them. One story had a dragon taking a man apart, de-boning him over a period of four days, before eating him. No, I really did not want that to happen to me. If I was going to do this, I needed a way to bypass the purported alarms that Anolyn had up, and find some way to hide from him so The Way could start running people off of Prince Edward Island again.

I had to get in without being discovered, get back outside the barrier, go back in again, find someone who wanted to escape, and help them escape. It wasn't enough to get in and out; it had to be repeatable. Once I could do that, and prove it to Cobb, my service would be done. The smart thing, however, is to make sure you've found everything you can before trying something this crazy.

I investigated the other white phone booth, and found that all the books there were illegible. It was frustrating, but I brought one book back with me to see if I could find anything that might match up with one of the English books. After a half hour of searching, I found one that had the same type of covering and the same embossed sigils on the front, which meant to me this one was probably identical in content to the other, just translated to English from the original.

I put the original book down on the reading table, next to the translated copy, and turned both to the front page; two identical English translated pages sat in front of me. I about fell out of the chair in surprise. I could have sworn it was not translated. I went over to the shelf, pulled a book at random, and looked at it. It was complete gibberish. I returned to the circle, laid the book down on the desk, and opened it. Elegant English script flowed across the pages. The circle must hold a spell that translated the books to English, or maybe to the main language of the reader, as long as she was inside the circle.

I decided to go against my instinct and look with my mage sight; I just about went blind. Everything glowed, and glowed fiercely. It hurt like looking at Cobb had hurt. Everything seemed to have magick pouring out, forming a glowing haze that surrounded me like a bright, blinding fog. I shut my eyes and waited for the after flashes to go away. I hate it when my instinct is right and I ignore it.

When the images finally faded and my eyes cleared, I went back to the book and looked it over. The book I had pulled was one on romantic poetry. I began checking the shelves to see where the books had resided before being placed in that pile by the desk. I found all eighteen locations. They were clustered on three shelves, which made me think the shelves were organized in some way. I took all the books down from those shelves and set them by the desk.

Just as I got ready to look through the first of the books, Cobb came in and looked around. "Are you done yet?" Now of all the times to ask. I think he did it deliberately.

I had to bite my tongue to keep from tearing into him. I forced a mild smile over my gritted teeth as I asked, "Why didn't you tell me this desk translated the books? I could have gone through them rather than trying to find English copies."

Then I smelled something different from him. Chagrin. He actually felt embarrassed that he had forgotten to tell me about the desk. He gave me an explanation sounding like he was bored, but there was a definite odor of embarrassment.

"To use the magick here, you just place the book on the table, and it changes the script to what you are used to reading. You can also ask the table to collect particular books by saying out loud the information you want," he finished, and left hurriedly.

That was way out of character for Cobb, and it bothered me to think that he might be trying to manipulate me even now that I was working on this service he'd tricked me into. I set aside the books, exited the room, and went back home to get some food. I decided to stop by Larry and Fawn's to see how their luck researching things had gone. We arranged to meet at a small restaurant called "Hole in the Wall" near his shop. We sat down, ordered our food, and then got to talking business.

"Dragons are a serious piece of bad news, Fernie. I have everything I could find out so far here." Larry handed me a spiral notebook. It was about a third full of notes. "You can look through it, but most of the stuff isn't in any kind of order, so it may not make sense. I think I'll need about four to five more days to go through the basic stuff. Probably another month to track down all the esoteric entries and collate my notes into a readable report. How about we set up a time each day to compare the notes we have?"

I looked over at my brother-in-law. The thought of Cobb using him to open The Way back up really angered me. That he had tried to use me to make that happen angered me more, and that helped keep me focused.

I shoved those thoughts aside, got a smile to my face, and said, "Sounds good. I'll bring mine tomorrow. Meet at the downtown library?"

"Yeah, that's great, Fernie. I can work until you get there. I have a few friends watching the shop for me while I'm doing this, so I'm not losing any business." He chuckled and looked at me with his lopsided smile. "I'd forgotten how much fun it is just to do research. Thanks, Fernie."

"Thank you, Larry. Without you, this would be a real pain to do," I told him.

The waiter brought our meals, and we tucked in to a good dinner. I beat Larry to the check. I'd hired him after all, and it was fun to see him grump about me paying.

I went back the next morning, and Cobb again escorted me to Underhill and to his mansion. He didn't say one word to me the whole time, which didn't bother me at all. Talking meant he was trying to manipulate me, so I enjoyed the silence. I went back to the first white phone booth and stepped through. The books had been stacked neatly next to the table. The torches flickered, and shadows danced on the shelves, as I walked to the desk and set my backpack down. As I straightened, I caught a glimpse of something that flickered and sped towards me. Instead of bracing for an impact, I pulled the same trick I had used before: dive into the legs. I passed through something that felt dry, cold, and cobwebby. I rolled to my feet and took a step towards my backpack, then abandoned it and sprinted for the doorway.

I exited the room just as something shredded the back of my sweatshirt. I felt a cold impact that had no force and then a wet trickle down my back. Then the pain hit, and I screamed in agony and managed to stagger away from the phone booth. I looked behind me, and there was a thick, glistening blood trail leading to a puddle around my feet. Just inside the door, a vague outline of blackness hovered for a moment, then flicked back into the room and disappeared from view.

I tried to stagger back towards the entrance, my body going numb from shock. My arms and legs felt leaden; the wounds felt like fire. My scream was a dry croak. I found myself on hands and knees, trying to crawl away from the door. The fire in my back, and the shock, made the room spin. I fell to my side and into the dark of unconsciousness.

9

I WOKE UP A LITTLE LATER to an argument going on nearby.
"She is incapable of performing the service, and the debt remains. Either her sister picks up the service, or a volunteer. Or I have my choice of compensation!" I heard Cobb snarl out.

"She was attacked on your premises, wounded in your house, and was under your so-called protection when the attack occurred. It seems to me that the Judge may see that as not fulfilling your end of the agreement, even to the point of deliberately allowing her to be attacked so that you could coerce someone else into accepting the service," said a familiar voice, which I recognized as Larry's after a few groggy moments.

"Who's imacabipple of tahrner?" My mouth was obviously not on the same channel as my brain was. It took a few more moments for everything to start working together. "Who's not capable?" I said again, much more clearly, and the argument outside my room ceased like a light switch being flipped.

Judge Kaddus stepped through the open doorway and walked to the side of the bed. "Ms. Fatelli, it is good to hear that you have awakened." He smiled as he talked, and I smiled back — or I think I did. "Do you remember what happened, Ms. Fatelli? I was unable to find a trace of anything except your blood starting at the doorway."

I sat up slowly and, despite a pounding headache, told the Judge, with Cobb scowling behind him, the details of what I remembered: diving through legs that felt like cobwebs, the flickering as the attacker moved around, and the shadow at the doorway after I escaped the library and got back into the main room. My little finger began to throb as I recounted what happened. I rubbed it to ease the ache, thinking of Zhirk, and wishing he was here to talk to. What happened was pretty random, and whatever attacked me hadn't followed up the advantage.

"What I want to know is what the hell it was, and why it attacked me. This doesn't make sense at all. What am I digging into that's got somebody so nervous?" I mumbled woozily.

It was hard to focus with the headache driving a nail in my skull. I wanted to go back to sleep, but a stubborn part of me wanted to stay awake just to hear what Cobb was going to say, so I could try and figure out what was really going on. Stubbornness, unfortunately, doesn't trump medication. I really don't remember passing back into sleep.

I woke again a few hours later, and levered myself back upright in the bed. The room was hexagonal in shape. Ornate columns that looked of carved marble stood at each corner. I didn't know any human hospitals that looked like this, so it seemed that I was still in Underhill. A quiet hum to my left caught my attention. A small sphere hovered just next to my pillow. When I moved to get out of bed, it rose away from the bed and floated out the archway. I felt the breeze of its movement as a brush along my entire body, which is when my slow-on-the-uptake brain realized I was completely naked in the bed.

Gingerly levering myself off the bed, I got unsteadily on my feet, then looked for my clothes, or some kind of robe, to put on. The bathroom didn't have anything other than a towel, which I quickly wrapped around me. When I re-entered bedroom, I found my sweat suit laid on the bed, completely repaired. I hadn't seen or heard anyone. I shrugged, putting it down to magick. Underhill is full of it, I suppose.

All this time, I listened for other voices or activity, but I only heard my own breathing and heartbeat. Things were way too quiet for my liking. I walked out into a well-lit, greyish hall. Everything — floor, walls, and doors — had a wispy, ethereal quality, as if the first breeze would tear it all asunder. My room was at the end of the delicate hallway, so I walked towards what I hoped was the exit.

An opaque curtain covered the archway. I brushed it aside and stepped ... out of a phone booth, and back into Cobb's main hall of doors. Cobb emerged from another booth next to the one I had exited, faltering for a moment in surprise. He quickly recovered his poise, but I could smell the faint cinnamon of embarrassment emanate from him.

"I didn't expect to see you active so soon after being wounded as you were. The human doctor indicated that you would need a lot of rest to heal properly."

"Thanks ever so much for your concern," I said acidly. "Now how about you tell me about that place you had me in?"

He looked at me with a very neutral expression, apparently trying to decide whether I had really just tried to insult him. "It was a bedroom. Nothing more, nothing less. Was there something wrong with it?"

I ignored his question and threw out another of my own. "What was that silver floating ball?"

He looked at me for a moment, and I smelled something that my brain recognized as speculation. "That is a monitor, easily given simple commands to perform, such as waking one up at a certain time."

"So why was it hovering next to the bed I was in?"

"It was there to alert my servants that you were awake and to place your ..." his lip curled slightly as he looked my sweats over, "... garments on the bed so you could clothe yourself."

"So how long has it been since I got hurt?" Keep firing questions, maybe I could sneak one in that would give me an idea what he was planning next.

"It has been four days, quite a fast time to recover from a nearly fatal attack."

"Nearly fatal?" That caught me off guard.

"Yes, the doctor said the attacker stabbed between your ribs and nicked your heart. It took all his magick to repair it, and hours of work to stitch everything back into place, before he was ready to have his assistant encourage healing."

I guess I did get lucky. "Must have been a good doctor to get me up and ready to go so fast."

He looked at me. I mean, really looked at me, like a parent would to an idiot savant. It smelled like desire, contempt, and fear all rolled together. It made me wonder if he smelled me here. He said carefully, "The doctor said that your wounds would take weeks to heal properly. That it took only four days is interesting."

"Meaning what?" His unblinking stare was unsettling. He waited, deliberately stretching time out before he answered.

"Meaning: nothing at the moment. Maybe something later." He turned, and went back into the booth he'd appeared from.

I started to follow, intending on getting a straight answer, but ran into a solid wall of force, blocking my pursuit of Cobb.

So much for continuing the discussion. I hadn't gotten to asking about what attacked me, which made me wonder if Cobb didn't want me asking that question.

I decided to go talk with Larry and see if he'd found any new information about dragons and, if he'd gotten lucky, maybe Anolyn. It took what felt like an hour of aimless wandering before I ran into one of Cobb's seldom-seen servants, who directed me out of Underhill. I wanted to see Fawn and Larry. I was fairly certain that they both were concerned that I hadn't checked in with them in the last four days.

When I pulled up in front of their house, I found Larry had tried to get into Underhill the last two days, but had been stopped by Judge Kaddus.

"Miserable hoitey-toitey elf wouldn't let me in. He said I'd pollute Underhill. I can't believe those arrogant pointy-eared …" Larry paused his rant. "Sorry, Fern. If you'd been gone any longer, Fawn would have had the MaRS Unit storm the metaphorical ramparts." He took a deep breath and let it out. "I am so glad you're here. You look great."

Larry led me inside, and we sat down to discuss and share our information. I relayed the situation with the shadows, which had Larry clenching his fists and closing his eyes in frustration. To break the mood, I asked how the dragon research was going.

"Nothing much new here, so far, but I'm only about halfway through the books, so we might still find something out."

When Fawn had gotten home, she grabbed me in a tight bear hug and didn't let go for a full minute. She listened intently as I recapped what I'd told Larry, and suggested I come back out to the gym to practice my self-defense, in case I really needed it. It was a good idea, and I promised Fawn I'd see her after I was cleared by the doctor for that kind of activity. No sense in pushing things too much.

Fawn shooed Larry off to start dinner, and she and I sat down to discuss what might have attacked me.

She asked me to turn around and lifted my shirt to look at the scar. "Uh, Fern, I can barely see the scars. They must have used some pretty potent magick to fix you up."

"Honestly, Fawn, I'm not sure. That Cobb guy acted surprised that I was up and about so soon."

"Well, I can't tell what attacked you from the scars, but whatever it was had to be very sharp. I don't see any tug marks at all."

"Maybe that's why some of it healed faster, no tears or rips."

"Maybe, Fernie, but it doesn't answer why you were attacked. Just that you were," Fawn answered me.

She had shifted into cop mode. She picked up a piece of paper, had me turn around and take my shirt off, then lay the paper over the scars, and began tracing the scars on my back while we talked. She finished the first one and moved lower to the next.

"You said it was flickering? Was that because of the lighting, or was that the creature itself that was flickering?"

"I think it was the light," I answered, as I thought about it. "Though when I looked at it when it was in the archway, it seemed to flicker with the torches."

Fawn shifted behind me, and started on another scar.

"Best guess, without seeing, would be some kind of shade then, which would also make sense, as it needs shadows to exist and move about. No shadows, no shade. You said it felt like cobwebs when you passed through it?"

"Yeah, it was like running into a dense bunch of spider webs." I shivered involuntarily at the memory.

Fawn finished tracing the last scar, straightened and stretched her back, then handed me the paper. Three thin cuts ran parallel to my ribs, right in between them. Who or whatever did the cutting knew how to aim, or was just plain lucky. I figured the former. Always figure skill over luck.

"So if it's a shade, like you say, what can I do to protect myself against it?"

"Holy water works best on shades, I remember. We've dealt with only one since the unit was drafted; they're fairly rare. But usually they don't attack so much, as try to frighten people away from whatever they left behind. Hmm, I do remember one case where a shade was forced to guard a wooden box."

Fawn shrugged her shoulders and looked at the kitchen archway, from which some savory odors had started to waft out. She turned back to me and said, "It's a bit of a stretch to think that you were specifically targeted with the shade by someone. If that really is the case, then there must be a reason."

She raised her left hand to tap her chin with her index finger. I was thinking more a guard, but as a specific target? That gave me a chill that wasn't from a cool breeze.

"You think Cobb tried to put a hurt on me to get to you and Larry? That would really be the pits, Fawn." I was not happy with this thought.

She looked off into space as she thought about that. After a moment, she shook her head. "I don't think so, Short Stuff. If you are hurt or killed while on his grounds, he is responsible for your death, and, if I'm remembering the articles right, he would owe Larry and me something for your dying," she finished.

"So if I die, he gets screwed?" I mused.

A situation like that sure didn't make Cobb a very likely person to have called up the shade. If I had been a bit slower to the door, it would have gutted me.

"Comes back to the question: why? What's the motive? Who would want the whole service screwed up?"

That made me think back to Judge Kaddus and his little conversation.

"I do not like … Mr. Cobb. We have crossed in the past, and now I find I have an opportunity to ruin a plan of his. Your knowing changes the situation beyond his ability to control, and he hates losing control of anything."

He had a motive, to my thinking, but me, not being the cop in the family, I told Fawn about it, and she decided to look in on the Judge. I went back to the books, but with a little equalizer. I can do spells of my own, and one I do know is the circle of protection. I don't like casting spells, as it takes me a long time to set up and invoke them, but now, the time was worthwhile. I did not want another set of razor cuts along my back — or something worse. I made sure I had all the materials for the spell, before slowing down to get a meal and some sleep. I wasn't under a time limit, and I didn't like Cobb, so making him wait another day was fine by me. Yeah, I'm petty. So sue me. Don't tell me you wouldn't do the same to someone who screwed you over.

The trip back to Underhill felt more like walking into the proverbial lion's den. I knew what was likely waiting down there. The circle should be able to keep it out, but there's that small voice that keeps whispering doubts. You may think you've got it all figured out, only to find that you didn't. That's when things get very bad, very fast. I hoped to avoid "very bad, very fast", if at all possible.

Larry offered to drive me out to the entrance, and me, being the scared and lazy sort I was, agreed. I say scared, and I was, for the reasons I outlined above. Plus, it was a comfort to have someone to talk with, if briefly, before I had to go back Underhill.

Surprisingly, Judge Kaddus was the one who met Larry and I at the entrance. Larry scowled at the Judge, who ignored him. His gaze turned to me. I'd gotten back into the gym sweats, this time in neon pink that was a size too large. That was because Fawn gave me a ceramic vest the Special Unit used. Its weight was a comfort. His gaze picked out the bulky edges of the armor, and nodded slightly. Then, with a gesture of his hand, he indicated the path. He never spoke to me at all. I wondered why, but let the thought go. I had more pressing concerns in Underhill.

Cobb's servants met me once I'd crossed the threshold, and guided me to the room of doors. From there, it was a short walk to the door, and another slightly longer walk to the library archway. A quick look inside showed that all the books had been left as they had lain when the attack occurred. The first thing I did was take a deep breath, and step in the room. When nothing jumped out and tried to attack, I got busy picking up the books.

I made two neat stacks next to the desk. I scanned the room constantly, watching for any kind of flicker, shadow, or movement. It took me twenty minutes to draw the circle using chalk, and add the runes and five-pointed star around the desk. The center was large enough to hold the desk myself, and the stacks of books.

Once I'd gotten that done, I sat in the middle of the circle to focus and invoke. For charms, I had only a small piece of glass and a handmade candle. My ability to concentrate was crap, so it took me about thirty minutes to do a five-minute spell. But once I was done, I felt the fuzzy hum of the magick. I walked over to the desk, and sorted through the books I'd set on the floor next to it earlier. The one I wanted was three down from the top.

I took a deep breath, and placed the book back on the desk, and tensed, adrenalin surging as I anticipated an attack. Nothing happened, and I let my breath go. I had thought the shade might have been with the book, and, if it had, my picking it up ought to have called it forth. The book was on dragon lifecycles, and some of what I had read had been paraphrased from this text.

Dragons, it began, *were conceived outside of the magick, and yet part of it. Zagyg speculated that dragons were the source, but later experiments ...* and my ward suddenly pressed on me.

It squeezed me hard enough that I couldn't draw a breath for a moment. I saw at the corner of my eye a darkness that was propelled out of my circle. Just as immediately, it started tearing at the ward to get back in. There was a sense of the book trying to shift towards the darkness. Insight hit. Its source was the book and, when it materialized, the ward thrust it bodily out of the protected area, pushing it into the bookshelves. I felt the pressure on the ward increase, and turned to watch the shade struggle and claw at the ward, but it couldn't force its way to me. Only if I left the circle, or if someone smudged the circle of salt, would the enchantment break.

I sat for a moment, and tried to decide what to do at this point. It couldn't get to me in the circle. Running out into the room would break the enchantment, and leave the shade free to continue guarding the book. Taking the book with me, and reading it out in the main room, was out of the question, I had no way to translate the book. Dispelling the shade would be the best solution. The question was how.

My thoughts were interrupted as the pressure on the ward increased from an itch to painful. The creature, mad to return to the book, had started throwing its entire being at the ward, which had begun to weaken. I edged towards the door, wishing Zhirk was here. The ward flared from yellowish to pink as the creature tore ferociously at it. I hoped I was fast enough. I stabbed my hand through the ward and pushed the door open. I dove out, and into the hall, and heard a frustrated growl close behind me. I looked back, and watched as the darkness faded back to the book. Shaken by the nearness of the thing, I left Cobb's demesne and returned to the real world. I needed to talk to people smarter than me about this. It was time to talk to Larry about dispelling that shade.

I walked back into town, eventually calling Larry to pick me up after I'd found a convenience store and borrowed their phone. Once back at his place, he showed me how to set the circle around the book, the incantations, and the finish.

"You sure you want to do that alone, Short Stuff? I'd be more than glad to help you, and shades can be pretty tough to handle alone, even when you know what you're doing."

"You saying that I don't, Larry?" I asked him, throwing him a quizzical look.

He held up his hands in mock-surrender. "Okay, okay, I won't go with you. Just please be careful, Fernie. I want you around to watch your niece or nephew grow up."

I got the items I needed, and went back to the Underhill entrance.

Cobb was waiting for me again at the entrance and, when he saw what I had in the backpack this time, his eyebrows went up and said, "No, this will not be allowed."

"What won't be allowed?" I asked him.

He gestured at my backpack. "This, all of your items in there will not be allowed. I will not have you casting human spells in my house."

What. The. Hell? I couldn't figure the reason for this. There was a deadly creature in *his* library, and now, of all times, he decides to pull rank and "disallow" spell casting? I'd already done it once with the circle.

"I already did that, Cobb, and I plan on doing it again to get rid of that shade."

Cobb glared daggers at me. "You did so without my express permission, and you polluted my library with your magicks! It will take weeks to purify the library to rid it of your human stink! This is my home, Ms. Fatelli, and you work for me, not the other way around. You owe me the service, and *you* will perform it the way I see fit."

I got mad, no build up at all. Just incandescent fuckity-mad. He'd hit every attitude button dead-on.

"You want it done? I'll do it, but I don't have to do it your way. I just have to get the service done, and fuck-all if it isn't the way you want it. Now either let me back there, or call the judge and explain to him why I'm not finishing your so-fucking-precious-gods-damned service!"

He looked at me like one would look at a particularly disgusting piece of trash. I started to wind right up again, but he held up a hand. The hate felt like a wave rolling off him. For a moment, it was so palpable that I felt slapped in the face. Just as fast as it was there, it was gone again.

Cobb pressed a hand over his chest just below this throat. "I, apologize. This is a very difficult time. I have forgotten my manners. You are correct. I will allow the spell. This one spell, mind you. This one, and no others. I will assist, and I will be part of the spell, start to finish."

The smell of hate faded, but didn't disappear. Something about all this was starting to not add up in my mind. I just wasn't sure what it was.

But, if he was going to be there for the spell, that was fine by me; in fact, better than fine. I got to keep my eye on him and, if he pulled anything devious, it would be where I had a chance to spot it before I got surprised.

10

I T TOOK US A FEW MINUTES TO GET SET UP. Cobb was all over
everything. The book was placed unopened on top of the desk
the circle of protection was drawn around. Cobb finished the salt
circle, drew the chalk one about a hand span's width outside it,
then scrawled marks inside the ring the two circles made. I set
the candles — one black, one white — on the north and south
axis of the circle.

I lit the white one, left the black one unlit, and started the
chant. It was in Latin, so I have no idea what I was saying, but I
have a good memory. Larry had made me memorize the spell
before he let me pack off back here. As the chant built, the shade
whispered from between the pages of the book and solidified
inside the circle. It tore at the barrier, but with the reinforcements
from the chalk and the symbols, the shade couldn't escape.

As I got to the midway point of the spell, the shade began frantically throwing itself against the walls of the barrier, pieces breaking off of the apparition and dissipating like smoke. The barrier flared white and black as the shade attacked it. A sudden flare appeared to one side of our protection circle. Cobb swore as we saw a second shade, this one outside the circle, flicker into view momentarily, then disappear into the shelves. I did not falter, but two shades were a surprise. Our situation had changed.

If I had done this alone, I'd have been up to my eyeballs in trouble. As it was, both Cobb and I were in trouble, but only about chest high, instead of in over our heads. I kept the chant up. The trapped shade began unraveling faster, pieces drifting away like smoke. The other shade, whom the spell was also affecting, I could see it unraveling as it redoubled its efforts to breach our protective circle. Unexpectedly, its efforts were starting to show some effect.

There was an area on the chalk outer circle that looked like it was being erased by a strong wind. The shade had been worrying that point consistently, and the circle was weakening. You can fight a shade and come out on top, if you're prepared to do it, but my experience made me think, even if you were prepared, you're still going to get hurt badly beating one.

"Do not stop the chant," Cobb growled at me. As if I would without him telling me.

We both watched the second shade attack the barrier again.

"I can deal with this. Just make sure you finish that chant or we're fighting both of these creatures, not just the one."

Arrogant asshat elf. Telling me what to do after I'd gotten how to do it from an expert.

I heard him start up a chant of his own, and I kept at mine. The shade in the circle was weakening rapidly, and would soon be gone, but I almost faltered when Cobb cursed in fae, and I felt the outer barrier go down. One thing about spells like the one I was casting: they take time; they take time because you have to get the pacing right so that the magick works effectively. Too fast, and it starts expending itself before you have it focused. Too slow, and it doesn't build up properly and begins to dissipate before you're finished. So I had to keep exact cadence, or the spell would unravel.

Out of the corner of my eye, I saw Cobb step to his left away from the circle. He turned from me like he was facing something. It had to be the second shade. What my spell was doing to the trapped shade, it was also doing to the one Cobb was confronting. Hopefully weakening it and hurting it. Another step took Cobb out of my line of sight.

As I chanted, I caught quick glimpses of the fight. Although I couldn't afford to be distracted, I couldn't help but watch as Cobb stepped back into the edge of my view, braced and threw himself at the smoke, mumbling some chant as he did. I saw the shade freeze for a moment, then Cobb slashed a silver sword through the darkness, eliciting a scream that I couldn't hear, but surely felt: blind, hungry rage. The smell from Cobb was mostly anger, but also something else. *Magick.* He'd placed spells on himself. Cobb and the shade disappeared back out of my view, which was worse. Now I didn't know who was winning the fight.

I finished the chant with the proper flourish, and the last of the trapped shade sublimated away. I heard a muttered curse and a thud as something solid hit the floor. I turned and dropped to a half-crouch, ready to dodge if the shade came at me. I saw Cobb was on his knees, dripping blood from deep cuts all over him. He coughed wetly as I scrambled over to him and looked for the shade.

Cobb caught my look and mumbled, "Don' worry, it's … gone back to where it was called from …" and he fell forward, smacking the floor and not moving, his chest rising and falling with each wheezing breath. I tried to drag him out into the main room, and failed. Even with me being fit and healthy, I couldn't move him one measly centimeter. He felt like a solid two hundred kilograms or more.

I stepped into the main room and yelled for assistance. Two fae, who were on guard in the hall, came running and helped bandage the worst of Cobb's wounds. Then the two of them joined hands to make a fireman's carry. They lifted Cobb off the ground as if he weighed nothing, moving him out into the hall and down to another phone booth. I followed, and found myself back in the long hallway that led to the hexagonal infirmary/ bedroom.

The two fae pressed Cobb down on the bed gently, removed their hands and filed out of the room, pausing just long enough to make certain I exited the room ahead of them.

"Will he be all right?"

I felt a twinge of concern. The guy did, after all, put his butt on the line with me. That should count for something, even if he thought human magick was unclean. I couldn't let stupid prejudices get in the way; Zhirk would have been disappointed. It was an odd coincidence having a second shade hiding in the room, which just might have been guarding a second book, or waiting for a certain spellcaster to come back. I shook my head and threw the thought away. Cobb, Judge Kaddus, and their "feud" — whatever it was — had things so swirled up that I was getting overly paranoid.

I walked back to the library and looked at the book in the circle. It had been scorched, with several pages now having curled and blackened edges. I guess someone didn't want the book read by prying eyes like mine.

For the next week, while Cobb recovered from his wounds, I went over the books, reading legends from the dim past, and observations, both recent and ancient. Speculation upon speculation. I have to admit, the fae have a love of forming opinions and recording them in the most long-winded, obscure, and sideways manner. I had to take breaks every ten to twenty minutes to keep my head from aching with frustration as the writers slowly approached their subject, couching everything in flowery phrases and foggy passages. I suppose if you wanted to say that the author wanted to hide the real information in all that obscure language, and make it frustrating to read by the layman, I'd agree with you. I was certainly reinforcing that opinion with every book I read that fae had dictated or copied.

At the end of each day, Larry, Fawn, and I would go over to the police gym to do self-defense with Fawn and her team, and push weights to decompress. Then it was over to Larry and Fawn's to put all our heads together and see what we had.

After four weeks of research, reading, referencing, and more reading, we got what we thought was the best picture about dragons and their magick:

1. Dragons are very long-lived, possibly immortal, unless felled by illness or violence.

2. Dragons are highly intelligent and, coupling this with their lifespan, they could very well be way past human genius on the meter.

3. Dragons are easy to damage, but extremely hard to kill. This is because of their ability to hide the essence of their existence concentrated somewhere in their bodies. Unless you hit the right spot, you could theoretically blow them half to pieces, and they'd grow back in a matter of moments — which I'm sure is very painful, and would give the dragon a reason for burning the author of such hurt to a little lump of charcoal. They have scales like lizards and, in large dragons, these get tough to penetrate. Bullets will do the job, but also garner the shooter a lot of unhealthy attention.

4. Dragons have many dangerous natural weapons. Don't laugh. Claws as big as your thigh in the really big dragons; teeth straight and needle-like and long as your forearm. And, yes, they breathe fire. Their mouths are set up like a natural combustion chamber. Three chemicals come together in the mouth: fuel, oxidizer, and one that gels. Mix together and whoosh! Napalm barbeque at two hundred yards.

5. Dragons are inherently magickal. They not only can concentrate their essence, but they can work spells. Two of the three dragon spells we cataloged were for body control, such as hardening of their scales, and giving their teeth and claws razor sharpness. The "fireball" magick is the scary one. The dragon works up a mouthful of two of the three chemicals, casts a squeezing and aiming spell on the material, and adds the third chemical. We found reports of thousand-yard shots of exploding dragon-fire in some of the personal accounts. There were a few modern records of Anolyn's fight with four Canadian CF-18 Hornets, resulting in a wounded, pissed-off dragon and four obliterated aircraft.

6. Dragons seem to prefer intelligent prey, and more than one ancient scholar speculated that this was because the dragon saw intelligence as a personal threat, and thus killed anything showing any problem-solving ability in its territory. Others thought it was just that dragons saw intelligent creatures as more sporting to hunt. And I was going to invade the territory of one of these things, find whatever it was we were supposed to be

looking for, all without becoming a burnt and crispy dragon snack.

7. Dragons are sensitive to magick and magickal weaponry. Such weapons and powers can kill them without having to strike their essence. This was the information out of the scorched book that I'd given to the Halifax police. Their forensic methods were able to pull legible writing from the burned pages. They'd copied each page faithfully in the language in which it was written, and I took the pages back to Cobb's library where the desk translated them for us.

8. Dragon magick is subject to different rules than fae magick and human magick. This meant that my magick might not be able to combat Anolyn's magick, unless we were able to find a way that wouldn't take him head-on. The plus side is that human magick affects, and is affected, by every other magick. It's kind of like human magick is the base, or origin, for the others. Just a guess on my part.

Basically, Dragon magick came from the dragon itself, so dragons had a big mess of magick to draw from. Their spells were both complex and extremely powerful.

The advantage is that dragon magick had all the advantages. I wondered how whoever fought him was supposed to beat that combination of power, size, and magick. The only way seemed to be by being sneakier, or getting lucky and stumbling onto something Anolyn overlooked when he made the barrier. Our research said that dragons used internal magick exclusively, meaning they never tried to make bargains with outsiders, nor did they borrow from the world itself. That bit about the magick might be something else we could use.

What bothered me was how the shades were placed on two books that both dealt with some specific dragon information, and could be used against dragons, if it was known.

"What if dragons can change form? I mean, you're already saying that their magick is mostly internal already. What if that's another skill they have?"

Larry and Fawn looked at each other.

Fawn finally asked, "Can you try and find some more books that have been warded? I think we can remove the shades, or whatever the ward is, if we can deal with it out here."

"I'm not sure, but I'll ask. Cobb was cut up pretty bad, and I haven't seen him since we banished the shades." Thinking for a moment brought a possible answer. "Cobb said that other fae had books I might be able to borrow."

Larry spoke up. "I'm going to make a magick finder. I wish I'd have thought of it sooner. I can set it up to show you if there's magick on an item, though that may mean you may get a lot of false alarms. I remember some of the fae I talked to made mention of having some books being preserved magickally."

"It beats having to open each book and see if I get attacked again. I can put up with false alarms," I told him.

"Okay, it will be a day or so. I'll see you then, Fernie."

"Okay, Larry. See you later."

I drove on back home, in a better mood than in a long time. We'd made some solid progress, identified some possibilities, and maybe got a device that would keep me from getting bit by magick.

I sure hoped so.

11

THE NEXT DAY, I drove back over to Fawn and Larry's after Larry called and said he wanted to have me test the new magick finder. Larry laid out four books, then handed me a pair of reading glasses with plain glass where the magnifying lenses normally were.

"Put 'em on and tell me what you see."

I did as he asked and looked at the four books.

"That one has a yellow glow." I pointed to the one on the end to my left.

"Good! That's one of mine I put a screamer on. Not a big piece of magick, but a loud one," he said with a grin. He rubbed his hands together. "That test worked, so why don't you go back to Cobb's and see if there are any texts that have some magick on them that didn't fry in your little shady fight."

I just about punched him for the bad pun.

I went back to the Underhill entrance and Cobb was there, waiting for me.

"How'd you know I'd be coming?" I asked him as I got out of my Saturn Vue and shouldered my backpack.

"I knew that it was time for something here, but I didn't know it would be you." Face unreadable, he just stated it blandly.

Fae. Cryptic as secret codes. I really didn't like that. Magick makes all sorts of wild coincidences possible, and with Cobb being here at the exact time I should be showing up to go back to Underhill …? I didn't think it was much of a coincidence. The three choices I had were: a) he had me followed, b) he got lucky, or c) something got him here. I was betting it was that last choice.

Now I really didn't want to go back to Underhill. Things got messy every time magick began throwing out coincidences and portents. It hadn't been up to now, so it made me wonder why the sudden coincidence? I hadn't done anything, except get Larry to make the glasses, which suddenly made a little more sense as I thought about it. Cobb just watched me as I stood there trying to puzzle out something that was bothering me.

"Hey, Cobb, you believe in coincidence? Please say 'yes'," I told him. "I need a good laugh right now, and that would do it for me."

He frowned as if he was trying to puzzle it out, but after a few moments he gave up and moved to lead me back to Underhill without giving me a yes or no.

"Any chance you'll let me take a few books back to my world for reference? It would help me a lot."

He frowned at me and said with a touch of sarcasm, "I know you remember. You can't read the texts without the desk to read them on. Cease this lying and ask me straight out what you want. It will save us both time, unless you want me to say 'no' now, and we can forget about whatever it is you are lying to me about."

Directness from a fae. Well, wow.

"I want the books so I can have them checked to see if others have shades on them or some kind of magickal trap. I want to do it out here where people I know have better skills than I do, and can maybe not have the book blow up in my face, or get another shade trying to do me fatally, like our last little dispelling did."

That was Cobb, getting me wound up again. How one question can do that, I don't know, but I was upset with him.

"Besides, how the hell did those books get in a library like yours without a spell caster such as yourself knowing about the damn things?"

"Spell caster such as myself? Great gods woman, that thing surprised me as badly as it did you! I had no knowledge of it, or the other, until you brought it to my attention!"

"Why is that?" I shouted angrily back. "Don't you even know ..." and I saw pain in his eyes. It was a kind of pain that just is, and cannot be faked. He didn't know. He really didn't know about the shades.

He started to speak, then changed his mind and ushered me into Underhill. We moved at a speed and recklessness that he had never used before and, in mere seconds, we were inside his halls.

This display of recklessness and high emotion coming from Cobb had me more than a little worried. Was this going to be another maneuver on his part to get me to hand off the service? He turned and walked off a short distance and stood, as if he was contemplating something. The tension in the air almost smothered me with a smell like burning paper. He straightened and the smell spiked. Then it evaporated off like it never existed.

"My apology, Ms. Fatelli, for being so abrupt. Continue your service. You may take the books you choose back to your world."

I could smell a desperate anger, like burning pine, and a hint of lemon, like ... desire? The scent was distracting, and I almost missed what he said next.

"You only get to keep them for one day, then they must be back in the library." He quirked a smile. "You can always take them out the next day, but they will be back in the library by sundown on your world."

He turned towards me and I smelled something dry and dusty like chalk. He'd walled himself up emotionally. That saddened me for some reason, and then I got angry with myself and shook the mood off. The thought came that, if I could smell their emotions, they might be able to smell mine. If so, I was giving away information that he could use to manipulate me. I pulled a page from Cobb's playbook, and focused mentally on a blank chalkboard. After a few deep breaths, things felt a lot more neutral.

I glanced over at Cobb for a moment before I answered. "Deal. We'll try it for a few days, but I may need a book longer than that."

"Only for the day, Ms. Fatelli. And only in your possession. That is the deal."

He walked off and was gone before I could get a word in to argue. I wondered if a skill like that could be learned. I snarled irritably, put the glasses on, and went into the library.

The glasses worked all right. Larry was right too. *Everything* in the library had magick on it. But on the books, the magick was subtly diferent. I could pick faint shades of difference. I mean, it looked all pale yellow, but some of the yellow graded more towards ivory, and the shelves glowed with a richer, deep, almost saffron yellow.

I took a full shelf of twelve books and laid them on the floor, much like Larry did to show me how the glasses worked. With the glasses on, I looked down at them. They all glowed, but one book at the left of the line seemed to glow oddly compared to the others. I chose that one, and two others that seemed a different hue than the background magick of Underhill. Whether or not it meant anything, I'd figure out when I got them to Fawn. I think that "only in your possession" meant that I couldn't leave them out of sight, which was fine by me. If the fae want to parse sentences, I can do it, too. Besides, I wanted to see how they, meaning Fawn's hired wizards, would study these books. It was the perfect excuse to tag along.

I left Underhill and drove back to Halifax to meet Fawn at the police station. It was way earlier than anyone expected, so I had to wait for about three hours with the books before they could set up a room the way the wizards wanted it.

I walked into one of the interrogation rooms. Iron mesh hung on all the walls. Each wizard in the room had a machete plated with silver, like mine, hanging from their belts. Two large tables were pushed together with a piece of black paper covering them. On the paper was drawn a salt circle, and then a chalk one with the protective sigils in between the two, just as I had done.

One book was placed in the center of this circle, and the other two were, at my insistence, placed in a second small circle in one corner away from the main circle. The wizards then began a low, slow chant. From the few words I caught, and Fawn later confirmed, they were trying to slow the magick down, and carefully unravel it whole from the book, so it could be understood. As they got further into the spell, I put the glasses back on to better see what was happening.

The spell or magick was slowly coalescing above the book, which had started to suddenly get a worn, tired look, as if years of time had finally started to wear it away. As the spell extraction progressed, the book aged before our eyes. There was a magickal echo of what the book had been, and what it was becoming, as the magick was pulled away from it. Fawn called a stop before the magick was completely pulled from the book, and it snapped back into place like a rubber band. The book looked clean and well-cared for once more.

The wizards looked at the other two books. I took off the glasses and used my mage sight. The top book of the two seemed to have a slightly whiter glow to it than the other one, and the wizards chose that one next to try and tease apart. The circles were checked before the book was placed. Once the three wizards were satisfied, they began the chanting again. My mage sight was more sensitive than the glasses, so I left it up, and watched as the whitish magick was slowly teased out from the book.

In Japan, white is the color of death, I once read, and, looking at the whitish fog of magick above the book, I had to agree with that idea. If ever a spell looked lethal, it was this one. The white color pulsed as if it was pulling things in, bleaching everything it touched into a dry brittle color that would powder away into nothing.

The wizards also saw this white magick, and their cadence slowed. They took extra effort in pronouncing each word with more clarity and care — this from a trio of already careful wizards. This was one spell I instinctively never wanted to see activated. After about forty minutes of careful teasing of the spell, it was finally free of the book. More careful chanting and mystical tests revealed what the spell was supposed to do. Once the intent of the magick was known, the wizards aggressively unraveled it. I understood, as everyone in the room did, that the spell would have aged the opener of the book to powder. Under their assault, the spell pulsed a brittle white and faded. Score one for the good guys.

The last book was like the first one, a spell to keep the book intact and clean. So, of the three, I believed the one with the aging spell on it was the one we wanted to look at as soon as possible. I thanked the wizards, gave Fawn a sisterly hug, and went back over to the entrance to Underhill, where Cobb was waiting to escort me to his library. Once back in the library, I placed the book on the desk and began to study the pages inside.

After finishing the book, I could add two more pieces of information to our list about dragons:

9. Dragons have inherent shape-shifting ability, being able to mimic anything from a large dog to another dragon. They could never go bigger than they are, but they could obviously go quite a bit smaller. Plus, while shifted, they were as vulnerable to damage of any kind as the creature they mimicked. Which meant to me that dragons didn't shift unless there was a real reason to do so. That reason was so that they could cast external spells. Dragons were magickal in their own body, so magick could not be cast from them. A dragon had to change shape to make a casting like the one Anolyn did. Something really to keep in mind.

The last one really was an extension on our fact number 6:

6a. Dragons prefer magickal, intelligent prey. Like certain other creatures, dragons can absorb the internal magick that their prey holds, and add it to their own, thus increasing their own reserve of magick power. This is why dragons are known to actively hunt intelligent prey, because of the magick inherent in most of them. I had a huge mass of magick attached to me from Ahiah. That would be a mother lode for a dragon. This was definitely not something that was fun to know. Don't get me wrong: I'm really, really glad I knew it; I just didn't like that I had to know it.

The rest of the week was spent bringing books to the police station, and those three wizards, bless them, never complained about the job at all. Fawn told me later that it was a break from their normal routine, and they had really gotten into the work. I wasn't sure what I could do to thank them properly, but Fawn smiled and told me not to worry about that until after I'd gotten The Way open.

Which brought up the next order of business: how the heck to open The Way in the first place. Anolyn had made the barrier not so much impregnable, as simply absolute death to cross. You could go through it any time you wanted; it's just that you would be dead when you got through it, regardless of what you went through in. Anolyn had set the barrier to kill anything that wasn't the rock the barrier rested on. That was why the clamshell rock boat had worked; it was made of the same rock the spell was anchored on.

The clamshell rock boat, and the knowledge of its last resting place, were lost to us, so that meant starting from scratch. I really don't like reinventing anything, especially when it has a chance to so seriously kill me if I screw it up. The next thing to do would be to look at the barrier.

I drove to the coast town of Pictou, which had been at one time the Nova Scotia terminus for the ferry that ran between it and Wood Islands on Prince Edward Island before it had been walled in by Anolyn. The barrier could be seen, a whitish curtain that went up and arced back over the island, creating an irregular dome over the whole of Prince Edward Island. Nothing went in alive. Nothing came out alive. It got me to wondering: why would a creature like Anolyn want such protection?

I thought about that for a moment and threw it away. My job was to re-open The Anolyn Way and, beyond that, I had no reason to think of anything else. If I got this done, and if I lived, then I had things to think about.

That's me: just little sweet sunshine.

12

THINGS WERE PROGRESSING QUITE WELL, considering my "real" job as a "sting" provider and a private investigator of some ill repute. My normal jobs, though, tended to be quiet, up to a point, then all too often all hell would bust out. I'm sure it's the magick Fawn and I both carry. Zhirk had pointed out that both of us had all this magick, and that magick itself saw that as a kind of imbalance, so to "balance" things, weird stuff kept happening around us. It still brought an ache to my chest knowing he was gone. I really wished he was around to help me with all the "weird".

Anyway, I really hated that explanation about magick and coincidence, but it made sense. I had two other acquaintances in the business, and neither of those two women ever had to contend with all the weird coincidences that went on in my jobs.

You'd think that, with my kind of reputation, I'd have gone broke long ago, because people generally are scared off by the weird and unusual. Not the case with me. I always had a backlog of better-off-than-average clients. Blame that on the magick too, I guess.

I was driving back to Halifax when the attack happened. It was so fast and powerful that I didn't recognize it as an attack until it was all over and I had a moment or two to think. I was on a gentle curve when a deer flashed in front of me. I instinctively swerved the car to miss the deer. I think that's what likely saved my life. A blow to the Saturn lifted it off the road and threw it into some pine trees. I felt a cold draft hit me and a tearing sound came from behind the driver's seat somewhere. I had my seat belt on, so I wasn't thrown from the wreckage, but I ended up being tossed about like a rag doll as the car fell through the trees, hit the ground, and rolled next to a stream.

My half of the Saturn hit a rock and came to a sudden rest. I sat in the car for a long time; I'm not sure just how long. Something told me that I needed to stay absolutely still and, for a wonder, I actually listened to my instinct. Fear helped a lot. You don't know what you can do until something scares you bad enough, or threatens you enough, that you act. My act was to play dead.

When my fear finally subsided, I slowly pulled myself out of the wreckage, alert for any sound that meant my attacker was nearby. When nothing happened, and the local birds began calling, I relaxed and looked the Saturn over before walking to the road. The rear half of the car had been torn off by something big, and was back up the hill a ways. The front end looked like a ball that something chewed up and spit out. In all that metallic carnage, I did not sustain a single scratch. I had a hell of a lot of bruises, though, and ached all over.

It was going to be a long, uncomfortable walk back to Pictou. I needed to call Fawn and Larry, and ask them if they could pick me up at the bus station in Halifax the next day. Luckily, after about ten minutes of walking, a patrol car spotted me and stopped. The officer took my name and drove me back to the crash. Once we got back to the site, he looked it over and, while he took my statement, we waited for the wrecker to come and begin cleanup. Once the wrecker arrived, the officer drove me back to Pictou and dropped me off at the Northumberland Gate Motel near town.

I walked to the bus depot the next morning and, four hours later, I was in Halifax, where Fawn picked me up.

"Fernie, you okay?" she asked me as I tenderly settled into the passenger seat.

"I guess. I'm going to need a new car. Whatever hit my Saturn tore it in half."

I looked over at her, and she flicked her eyes between me and the road as she drove. I must have looked a mess. I pulled the sunshade down, and opened the vanity mirror to take my first real look of the day at the damage. It took me a moment to recognize myself.

Last night, there had been no real visible bruises. Now, my face sported large yellowish-purple splotches on my chin, forehead, and cheek bones. The bruises didn't hurt, yet, but my face felt hot and the skin felt taut over the bruise.

"I have some bruises, but I don't have any broken bones, so that's something to be thankful for."

"I'll go with that," she told me, and I could hear some of the tension in her voice leak away.

I smiled at her and put a hand on her forearm. She smiled and relaxed a bit more, and we drove in a comfortable silence back to my office.

After Fawn dropped me off, and secured a promise from me to call her, I went to the small washroom, had a quick, cold shower and got a change of clothes. I had thought about The Anolyn Way for a good while on the trip back from Pictou. Using the ferry was not a possibility, but there was the bridge that used to lead to Prince Edward Island. It had been devastated by Anolyn as his first step in isolating the island. The dragon fire had destroyed the bridge, melting large sections of it all the way to bedrock. I wanted to go up to the site to look at where the remains of the bridge were and to test an idea that Cobb's books had given me.

I'd noticed that the book had changed when the magick had been teased out of it, but that some magick still remained — an echo of the book's original form, for lack of a better description. Maybe the bridge would have a similar echo that could be strengthened in some way to make a way passable onto the island. After my shower, I got dressed in good blue jeans and a dark blue t-shirt, then went back to the Troykin. Again, the opportunity to get some good points with Larry helped me immensely. Zik'k was available, and it wasn't past me to work on his guilt about abandoning me and rehiring him.

Larry was also a great source for a new ... well, a good used vehicle. Larry had an old Dodge Dakota pickup he used for hauling. I got to borrow it until I could find myself a new car. The thing was a garish lime-green that Larry had spray-painted on so it would stand out in a parking lot. He may be a smart man, but his sense of where he left a car wasn't part of the smart. He could lose a car by simply turning around, sometimes. The outrageous color made it easy to find.

"Why'd you brig meeb adlong for dhis trib, Mb Fatelli?" Zik'k asked me as we got in the pickup.

"Something attacked my Saturn, and would have killed me, if not for some blind luck. You're muscle in case something unpleasant shows its face."

"Bobdyguad," he said past his allergies, but I caught the spark of interest in his eye.

"Yeah, bodyguard."

"I cab do dhat." he said, and laid the seat all the way back, sliding as far as he could to get away from my magick.

I felt for him, but I felt for me more.

13

Zik'k and I headed west, towards the remains of the Confederation Bridge. It had been built between New Brunswick and Port Borden on the island. Twelve kilometers of melted concrete and steel. The bits of remaining concrete columns looked like broken, rotted teeth above the waters of the Northumberland Strait. Anolyn had done his best to make sure it could never be used again. I was hoping that his best hadn't.

Four hours later, Zik'k and I stood on the point where the bridge had once reached over the water towards the island to the northeast. I grabbed my backpack and walked over to the bridge. We searched until Zik'k found a piece of concrete that had been cracked loose from the bridge. He smashed a rock against the remains, broke off a fist-sized chunk, and put it in the pack. We then ascended the bridge to its ruined end, about twenty meters above the ground. Zik'k handed me the piece of cement and I scratched a circle with it on the roadway. It wasn't pretty, being lopsided, but it was a complete circle which was all that was needed at this point. I placed the cement on the southwest edge, inside the circle. Using a piece of charcoal, I drew a ring around the first ring, inscribing two runes on the northwest and southeast of the circle, roughly in line with the direction the bridge had extended.

I set up a slow chant, like the wizards at the police station used, trying to pull anything up that might still hold a resonance of the bridge. It was really slow work, and the sun had started to go down as the spell finally produced a result. A wispy, shadowy form could be seen, just barely, with my mage sight: an echo left of the magick. I chuckled softly as I realized that there would have been no echo to use if Anolyn hadn't destroyed the bridge with magick.

Because of that magick, there was an echo. Now all I had to do was stumble on a huge amount of luck, and maybe we had a method to get The Way open. I had a few thoughts that needed discussion with someone smarter than me. That meant talking with Larry. Truth be known, I was expecting something to try and attack again. That nothing had happened made me even a little more paranoid. Anticipation is always worse than the situation.

We got back to the pickup as the sun was setting, a glowing hemisphere of brilliant orange-red that painted the sky and clouds a bold orange and violet that about took my breath away. The beauty of the scene transfixed me. I stared for a moment, and caught a motion just on the edge of the sun, and that fear I felt came back. Zik'k had stiffened and peered towards the sun, as well. He'd felt it, too. He blinked, then turned abruptly towards me. His strong hands grabbed my arm as he pushed me towards the forest.

"Trees! Now! Run!"

He got no argument. He released my arm as I bolted for the pines as fast as I could go. I heard Zik'k bellow, heard the pickup door open and slam shut, then I heard the door open and close again. I didn't look back, but hit the trees and kept going in. I was scared almost witless by whatever was coming. A metallic tearing crash, and I heard someone's footsteps pounding along the earth. I saw a patch of dense brush and dove straight in, not worrying about any thorns. I huddled deep in the brush, covering my mouth and nose with both hands as I desperately swallowed a scream. The footsteps pounded by, receding into the distance.

An inhuman scream came from back up the hill, and I heard more steps. The ground vibrated with each of them. I started to panic and shifted to dive deeper into the brush, then instinct kicked in. My body froze, like a rabbit trying not to be seen. The ominous, heavy steps were accompanied by a harsh snuffling sound. A moment later, a vicious roar almost made me bolt from cover, but the terrified need to freeze overrode it. I stayed put, just barely. My heart was beating so fast I felt light-headed. Terror choked my throat. The creature roared again and then took flight with a heavy, wet, flapping sound. As the noise faded, so did my fear, and, after a few minutes, I finally dared move out of the bushes, remembering that I had come with someone. Zik'k was still somewhere in the woods.

Guessing that the footsteps were his, I tried to determine the direction that he had run. I turned to my right, and began walking. The darkening sky forced me to stop after a few minutes. I could barely see and, with the cloud cover thickening, there would soon be no stars to follow. The sky had gone overcast while the creature was hunting us, so the smart thing to do was stop moving and wait for sunrise. Hopefully, things would look better in the morning. I just had to spend a cold night. Out here. In the dark. With something that wants to kill me. Life's a bitch.

Miserable was a good word. On second thought, "miserable" just scratches the surface. I started shivering in the sub-zero weather around three o'clock, and spent the rest of the night doing my best to stay warm. I didn't dare light a fire, fearful that the creature was still around. A light at night would draw it from miles away. So I hid in the wet brush, shivered, and silently cursed the whole situation.

About four in the morning, a rustle nearby had me wide awake and frozen in terror. Had it come back? A minute dragged by like it was hours. Whatever this thing was, it didn't generate the gut-wrenching fear the monster did. This was something else. The next-to-last thing I wanted to meet in the woods was one of the black bears that populated the area. They may be a "small" bear, but they're still bigger than me. Slowly, quietly, climbing up the first tree I could, I went as high into it as the branches would support.

Perching precariously in the upper branches was anything but fun. If it was a bear, hopefully all it would do is sniff and move on. Zik'k was still out there somewhere, hopefully not having as bad a night as I.

"Ms. Fatelli," came the harsh whisper from below me. "Come on down." The harsh whisper nearly startled me out of the tree.

"Zik'k, dammit, you scared the hell out of me just now," I answered back with an angry whisper of my own.

"Don't worry, hell's not looking for us, and it scared the bears, too. I only saw one big bear and one little one together," he stage-whispered back.

I climbed back down slowly. Going up a pine tree in the dark is pretty easy. Climbing back down, even in the light, not so easy. It took a slow ten minutes to climb back down thirty feet and join Zik'k at the base of the pine. He gave me the short version of his night.

"Thing scared the hell out of me. I couldn't stobp rubnning abfter it gobt so clobse. All thabt mabbttered was gettin' away frub da ting ... WAACHOO! ... Ub Mb Fabtelbi, Iba goad ober her abnd tabe a nab. Kibk meh ib you hear subding."

He walked a short distance away and curled up next to a large pine, and actually drew the needles up and around him like a small nest, and passed out after another sneeze. I stayed awake the rest of the way-too-early morning, making certain I stayed a good thirty feet away, so he wouldn't start sneezing. Once the sun started peeking over the horizon, I tapped Zik'k awake. The sky had cleared, making it easy to figure out direction. We trekked north, and found the road after about a ten-minute walk. Orienting on the bridge, which was the tallest thing that jutted out over the water, gave us the direction to the pickup. When we got back to where I'd parked it, what we found looked like it had been chewed up and spit out. For all we knew, it might have been. Larry was going to chew me out for trashing his truck.

It took us another hour to walk into town. I went over to the first public telephone I could find and dialed Fawn. She answered on the second ring.

"Hello?"

"Hi, Amazon, it's me. Can you pick me up at the bus station tomorrow? Something messed up Larry's pickup, and the bus doesn't run until tomorrow morning."

"Oh, gods, Fernie. Again? Sure, I can ask Larry to get you. Same time as yesterday?"

"Yes," I said and hung up before my shakes got real bad. Now that I felt safe, my body was reacting to the dump of adrenaline wearing off.

We managed to book two rooms. Luckily, the manager was one of those folks that didn't care what you were, so long as you paid for the room and didn't try to trash it.

We caught the bus the next morning, and Zik'k rode in the back so that he wouldn't go into paroxysms of sneezing while we rode back to Halifax. Larry met us at the depot in a little Honda Civic, and together we drove a suffering Zik'k back to his home, and then Larry and I went back to the house.

"So what is this thing that trashed your Saturn and my Dakota in the last four days?" Larry asked me as he got me a cup of coffee.

I winced as I heard a slight emphasis when he said "my Dakota". He was upset, but thankfully didn't chew me out. I shrugged and shook my head.

"No idea. All I know is that it has wings, and that it scares the hell out of me. It's like it spreads fear just by being there. You should have asked Zik'k when you had the chance; he was the one who kept me from getting killed. He told me to run, and then drew its attention away." I shuddered. "I don't know how he handled being so close to that thing."

"Troykin have got that touch of outsider to them. They can handle magick a lot better than most people realize. If he took off running, like you said, then it was a very nasty piece of work sent after you. You're right, I should talk to him." He looked at me and favored me with his lopsided smile. "I just couldn't help but feel sorry for him with the two of us in the car. Thank god you left the windows open, otherwise he'd have never got his head out in time."

I winced at remembering Zik'k, hanging half out the window and trying to get rid of last night's meal while we drove. Yeah, I had to feel for the guy too.

This time, I spent a small fortune getting a surplus Hummer. It had the removable roof and canvas replacements, which I threw in the back. The stand-up hatch was in place and, although the swivel had been pulled, a little work at a friend's body shop would fix it so someone could stand up and fire a weapon, if need be. I hoped that never happened, but, considering the last two cars, I wasn't taking any bets against it.

I went back over to the Troykin section of Dayning again and found Zik'k.

"Hey, Ms. Fatelli." He smiled, and walked over to the Hummer. "Needin' body guarding again?"

"Not this time," I replied. "I want to ask you about that creature that trashed the pickup. I didn't earlier, and I want to know more about it."

"That thing? I've never seen anything like it. I sure as hell don't want to. It tore your car apart like tissue paper. The only reason it didn't catch me, I think, is that it's pretty stupid. It tore the car into tiny chunks, and the fear it generated kept me running for an hour at least." Zik'k got a serious look on his face. "That thing was definitely an outsider, I could feel it in my blood. I think it could feel me too, but once it lost sight of me ib couldn't find me abgain, so Ib dobn't thibnk itb canb smellb anyone. Ib neebds to seeb wab ibt's chabsing." His allergies were kicking into gear.

I moved downwind and a few steps away, hoping it would lessen his allergy.

"Well, the biggest question is what it looks like. Maybe Larry and I can put our heads together and figure out what it is, so we can do something about it next time it shows."

"I hobe you can, I do not want to fabce itb at all, but if I hab to, I want sombething ob my sibe." He sneezed and stepped back a ways to clear the zone of magick that was around me. "That's better," he sighed. "What it looked like was a flying zombie. Flesh was falling off of it, and its wings looked like large flaps of wet skin. I don't remember much more. I was too busy running away to care."

That sounded pretty descriptive to me. I thought we might be able to figure out what it was with that information. I know I never wanted to face it straight up. Now the thing I needed to figure out was how feasible my idea was.

14

"YOU WANT THE GOOD NEWS or the bad news first, Fernie?" Larry asked me after I'd outlined my idea.

"Just skip the 'good news, bad news' shtick and spell it out."

Larry gave me an irritated look, then sighed and explained it to me. "First off, it's a good idea. Sympathetic magick makes things like making the tunnel along the bridge route feasible; the downside is the huge amount of magick needed to do it. You cast that spell, and everything within fifty kilometers will know something big is happening. Anolyn would be certain to know where it was happening. You couldn't hide that." Larry plowed on before I could break in. "That doesn't mean it can't be done. We may be able to do the spell a little at a time and, with some manual labor, we could do the job."

"But what about that creature? Both times I was up along the strait, it came right at me. You think Anolyn knows somehow about The Way maybe re-opening?"

Fawn snorted, "How could that overgrown lizard know anything? He's kept that island isolated, and the curtain is death to anything trying to cross … wait … you said that thing Zik'k saw looked like a flying zombie?"

"Yeah, that's how he described it: a flying zombie," I replied.

"Okay, assume he knows something is going on, and sent a dead thing through the barrier."

"Not so fast," Larry said quickly. "That barrier destroys anything going through it, and zombies would de-animate when they hit the barrier, so it has to be something someone conjured up on this side of the barrier."

"Or," said Fawn, "maybe Anolyn has a secret way through his barrier?"

Larry stopped and stared at his wife. "Fawn, baby, I think you may have something there. Trouble is, that barrier is huge, and finding the hole in it would be like a search in a haystack for a wooden needle. We could spend years looking." He got up and started pacing as he thought about the problem. "I don't think the service is supposed to take years. Anyhow, we need a better answer. Even if we found Anolyn's secret way, he'd have that guarded. Best thing to do is make our own," Larry finished.

"So back to the question, how do we do that?" I asked grumpily. "I mean the shortest distance is the bridge, and making a walkway would re-open The Way the quickest. And making it, and the people on it, invisible would keep them from being discovered easily. It's the best all-round solution."

I finished speaking and, in that moment of quiet, we all heard a heavy, wet flapping sound. I just about crawled out of my skin, I was so very frightened. Larry and Fawn looked at me oddly, and then, a moment later, both of them felt the fear. Larry grabbed Fawn and dashed into his work room. I followed hot on their heels.

Larry got Fawn into a silver circle that he used for his experiments, and muttered a quick activating spell. I felt the spell go up just as the front door was ripped loose from the frame. That same unearthly roar that I'd heard before blasted through the house. I dropped to my knees in terror as the thing battered at the wards protecting the room. The sound seemed to press in upon us physically. Then there was a pulse of light, and we felt heat waft over us. A scream came from the front room. The terror eased slightly, as pain entered its voice. There was a second voice, one I recognized: Cobb. The elf was somehow on Larry's doorstep. I heard him chant harshly as another waft of heat and light sprang to life with a muffled roar in the front room, eliciting another bark of pain from the creature. There was a heavy, wet flapping, and silence fell around us. I heard a footstep crunch some glass, I think.

"Ms. Fatelli? Is anyone here?"

Cobb's voice. I started to call out, but Larry grabbed my arm. Cobb had shown up here? He was pale and shaking.

"Hang on, Fernie," Larry whispered. "We don't know. It could be a trick. Wait."

We heard a shuffling in the front room, and then the steps became louder. Cobb stepped into the warded doorway of the work room. He started at seeing us huddled against the far wall. Cobb brought his hands up, placing them on the barrier, like he was testing its strength. Larry raised his hands and began a measured chant, reinforcing the barrier as he watched Cobb. The elf lowered his hands and waited. Larry relaxed as he got a good look, and lowered his hands to his side. After a quick second spell to spot illusions, he dropped the barrier. Cobb started forward, a half-smile on his face, only to stop abruptly after two steps. The half-smile died. His features once more returned to a careful neutrality, and then he pulled up short and straightened, becoming once again the tall, odd fae.

"I came, Ms. Fatelli, to determine your progress on re-opening The Way." He seemed oddly unaffected by the fight with the creature.

I responded in a similar calm manner, surprised that my voice didn't waver as the adrenalin dump still surged through me. "I think we may have an idea, but it still needs the details hammered out," I said to him.

Larry added quickly, "Thanks for driving that creature away. How'd you do it? That fear it exuded left me barely able to think."

"Fae are privy to some powers more effective than yours against such a creature," Cobb said haughtily, and made a dismissive motion with his hand.

"Yes, I understand that, sir," said Larry. "But if you could tell me, I'd like to at least try. Fernie, er, Ms. Fatelli, has been attacked twice before by that creature — or one like it."

"I said, Mr. Potter, that my magick is more effective against it. Your type of magick would at best create a stalemate. There is no more to discuss," and he made that dismissing hand gesture again.

Larry looked at Cobb for a moment, and let the conversation go, though he clearly wasn't satisfied with Cobb's answer.

Cobb walked over to me as the last of the spell dissipated. "Ms. Fatelli, I would like to know what this solution you hinted at consists of."

I looked at him, and decided just to be ornery. "When we get the details figured out, you'll be the first to know, I promise you."

I turned to look at Fawn. She was watching both Cobb and I with that "cop look". She had sensed something, and was looking for clues to what it was. Cobb noticed her attention, and his whole demeanor changed. He stood straighter, and a haughty sneer formed on his face.

"I do not care for human promises; I care about The Way being re-opened, Ms. Fatelli. That is your service. And that is all I care about." The words grated out at odds with his bearing.

What was he mad about? I'd think the fact that we actually had an idea might have made him happy, yet here he was berating me because of something, and I had no clue what it was.

"Thank you very much for showing up to yell at me. Now, could you go back to Underhill and get out of my hair? I'm working on The Way. If it's not fast enough tough if you don't like it. I'm getting the job done; that's what the bottom line is."

We glared at each other for a few moments, and I caught Fawn smiling out of the corner of my eye.

I started to turn to snap at her, but Cobb snarled, "Ms. Fatelli, I expect to be kept abreast of developments. I expect a report first thing tomorrow morning."

He stepped out of the room and stalked to the front door. I started to go after him, but Fawn grabbed my arm and held me back.

I turned on her and pulled my arm free. "What the hell are you doing? I'm going to go rip his face off!"

"Ease up, Fernie," Fawn said, almost chuckling, but she grabbed my arm again. This time held on hard enough that I couldn't get free. "Oooh, has he got it bad," she said with a laugh.

"What are you talking about? Oh, I know, he's got an attitude that badly needs someone to smack it around the block a few times," I snarled at her.

"No, Fern, what I mean is that he's got a crush on you! I'd never believe it if I hadn't just seen it. A fae ... mooning over my sister."

I stared at her, slack-jawed. Cobb infatuated with me? What the hell for?

"You have got to be kidding me. That guy hates my guts. He backed me in a corner so I had to take the service, or he'd have made you and Larry do it!"

"I know, Shorty, I know," Fawn said soothingly. "You told us that already. But he is definitely after you, Fern. I think you ought to talk to him some more. Maybe you can get him to help with that plan of yours." My sister, the matchmaker.

"Don't even think it, Fawn. That guy is an arrogant prick that needs his ego shrunk seriously before I even think about something like that. And just where do you get off telling me that anyway? We just about got ourselves killed here, if not for that idiot —" and that brought me up short.

We did probably owe our lives to Cobb showing up. I kind of felt bad about the fight now, looking at it from that point, but what'd he expect us to do? Thank him? Yeah, that's exactly what he'd expected. And he got miffed when we didn't. I did owe him thanks, but it left a sour taste in my mouth. You don't expect thanks; you just enjoy it when you get it.

This was going to make working with him harder than ever. Now I had to do the job, and not lead him on in any way. Everything I did would be magnified according to what he thought I meant. Gods, what a stupid thing to happen. I just did my best to put it out of my mind, and started helping Fawn and Larry clean up the mess in the front room.

As soon as we finished, Larry cast a barrier to keep the cold and the unwanted visitors out until he could get a new door. I went back to my office to get some sleep before I went to see Cobb. I like my office, especially when I want to think. Home, well … it's too homey. I like the edgy feel of my office. And with what Fawn was hinting at, I really wanted to think.

15

I WENT TO UNDERHILL NEXT MORNING AT SUNRISE, and Cobb was waiting for me. He took me back to his territory in a sullen silence. Apparently, he was still angry with me about the conversation last night. Once he had gotten me to his place, and into the phone booth room, I stopped and waited until he turned to face me. He started to speak, but I started first.

"I know we should have said it last night, but everything was still too unsettled for any of us to think clearly, so I want to say thanks for helping us out with that creature."

Cobb looked at me, and I smelled satisfaction come from him like pine. "You are quite welcome, Ms. Fatelli. Now if you would please update me on your progress. I would be most interested as to what you have found so far," he said with a smile, and a slight bow to me.

Well, if he was going to be so accommodating, I suppose I could live with the situation until the job was done. "Thanks. Now let me start with what we found in the books ..."

For about fifteen minutes, I gave him a detailed outline of the data we found, and how the aging spell was found and counter-spelled by Fawn's on-staff wizards. He listened with apparent interest, even asking a few questions about the spell, and a little more on how it was extracted. I didn't know the details, but told him I'd ask Fawn about it, that she would ask the wizards and get back to me.

He leaned back against the wall he was standing next to, as I detailed the information for him, and crossed his arms. "Very interesting report, Ms. Fatelli," he said, when I finished. "Now, do you have any idea of the creature that attacked you?"

"None at all," I responded. The memory of the fear it generated around itself made me rub my arms for comfort. My missing little finger ached.

"Do you wish help in driving it away?" He said that in a peculiar way, as if there was something of a ritual in asking.

I looked sharply at him, saw the hunger in his eyes for a moment, and I went cold. Fawn had seen something, but she got it wrong. I could feel his eyes boring into me, almost willing me to say "yes", so that he could claim something he wanted — and he wanted it so very much. I could smell the need coming off of him like a thick wave of musk. How had he kept this consuming hunger under iron control before? Or was it something that was new? Something he had just discovered? Regardless, he wanted an answer now.

"I can manage the creature, I'm certain, and I have to finish the service you so neatly maneuvered me into. So, no, I do not wish any help in dealing with the creature," I told him.

He reacted with an enigmatic look, but accepted the answer with a quiet, stiff bow. I could smell the disappointment and frustration.

"Very well, Ms. Fatelli. I will leave you to your work. Please keep me accurately apprised of your progress," he said, with almost no inflection at all. His smell was like a faint whiff of dust. Dry and irritating in the nostrils, and without scent. Whatever he was feeling and thinking, he buried it deep suddenly.

"Yes, I shall do so," I said, and suddenly I wanted out of Underhill very badly.

The place now had the feel of a prison, rather than a place to visit. It also made me wonder if he could actually smell me the same way. If he had, I didn't remember noticing any reactions. Was he that controlled, or was it that I was a human in Underhill?

Cobb's smell changed again. Now it was like burnt hair and death. I caught a very faint whiff of rotting meat under the scents, and it caused me to think of Cobb as dangerous. I had thought him manipulative and petty, but not truly dangerous — not until I smelled him this time.

I kept myself firmly under control until I got back to my Hummer, then I threw it open and scrambled in and drove wildly away. Cobb had scared me at the end, and I needed time to sort out what had changed, to try to figure out why. I was going to take on a very dangerous spell soon, and that needed all the concentration I could give it. We had to be subtle, and the power of the spell would be anything but, if we didn't control it absolutely.

16

"IT ISN'T GOING TO WORK," LARRY GROWLED. He stood up by the table, wadded the papers in his hands, and then threw them at the wall of his work room. They splashed against it, scattered, and then drifted down like large white snowflakes. Larry muttered something unintelligible, and then walked around the table and started picking them up.

"Why not? We know how to do the spell. We've got the echo of what was there before, and we've got enough wizards signed on that we can do the work in shifts like you suggested. So why isn't it going to work?" I was honestly puzzled.

"Because no matter how slow we go with it, a spell that big is going to be noticed. We need a powerful spell to hide the effects, and I don't know of anyone here in Halifax that has any idea of how to quiet a spell with a spell. Hell, I don't know how and, until we can, there's no way I'm going to let anyone risk casting it."

I grimaced in frustration. We had a solution, but without a solution to keeping the spell quiet, we were no better off than when I first was forced into service. I didn't want to talk to Cobb about it, knowing he would offer help again, but I didn't want his help. There was a feeling there of knowing that accepting his help would come with incalculable expectations and consequences. I hated the first, and was worried what the second might be. I had resolved never to find out if it could be avoided.

Cobb had gone from irritating to downright scary over the last week, as we got the materials together. His demands for updates to the situation were now daily, and his eagerness was bordering on fanatical. He was like one of those crazed zealots. If it wasn't how he envisioned it, then it was excrement. More, I was thinking past the service, when I could get away, rather than focusing on surviving. That could be lethal, especially with the spell we were trying to cast. There had to be a way to silence the spell. There was, but it meant looking up something that had haunted me for years. I could try finding the entity of the Dark. Really, it was one of the last things I wanted to do in this lifetime. However, those things are precisely the things that find you when you least want them to.

I went over to where Anne Maystack resided. For a while, she stayed well hidden, fearing reprisals from those that her husband turned evidence against. Her husband, before he died exposing a smuggling ring on the airbase, had hired me and Zhirk to kidnap his wife and daughter, to keep them safe when all hell broke loose. We managed to do that, but it took calling the entity of Darkness, and borrowing some of its power for a while to do it. Once the ringleaders had been caught, and the smuggling operation dismantled, she was able to come out of hiding. But her daughter had made her own pact with the

Darkness, and she was angry and impetuous. She didn't think it through. The Darkness caught her in that bargain, and got itself a permanent slave.

I tried to find out the details after we'd stopped Ahiah, but the mother refused to talk to me then. She and her daughter disappeared for four months, until the mother resurfaced and bought a small house near Dayning. I'd heard through the professional grapevine that she'd hired an investigator to find her daughter, who was supposedly here in Dayning somewhere. The investigator found her, and mother and daughter were reunited. I'd heard the daughter had been changed by the Darkness, and not for the better. I wasn't sure what I'd find, but in lieu of calling the entity up, I wanted to talk with her.

Anne opened the door when I rang. Her eyes went flat and ugly when she saw me. This didn't seem all that promising.

"Mrs. Maystack," I started to say, but she interrupted me.

"I remember you. Leave, or I'll call the police." Her arms were folded across her chest, fists clenched. Anger rolled off her in waves. I took a deep breath, and tried to project calm.

"Mrs. Maystack," I said quietly. "I need to talk to Megan. Could you please tell me where she is?"

This made her even more hostile. "You don't need to talk to my daughter. You need to leave right now." She shut the door in my face and I heard her start talking loudly.

"Mrs. Maystack, please. I need to talk to Megan. It's very important." I paused. "I know of a way to get rid of the entity."

The door jerked open, and she was there, angry eyes flashing. "I'm listening. Explain to me how you're going to do that, to get rid of that darkness in her."

"I'll take it. I'll offer myself in trade to the entity to make it let her go."

I spoke the words and knew that there was no other way. The entity wanted its time on earth and Megan, the angry impetuous child she had been, was a perfect choice. It wanted me though, that had come through loud and clear when we'd bargained. It had always been angling for more. I wondered if it was the magick that our parents had cast on Fawn and I. I was thinking that the creature wanted me the last time because it thought it could tap that magick. Why, I didn't know — and probably didn't want to know.

Why offer myself? For starters, Megan was under my protection when she was possessed, and I felt responsible — and a lot of guilt — for what happened. I know that she made her own choice, but still, it was an uninformed one, and she had paid for it for a long time now. Plus, with Cobb breathing down my neck, and absolutely crazed trying to open The Way, I wanted something big in my corner so that if push came to shove, I had serious firepower. But mostly it was because she had been hurt when I was supposed to be protecting her.

Anne started to turn, then stopped and faced me. "You're going to offer yourself to free Megan?" Her gaze hardened again. "Why now? You could have done that months ago, when you got her involved with magick. I want to know why." It took me a moment to form an answer. "There wasn't time to figure out what to do. The entity answered so fast I didn't know what happened until it was too late. I've got a plan now. One that I think will keep it from getting me or Megan." Okay, that was a lie. I had no clue what to do about the Darkness. Negotiations always are improvisation as the entity and the caster haggle like vendors at a fish market back and forth trying to get the best deal possible. I knew I was lying, but I need Anne to believe me. I needed Megan's address, so I could find and talk to her and The Darkness.

Anne was quiet. She folded her arms across her chest as her gaze softened from the hard, suspicious glare to something akin to hope. "Swear to me you'll bring Megan home to me." Her gaze hardened as she said the words. Longing and fear were so mixed in her voice that I could tell it came straight from her heart. She wanted her daughter back, desperately. I looked back at her, and swore I would. Anne disappeared back into the apartment, then reappeared in the door a moment later with a slip of paper in her hand. "That's her address. Bring her home to me, please." I pocketed the address as she told me Megan changed locations often due to the entity. This was the most recent address she had for her daughter. The only way to find out was to go check it out.

I ended up at an old section of Halifax near the dock area. The buildings here had been partly rebuilt, and then left to rot when whatever project that got started lost its funding. There were squatters all over. Most, but not all, were human. I'd come down here to find Megan, so that's what I was going to do. It didn't stop me from wishing I had Zik'k along. This would have been exactly the place that would be great for having a bodyguard to watch your back. Unfortunately, I didn't.

I walked into the semi-converted building that I think may have been an attempt to create a loft apartment. The address led me up to the sixth floor, and the second door in from the stairs. I looked out over the street, and felt the wind come through the steel mesh that enclosed the long balcony-like walkway in front of the apartment doors. The cold wet air, the salt tang, and the faint smell of dead fish reinforced the hopeless feel to the place. I rubbed the nub of my missing finger, and screwed up my courage.

The lock turned as I raised my hand to knock: the door knob rotating slowly, and opening inward, disappearing into pitch black. Not just shadow, I mean the kind of absolute black you can only experience properly in a cavern.

The lizard part of my brain was screaming to run back down the stairs and leave, but my feet wouldn't move. The black in the doorway was absolute: no light in, and none out. Something no sane person would ever enter voluntarily.

I called out, "Megan? It's Fern Fatelli. Do you remember me?"

The voice I heard was never meant to come from a human throat. "Ms. Fatelli, it is a surprise to see you here and wanting to talk. Have you fared well since our last meeting?"

I swallowed drily, and heard the slight quaver in my voice as I replied, "Well enough, but I didn't come to talk of past happenings. I came to talk about opportunities and situations."

I didn't want to talk, I wanted to run. My feet though, refused to give in, or perhaps more properly, were too terrified to move.

The sepulcher tones of The Darkness had the hairs on the nape of my neck standing up in alarm. "Intriguing, Ms. Fatelli, but I sense there is much of each that needs a more direct explanation. So please elucidate your opportunities and describe your situations."

17

"WHAT THE OPPORTUNITY IS, is a new body to act as a conduit, and the chance to challenge an established power on earth. One that may even be a true challenge to your ability."

There it was. I didn't name the volunteer, but we both knew what I meant. The entity decided to let me squirm on the hook. I could feel the malicious joy emanating from the cold dark. My skin wanted to crawl off my bones.

"An interesting and intriguing proposal, but vague," the Darkness mused from inside the room.

I heard Megan's breathing: loud, steady, and very slow. The power in each breath seemed like a drum, and my body felt pressure with every exhalation.

"What would be the terms of this 'proposal', Ms. Fatelli? I wonder about the details."

I took a deep breath. You know how I jumped right into this idea of letting it use me as a conduit? Think that was fast? Wrong-o. I'd been thinking about this since Megan got taken, but I had only very recently decided to propose it. I'm likely to be taking on a big, evil dragon in a short while, and I'd need all the juice I could get on my side of the fight. You have to survive to deal with the consequences, and I wasn't sure that, even with the entity on my side, I'd survive it.

On the other side: this was a really, really bad idea. I did not want to do this, but it was a chance at redemption for the past screw-up. Scared as I was, I was certain that I needed redemption more.

"I'll take Megan's place as your conduit for three months, and in return, you help me open up The Anolyn Way.

"A very interesting proposal, Ms. Fatelli. Very interesting, indeed. I have not pitted my abilities against a dragon, especially while in a form that has such ..." The Darkness paused, the barely concealed satisfaction in its voice as it continued, "... limitations upon it."

I thought I felt Megan shift slightly through the dark that enveloped her room. The dark rippled like obsidian water. It was like looking at a muffled scream.

I stepped back involuntarily, and gave The Darkness a bit more room. I fought the impulse to shrink away from the ominous presence in the blackness.

"I would know more about the limitations you propose, Ms. Fatelli. After all, a smart human wouldn't leave me free to wander in a conduit for so long, would they now?" I felt its gaze like a heavy weight on my shoulders. "Feeling guilty are we, Ms. Fatelli? That such a young child should be so ... ill-used by one such as myself? Is that what you're thinking, Ms. Fatelli?"

That had been exactly what I'd been thinking, and that the entity knew my thoughts made the whole bargaining a lot more hazardous. I needed its power a lot more than it needed me as a conduit. Unless I could think of a compelling reason that would sway it, I was likely to condemn Megan to further manipulations by the Darkness. The one bit of breathing space I did have was time. If I played that advantage correctly, I might get it to relinquish Megan.

"Yeah, I was thinking that actually, and how easy it must have been to lead the girl the way you wanted. I hope she's still sane enough to make up her own mind when you let her. 'cause if she's gone round the bend, she's of no use to me to negotiate for her release. And yes, I want redemption. I want to make things right here between me and Megan, her mother, and between me and you. You have a stake in this, too. If we can find a mutually agreeable setup, we can all benefit. That's what I'm after."

I spoke the words strongly, and with as much conviction as I could project. I had to make the Darkness believe that I was working for my own interest — and its interest as well. If I did that bit of acting well enough, it might not pay close attention to the terms — if and when we made our bargain.

"I am intrigued by your bluntness, Ms. Fatelli. So few of you humans are willing to be blunt; it is refreshing to encounter it on occasion. What are the specifics of the proposal, beyond the three months with yourself as a conduit? What would I get, beyond just the chance to operate through you, Ms. Fatelli?"

"A chance at a different perspective from me and a different identity. Plus, I'm not as likely to go crazy with you riding me." I wanted to stop, but it was like an idea sprouted as I spoke. Pieces seemed to click into place with each word that tumbled from my mouth as I continued, "I'd think Megan is pretty close to the end of her ability to handle things realistically and, like I said earlier, if she's gone mad while you've been inhabiting her, how are you going to find a new host? She can't listen to you as a vegetable, so driving her mad just locks you in a prison until she dies, I'm believing. Which gives me incentive to maybe drop the deal and see if that's true. I hear that once a contract's accepted, there's no way for anyone else to call you up. Sounds kind of like, well, karma. Trapped in a madhouse you made. Of course, if she does go mad, she'd be of no use to me damaged like that. Her mom would still blame me like she does right now. Nothing would change." I swallowed my fear and stared at the doorway, imagining where Megan might be. I shrugged, then did my best *"I've got you by the short hairs"* smile as I said, "So what's it going to be: yes or no?"

I wanted it to feel pressure to make the decision right away. The more chance it got to think, the more it could negotiate for. I didn't want it to feel the advantage; I wanted it careless. But, unfortunately, you don't get an entity being careless very often. Such was the case here.

"Ms. Fatelli, I do believe you are looking to sway my decision unduly. I do believe I need time to ponder all the ramifications of the options and the information you have provided me. I will contact you this time tomorrow at your office. I will see you then. Watch your step on the way downstairs, as there's loose material all around."

My bluff got called.

It was a long, depressing walk back down to my Hummer. By a miserable stroke of luck, all bad, I found it up on blocks and stripped down to its skeleton. Scorch marks marked the door frame. The Warding spell had been activated. Someone was nursing burned fingers from the electric shock they'd gotten without the proper magickal talisman in their pocket. Score one for prudence.

I called Larry and Fawn's house to bum yet another ride — which Larry provided. Once there, we settled on the couch to talk a little more about having an entity on our side to cast the spell. I thought it a good idea; I just needed Larry and Fawn to agree with me.

"Are you nuts?!" Larry said to me, after I laid out trying to get the Darkness to take me as a conduit. "It will agree, and screw you four ways to Sunday. That is *not* a good idea. It may like the challenge, but if you die, it just goes back to its own world, and temporarily loses a conduit to this one, until the next idiot that comes along and thinks it's a good idea to play with a power!"

"I'm not playing. I'm trying to correct an accident that happened. I'm responsible!" I shot back at Larry.

"No, you're not responsible!" Larry snarled back, and Fawn nodded in agreement. Larry pushed himself away from the table, and I stood up. He started towards me, shouting, "That girl made her own deal, and the only thing you did was try to help when she didn't want you to."

The crack of Fawn's hand slamming down on the table startled the both of us, and we turned to face Fawn, who was giving us both her best "cop look".

"Fernie, sit. Larry, go to the work room and play with your toys back there. I'll handle the midget from the black lagoon here."

I glared at my Amazonian sister. Six-foot-plus of buxom blonde-haired womanhood, six months pregnant, and in shape enough to turn heads even in the dumpy pair of sweats she was wearing.

"You quit riding yourself, sis. I mean it. You could no more have stopped her from doing what she did than you could make water run uphill. The only thing here was that she did it under your cute little button nose, and you're upset that she got away with it."

My faced burned as her words hit home. She was right to a point. Megan did make the attempt and made the bargain by her own self. The trouble for me was that I'd shown her how to do it by calling the entity up in the first place. She used the same technique to call it up herself. That was my problem.

"Listen up, Fern. If you keep dwelling on that, you'll lose the big picture and pull something really stupid like actually taking that girl's place. You think you need that? I sure as hell don't. We can pull it off. Hell, if you want to ask for help, ask that Cobb. He's really falling all over himself to help." Fawn was still trying to match-make.

"I'm not going to ask Cobb for anything. He's not interested in me; he's interested in something else and, whatever it is, I don't want to find out. Something about him has started to really creep me out. He's hungry for something, and maybe it's something to do with me, but after seeing his face the other day, I do not want him to be doing anything for me. He can take his help and walk it of the short end of a high pier!"

Remember what I said a long time ago about magick and coincidence? Well, I'll say it again: With magick, there are some mighty long coincidences that are not really coincidences. I was telling all about how Cobb creeped me out the last time I saw him, and we got a knock on the front door.

Both Fawn and I jumped at the noise. Fawn got up and went over to the kitchen archway. I went to the door. As I reached for the doorknob, the knocking started again. I growled, and jerked the door open.

Cobb took a quick step back in surprise, staring at me as if I was going to attack him. He composed himself quickly. I saw Fawn put something away out of the corner of my eye.

"Ms. Fatelli, it has occurred to me that since I am asking you to do this, I would be remiss if I did not lend my abilities to their fullest. So I have decided that I will take part in this endeavor.

You can come see me at the usual location tomorrow. I will be expecting a full report of your progress."

I stood there flabbergasted. He was stepping in to take charge of the whole thing after I had gotten us to a point where it would succeed? He apparently took the silence to be acquiescence, and swept back out the door, a self-satisfied smirk on his face, and disappeared into the night.

Before I could run out to catch him and tear a verbal strip off his back, he was gone. Frustrated, I stormed back into the house.

"God damn his little power plays and manipulations! I am *not* going to have that high-handed bastard messing up anything! He is a fuckin' moronic idiotic miserable pompous egomaniac and anything he —"

"Fernie, STOP!" Fawn shouted. My rant died in mid-voice, and I looked back over at Fawn, and heard, rather than saw, Larry come out of the work room.

"Don't you see? He's doing it deliberately. You came here to us when he put pressure on you, and you came over again when you needed those books rendered harmless. And again, when he started asking for 'regular' reports on progress. He's using you, making you jump to his tune and go where he wants. He wanted you to get to Larry, and now he's got him through you." She paused to let that sink in then hit it again. "I think he's hoping you will use Larry again as your 'expert' to cast the spell, just like he wants. I say make him do it. He wants in? Bring him in all the way! Make him earn that, and use his power to make the spell. I don't know much about fae magick, but it can't be any more noticeable than human magick when a spell's cast, especially one that big."

I stopped stalking towards the table, and really listened to what Fawn was saying.

"Let him help. He's expecting to watch you run off in the opposite direction. You want to screw him over? Take that offer, and make him hold his end up. I, for one, would love to see his face when you say yes, and then expect him to help."

Fawn was right, and it would keep Cobb where we all could see what he was up to. I still had reservations, since I was never sure what Cobb was after. Sometimes I'm not sure he did either. But Fawn was right. Keep him close, and make him work for us since he volunteered so nicely. Maybe tomorrow would be worth getting out of bed for after all.

I smiled at the notion, and went back to my office to meet with the Darkness. I planned to withdraw the offer and see what would happen. Gods and magick willing, it would just go away, or crater completely and let me dictate terms. I didn't think I would get either situation, but there had to be something in between the two extremes that could be helpful.

I started to go through what I thought we still needed to do for the bridge spell, when my office door disappeared in a blot of absolute black.

"I'm glad to see you had no trouble finding the place," I said to it, as I tried to slow my heart from the six thousand beats per second it had just tried to reach.

The Darkness receded enough for me to see Megan. Her face was stiff, as was her body. The few movements she made were like those of cliché television zombies. Her eyes were terrified, wide and glassy, and my heart tightened. That could be me. Dear gods, that could be me.

"I am here, and I am given over to listen further to your proposal, Ms. Fatelli. So please, remind me of the current offer," it said with a smug, mocking sound to its voice.

Time to spring the surprise.

"I don't think we'll need you to do this. You've undoubtedly ruined that child's mind long before now. So, thanks, but no thanks. You had a chance last night. In the light of today, forget it."

The Darkness expanded and enveloped the room, except for me and the small circle of light the Darkness left around me. In spite of the heater humming in the background, I felt half-frozen with such absolute Dark around me. I tried to steady myself mentally as it spoke.

"So you choose to withdraw the offer? Think carefully on your answer, Ms. Fatelli. Think very carefully, indeed."

The threat hung in the air, and I could feel the pressure of the Darkness start to creep towards me, like a vise squeezing down on an object.

I took a deep breath. "I really mean it! We don't need you for this. Someone else has volunteered to help. He has enough power to do what I want without having to strike a bargain."

The Darkness paused its advance, as if considering something. Then it was gone in an eye-blink, and all that stood before me was Megan. Her eyes remained pure black, and still conveyed that wide-eyed-edge-of-madness haunted desperation.

I felt, rather than heard, the Darkness chuckle possessively. "She is mine to do with what I will. The contract was flawed, and she is mine until I relinquish her. Quite an amusing situation, don't you think, Ms. Fatelli?"

Darkness tweaked my weak spots like the expert it was. It frightened me that it could find them so easily. The casual cruelty that I heard in the Darkness's voice started my heart speeding up.

My imagination started to run away with the possibilities of what it put Megan through during the time it had her as a conduit, and I had to work hard to quit thinking about the past and focus on the now. It wanted me, and it would crush Megan if I didn't acquiesce. Even if I did, I had to do the wording precisely correct, or it would find a loophole to create some kind of misery to me or to those around me. The thought of that thing riding me like it did Megan boiled up in me again like a monstrous fever. I was officially terrified. But there was still only one way to stop her torment, and that was to invite the Darkness into the conduit of my body.

I forced myself once again to try and ignore Megan. I had to do this right, or both of us would get screwed over badly in retaliation for what I wanted to try.

"Let's talk, then," I said to it, half-proud of myself that my voice didn't waver or crack. "My offer is three weeks as your conduit, and then you leave and go back to your own realm. You will no longer lay claim to anyone here ever again that has held a contract with you. You release them completely. In return, you will be allowed to ride me while I work the spell and confront the dragon if it shows."

"Oh, my. 'Hardball', I believe it is called. This will add spice to our negotiations. I will enjoy you as a conduit, Ms. Fatelli. I will not relinquish control, but borrow your body under my full control for the next nine years, or time being considered sufficient to my desires." There was unconcealed joy in its voice.

Great, it loved haggling. It should have been a fishwife, or got a contract with one.

We offered and counter-offered for the better part of three hours, way past when I was supposed to see Cobb at Underhill. We were deadlocked, unwilling to move on the final part of the contract. The concessions that I'd managed to get were that it would release Megan and hold no control afterward over her, and that I would be the conduit, but it would have control for half of my day each day. The downside was that Megan's contract would remain in effect until the end of my three-year stint as its conduit, then it would relinquish Megan and declare her contract null and void. She'd be free again. And I'd be stuck with the Darkness.

"No, this doesn't work," I said. "It won't work, and I'm not going to try and make it work anymore."

The Darkness watched me, and I felt the pressure of its gaze.

"Why not? You argued quite decisively, Ms. Fatelli, I find I have enjoyed this mental sparring much more than the terror I've invoked the past year with this young human. You will be an excellent conduit."

The confidence that oozed from its voice was disconcerting. I felt it trying to stroke my hopelessness, trying to convince me to give up, to let go, and agree to the negotiation, as is. Lose my identity to the Darkness. I was going to do it anyway; everything dies and enters the Dark.

I shook my head violently to stop the thoughts. This thing was insidious, and it wanted me as a conduit badly. Just how badly, though, was the question. It would have to wait. Maybe a delay would make it careless. Not damn likely, but I wanted to delay things some. At least give me time to think.

"I'll talk with you again tomorrow. Right now, I'm late for another appointment. Drop by tomorrow, and we'll pick this up again." I wanted to end this and get to Underhill.

"Agreed. I am savoring her hope and terror, Ms. Fatelli. This has been most entertaining. I will return tomorrow, at the same time."

The Darkness rolled out from Megan and I saw tears on her cheeks as it commanded her body to turn and face the door. Absolute endless black filled the room, then receded, flowing away like a wave retreating off a shore. The door was a black, square hole for a moment and then the black lightened to grey, and the door solidified.

I was alone in my office. I sat down and pulled a bottle of Scotch from the bottom drawer of my desk. I didn't indulge very often, but I wanted a drink badly. My hands were shaking so badly, I spilled twice as much as I got into the shot glass. I grabbed the glass with both hands and poured it into my mouth. The liquid searing down my throat helped focus me. I put the bottle back in the drawer for the next "emergency".

I got the blanket out of the Murphy bed, wrapped myself in it, and sat at the desk. I knew Cobb would be waiting impatiently for me, but I didn't want to go yet. I needed time to get myself composed and ready to face him. The nub of my finger ached, as did my heart. It was times like this I missed Zhirk the most.

It was about a half-hour later that the door rattled angrily, and I heard Cobb's voice, "Ms. Fatelli, answer me this moment! We had a meeting to update our situation, and I will not tolerate being snubbed in such a manner!"

I stayed in the blanket and shivered.

"I can feel you in there, Ms. Fatelli. Either come answer this door, or I shall break it in!"

Let him try, was all I could think when he said that.

I knew the door would hold against most human magick, and nearly all human thugs. Then I was up, and unbolting the door, before he could smash the glass. I don't care how apathetic I was at the time, having someone you owe things to lose fingers or an arm to cutting glass is not a good idea. It sours a working relationship.

Cobb stood on the other side of the door, haughtily looking down on me from his near seven-foot height.

"You did not show at the time designated, Ms. Fatelli. This cannot continue if I am to lend my assistance. I need to know everything so that I can …" he paused a moment, and I could hear the shift in his words, "… assist in an effective manner."

"Cobb, or whatever the hell your real name is, this is a very bad time to be trying to tell me what to do, or how to do it. In fact, it is a very bad time to visit and, right now, you want to leave. I will talk with you later."

I slammed the door shut hard enough to rattle the glass. Cobb kicked the door back open. I should have realized what kind of power he had back when we got his daughter out of the place she was held in the faked kidnapping. The door bounced crazily and the glass shattered. I ran back deep into the room. I did not want to be around when the glass reset itself. Cobb followed me in, more intent on catching me than avoiding the danger. He caught up and cornered me by the Murphy bed. He'd come in here uninvited and tried to lay hands on me. As he closed, I used what Fawn taught me at the gym. I stepped inside his reaching hands and planted a flat-footed side-kick in his stomach. His head came down, and my knee came up with a sharp crack. Cobb fell sideways, his nose gushing thick, red blood. I placed a second front-kick on the side of his head, and he went down, and stayed down.

Cobb's nose was going to need re-setting, and his ear would be tender until the swelling went away. I flashed a light in his eyes. Both pupils contracted the same amount, so I hadn't given him a concussion. He'd survive.

I went to the Murphy bed and pulled it open just enough to snag the pillow. I went back over and placed it under his head, and then covered him up with the blanket, and settled down to wait for him to wake up. I was in no hurry.

Surprisingly, when he'd fallen, he'd missed my desk, my files, and the breakable pieces of my authentic 1930's Private Investigator's office. Yes, I'm proud of the place. I love it, and I spend more time in it than I ever do in the small house I own. The house is more like storage space; that's about all I use it for.

After some fifteen minutes, Cobb moaned slightly, then surged to his feet with an angry shout. He spun in place until he turned enough that he faced me. His face was pale with rage. His eyes seemed to go totally black, looking unnervingly like Megan's eyes as the Darkness rode her.

"You dared to strike me?" he roared in outrage.

"When someone kicks my door open, comes into my space uninvited, and attempts to lay hands on me without my permission, you bet I do! Try it again, Cobb! You'll spend time in jail behind *iron* bars. Or did you forget who my sister is?"

That sank in, and I could see him think it through. He looked at me with a very sour face, then composed himself and straightened his clothes.

"I do sincerely apologize for my behavior, Ms. Fatelli. It was a mistake, and I shall not repeat it. Now, do you wish to call your authorities?"

"No," I told him. "I want you out of my office now. I'll work for you — I don't have any choice there — and I'll accept your offer to help, but I draw the line at taking your orders on things you haven't even bothered to learn anything about." I motioned towards the door. "Leave now, please. We'll talk tonight."

He looked at me as if the fight had given him a new opinion of me. I'm not sure I liked his contemplative glances, but I wanted him out of the office more than I wanted to be offended by the way he looked at me. He left at a slow, dignified pace, almost like he was trying to defy me or my desire to see him gone. Weird. Why did he hunt trouble like that? It reminded me of a kid trying to prove he was an adult, when all he really showed was how much of a child he still was.

I'd given that enough thought. It was time to work on the real problems of the day. Namely, getting the preparations set for the spell. We'd need a way to run the spell through the barrier to the shore, to protect and conceal the spell from Anolyn, and as many potential threats as we could figure out. Ideally, I could find a way through and cast part of the spell from the island, but that was not too likely.

I wasn't sure how Cobb would help, as fae magick had a number of differences from human magick, but in retrospect, and considering the effectiveness of fae glamour, his magick could be invaluable for possibly concealing the finished spell. Now we just needed to get in place, and avoid that flying dead thing, if it showed.

I called Larry to make sure he had enough time to gather materials, and to coordinate the others. I thought about how much Cobb had wanted Larry doing the work, and now, in a way, he'd conned me into getting him to sign on and help out. I knew he'd do it — we're family — but I really started feeling guilty and manipulated as I got further into the preparations. Larry needed to be cut out of the situation before Cobb figured out how to manipulate us more for his own ends.

18

JUST HOW I WAS GOING TO MAKE SURE Larry and Fawn were
kept out of Cobb's machinations was the big question, and I
spent most of the day in my office with Larry trying to figure out
exactly each of my and Cobb's steps in this little dance we were
in. I was still trying to chart it on paper when Cobb knocked on
the door. I was not going to take any chances, so I'd taken the
precaution of putting some iron nails in my pocket, and dribbling
iron filings around my desk, to lessen the impact of any fae
spells. Cobb entered as I stepped back and, once past the inner
door's threshold, he seemed to deflate slightly as his magick
encountered the cold iron.

He saw the filings on the floor, and stopped dead in his
tracks, just in the doorway to my inner office. I stepped into the
room and turned towards him, leaning back on the edge of my

desk. My left hand landed near a pouch of filings and my right hand on a heavy iron paperweight, which I could throw if need be. After his performance earlier today, I was in no mood to trust, or forgive and forget. I may have to work with him, but I don't have to be nice, or fake being polite, any more after our previous little "meeting".

"You're here. Now, what do you want to say before I tell you how this is going to work?"

His face hardened, and his shoulders hunched over like he was getting ready to attack. I moved my hand over to the pouch, ready to fling it in his face. He suddenly let go of the anger, and stood there, watching me.

"I believe I said that I apologize for our … misunderstanding. I do apologize, and it will never happen again." He tried to give me a sincere, disarming smile, which only ended up looking to me like a sour grimace.

"Yes, you did. I have to work with you, and I will to get the job done, but I don't have to like working with you or like you. So we work, we get this done; we go our separate ways."

I will have to say that he didn't get mad or pout like I expected. He considered the words and kept his temper in check.

"Very well," he said at last. "I will listen to your directions, and I will not have any rancor for you in this. I understand and accept."

That went a lot better than I'd hoped it would. The next job was to make sure that Cobb was willing and able to create the effect we needed. The last was to ask him how he stopped the creature when it attacked the house. Cobb got evasive about this.

"I will deal with it if it does show again. I promise you that, Ms. Fatelli. The pain I gave it the last time will no doubt cause it to stay well away from any group I am with."

"Maybe so," I countered. "But you can't be everywhere at once."

"I don't have to," he said with a smile. "I can glamour one or more of the other wizards with my countenance which should convince the creature to stay clear. My skill can ensure that every nuance of myself is duplicated on another. The creature will not be able to tell the difference."

I didn't like the idea, actually, but it did make sense, and, if it worked, that was great.

"What if it does? How will the others defend themselves from it? You may be willing to put trust in an illusion, but I'm not. That creature is strong enough to rip someone in half, and I don't want anyone dying because we didn't think things through. Why all the secrecy?"

He pulled himself up, stood straight, and stared at me.

"Those matters are of the fae and, rest assured, I will deal with the creature myself. If it should penetrate the glamour, I will confront it directly," he said, in a tone that said I was not going to get another word out of him about it.

I was really getting tired of "fae matters". A few deep breaths helped me get my patience back and not think about strangling His High-and-Mightiness. I told him when and where to meet us for a ride up to the bridge, but he refused, saying that he would be there directly through the fae paths. As long as he was there on time, that's all that mattered.

I used the spare time I had to go through telephone calls that had backed up, and do a little cleaning of my office. It was still dingy, and looked like a down-on-its-luck 1930's *film noir* version of a private investigator's office, but it's a tasteful dingy. Just to be sure I had some kind of warning should any bad things try to get into the office, I took the time to put wards on the windows and the thresholds. They might not stop a creature, but the spells would hurt it and slow it down, giving me time to either fight or run. I was a big fan of running. You don't get hurt if you're not around to be hurt. Once the wards were finished, I went to bed to catch up on some much-needed sleep.

It felt like I'd just closed my eyes when an insistent knocking on my office door woke me. My bleary eyes checked the clock on the desk: 12:02 a.m. What kind of sadistic person knocks at midnight? One that was apparently going to knock until doomsday.

The door rattled even more forcefully, and the knocking escalated into a heavy pounding. I did what any sleep-deprived red-blooded human would do. I turned over in bed and covered my ears with the pillow, which muffled the sound nicely. I burrowed deeper under the blanket, into its comforting warmth and darkness.

"Good morning, Ms. ..." came from under the sheets with me.

I was awake and all the way across the room in one long, adrenaline-laced, screaming-in-terror leap from the bed. I looked back at the bed to see Megan/Darkness sitting upon it.

"... Fatelli. It is nice to see you so awake and chipper," the Darkness finished, and gave me a smile that would have melted butter if the eyes had matched it.

It made my skin crawl. Megan/Darkness got off the bed, sidled over to the desk, and sat in the chair nearby. "You had said we should talk on the morrow, so here we are. It is the morrow, after all." The Darkness smirked at me.

"I had hoped to get in some sleep before we talked."

"You can't have everything, Ms. Fatelli. Where would you put it all?"

It made jokes. Bad ones. This felt like a deliberate ploy to lower my guard. Me, paranoid? You bet, especially with something like The Darkness. I clasped my hands to keep them from shaking after the adrenalin dump, and did my best to give Megan/Darkness a neutral face.

"Very funny. Now would you mind telling me what was so important that when I said we would talk 'tomorrow', you had to show up two minutes past the hour?"

Megan/Darkness smiled again, and said, "All is not what it seems. You should know how appearances deceive so thoroughly, Ms. Fatelli."

I about lost it. It comes here at two past midnight to spout clichés? I itched to grab it and throw it out the window, minus Megan.

"I can assure a complete situation of truth for you, Ms. Fatelli. We conclude our negotiations, Megan goes free, and I get you as a conduit, as we have tentatively developed as an agreement ..."

I glared at the creature.

"I said 'No' before, and I say 'No' again. The deal is not going to be made, so remove yourself, and let me get some sleep."

Megan/Darkness smiled, showing teeth like a predator.

"I shall go, and we will visit again, later today, after you have had time to rest. I look forward to concluding our bargain." Megan stepped into a shadow and melted away like a black mist.

I tried to go back to sleep, but saw Megan's terror-filled pleading eyes every time as I closed my own.

19

AFTER THE DARKNESS' VISIT, I gave up trying to go back to sleep, and ended up going to my chair. Wrapped in the blanket from the bed, I did a lot of staring out my window at the street below it. The sporadic traffic trickled by on the road, stopping on occasion for the light at the corner. A mist drizzled on the window, sometimes shifting to rain, then to fog, or simply fading away for a few minutes. The Darkness had let me see Megan's fear, and was probably tormenting her with the thought of continued servitude as a conduit, and that ate at my heart and soul like acid poured on skin. There had to be a way to help her, but for the life of me, I couldn't find it.

In two days, we would be going to the Northumberland Strait to start our attempt at reopening The Anolyn Way. I had to think past Megan. Gods help me, it hurt so bad that I couldn't help her. She had to wait. Getting Cobb off my back would give a little mental breathing space, and the time might reveal options I hadn't thought of during the negotiations. The big problem was that creature. It had shown itself twice by the strait, and once at Larry and Fawn's. It felt like a guardian, but that third attack seemed to blow up the theory.

Preparation was key. I wanted an ace up my sleeve against that flying bat-monster that had hunted me three times now. It was time to do a little hunting of my own. During my jobs as a tracer and trouble-shooter, I've found location spells to be very useful. I now wanted to find this creature, and learn how to either banish it or kill it; I didn't care which, so long as it was gone. To do that, I needed to find its lair, or where it preferred to operate. That might give a clue how to best work this problem. That being said, I needed to gather up the one thing that I knew the creature had touched: Larry and Fawn's front door. First, though, I needed to get another car.

The car was fairly easy. I wanted something tough and cheap. The Hummer, big as it was, had gotten totaled after only a few days of ownership, and the insurance hadn't had time to cut a check on it. That meant I had to dig into my dwindling savings to get something. After checking with friends of friends, I found myself the bemused owner of a beat-up red Chrysler PT Cruiser. The two back seats were missing, and the floor liner had been torn out. With my current luck with cars, this would be just fine. After paying for it, and taking a day to get all the paperwork filed, I loaded it up and drove over to Fawn and Larry's.

I'm sure Larry and Fawn's neighbors were rather puzzled by little old me grabbing the busted door off the trash heap in front of the house, and stuffing it in my car. Once I got to Larry's workshop, it was a bit of work to drag the broken solid oak door into the back room. I needed to use his circle to contain the spell. It took me fifteen minutes to get the door in place, and then catch my breath before I could cast the spell. A magnifying glass on one point, compass on another, flashlight on a third, a fingerprint pad on the fourth, a DNA test strip on the fifth, and a pencil on the sixth. I sat on the seventh point. I began the chant to focus myself and the magick I was calling to my aid.

The spell flowed easily and, almost immediately, I got the sense of a direction and distance. I had tapped in very quickly. I decided, on the fly, to try to modify the spell from search to *scry*, so I tilted the chant slightly to build the effect. Normally, doing something like this takes a long time, if you're able to do it at all, but I'd tried it, and found that, like anything, it got easier with practice. The big worry with a scrying is that, if you see the creature, and if it has a sense of the spell, it can look back at you and get your distance and direction as well. That's one of the reasons magick isn't used for scrying very often. It could blow up in your face, and show the target who was looking for it, along with handy directions to your location.

The spell-shifted with my chant, and began to clear after a few minutes of concentration. I couldn't quite make out the image, but there were two things in the scrying, rather than just the one creature. This gave me a bad case of butterflies. There was more than one? I dismissed that idea as the two figures were not identical in size. Since the creature — or creatures — in the attacks had been identical, it could only be either one creature, or a pair of identical ones. Since the two figures were not the same size, that blew my "twins" theory apart. I was seeing two different creatures, then.

I shifted the view line of the scry clockwise around the two, hoping to get a good angle on the faces. If I could see enough to identify the larger creature, I might have a clue about what I was dealing with. The larger of the two creatures straightened, and I gasped. The face was Judge Kaddus. He was talking to the creature. The thing's face became illuminated as Kaddus stepped away from it. My mind reeled.

Why would the Judge want to send a creature at us when we were trying to open The Way again, as he demanded in the details of the service? It just did not make sense. As I watched, Judge Kaddus continued to speak. His features were tight, his actions sharp and angry. The creature appeared to listen and understand. My best guess at the moment is that he was either berating the creature, or he was giving it instructions. Either way, I was going to find out the next time I saw him.

The two finished talking and, with a short, ungainly hop, the creature unfurled its wings and rose off the ground, soaring out of view. I tried to lock onto Kaddus by shifting the intent of the spell, but I did it too fast and the spell collapsed, noisily. Fortunately, the collapse also kept the Judge from knowing who had cast the spell, and that would give me some advantage the next time we met.

I sat in the workshop, and contemplated recasting the spell to follow Kaddus once more, but dismissed the idea as a bad one. He'd heard the first spell collapse and would be on his guard; I was certain of that. I tried to lock onto the creature again, and again it was easy to slip into the spell. The trouble was there was nothing to find. My magick couldn't locate the creature. There are a number of bad things that can shield themselves from locator magick. Nearly all of them lived in Underhill. The trouble was, Larry's pickup and my Saturn had been built with iron and steel, and that thing still tore it apart with no apparent ill effects.

There were a few creatures of Underhill that actually were not harmed by touching cold iron. The strongest and most dangerous were RedCaps. They were a race of fae that were able to stand the touch of cold iron, and actually preferred to make their weapons from it, when they could get their hands on it. They were from the Unseelie court and hated humanity. I canceled the spell and thought about the RedCaps. It was time for a little research.

Searching the internet got me the following: Redcaps are supposedly vulnerable to anything like a human is, and they generate fear in their victims. The fear aspect about clinched it for me. If we could find a way to get around that horrible fear, we could take it out. Other things, like Outsiders, were also vulnerable to "enough bullets". It's just that when an Outsider can get to the size of a high-rise building, "enough bullets" is a relative thing. Based on what I knew, the most likely answer was a RedCap.

I went over to Fawn's and was greeted at the door by Larry. Fawn was pulling her turn in the kitchen. Fawn is a great cop, and a great sister, but I was not going to stay and get poisoned. She had a deservedly lousy reputation as a cook. Larry, I guess, was a glutton for culinary torture. Either that, or he knew when to compromise about cooking.

"So what's the house call for, Fernie? Something new?" Larry inquired as he sat down at the circular dinette table in the kitchen.

He reached out and idly slid the salt shaker between his hands as he listened to me. I'd found that irritating before, but he always had his hands doing something when he talked or listened, so I'd gotten used to something going on besides talking. So, as the salt shaker slid back and forth on the table, I outlined what I'd discovered.

Fawn came over as I talked. When I got to the part about Judge Kaddus talking to the creature, and the RedCaps being able to generate fear, she put two and two together, like I did. She was ready to call on the good Judge, and have a little "cop chat" with him.

Larry convinced both of us that putting Judge Kaddus on guard was the last thing we should do if we wanted to find out what was really going on.

"He's gone to some pretty great lengths to set whatever it is up," Larry pointed out. "And if either of you start getting smart and asking questions, he might pull something more dangerous than he already has. Lay back and watch him. "

He paused for a moment, and then said, "You sure about that creature, Fernie? If it is a RedCap, that means we can do something about it."

"I'm really not sure, Larry. That was the most dangerous thing that I could think of that could handle touching iron or steel, so I was working from a worst-case situation." I paused as a thought hit me. "Though my research never said anything about flying."

"Hmm, that does give us something to go on. With a little more reading and research, we should be able to come up with a list and narrow it down from there. I can take care of that. Just give me half a day; it shouldn't be too difficult."

Larry leaned back slightly in the chair and looked at Fawn for a moment. My stomach tightened. It was so nice to see them together, and so wrenching to imagine either one of them hurt. I remembered what else I came to do, and it was going to be hard. I looked at Fawn and then at Larry. I knew Fawn would back me on this.

"Larry, there's something else we need to discuss now" I said to him. "You and Fawn both need to get distance from all this. The research is fine, but you can't go with me. This is dangerous, and I think Cobb has been manipulating things so that I have to rely on you and your contacts to do the job. Judge Kaddus is playing a game too. Maybe it's to screw up Cobb's plans, or maybe he has something else in mind. Call me paranoid, but that's what I believe. Because of that, you're not going with me up there. You're staying here with Fawn."

Larry looked at me without expression as I said my piece. The salt shaker stopped moving, and Fawn stiffened slightly. She knew he was upset, and I knew it, because I could tell when she was upset. Larry focused on me, laid both of his hands flat on the table, and stood up.

"Fern, I'll agree not to go along with you, but in return, you have to take someone along to watch your back. If you don't want me, you don't want Fawn for the same reason. I'd say go find that Troykin and hire him again. But understand that I am not happy. You're family, and if anything happens because you get stupid and heroic, I'm going to be really unhappy."

I held up my hands placatingly.

"I hear you: no stupidly heroic anything. Cast the spell, hide the spell, test it both ways, and get the hell out."

"Make sure you know where Cobb is all the time," Larry told me. "If you're right, that fae is playing something really close to his chest, and not knowing what it is can get you all in between a rock and a hard place."

"I'll stick a ring in his nose if you want. I don't trust him at all at this point. I'll be very careful; I promise you that."

Boy, would I ever. Judge Kaddus really worried me after that scrying earlier. If he was giving the RedCap instructions to "get" me, I would be hard put to just stay alive. Larry's acquiescence lifted a load of worry.

The "talk" had gone a lot easier than I expected. Larry is such a good reader of body language; I doubt it came as a surprise to him. It made me wonder why he hadn't laid things out for me like he usually did. It wasn't something to worry about at the moment. What was to worry about was that creature. I was guessing it would show when I started the spell, so I needed to figure out what precautions and bits of trickery I could come up with for just such an emergency. There was no way to figure what Cobb or the Judge were after, or, more ominously, why Kaddus had made that apparent deal with that creature. I hoped Larry found something tomorrow that could be used.

I went back to my house, rather than my office. The thought of having to talk to the Darkness again just wearied and depressed me. The house is a little thing: barely one living room, one bedroom, kitchen, and a bathroom. No basement. I'd gotten it when I was still in the Halifax police, before I found out how much I hated being told what to do. I never had the heart to sell it, and dropped by once in a while to make sure everything was kept clean and repaired. I didn't bother to go into the bedroom, but just turned the heat up and flopped down on the couch and went to sleep. For a change, my sleep wasn't disturbed by something coming by to ask questions, or wake me at ungodly hours of the night.

Next morning, I went back over to the office and settled in to do a little answering of the mail, pay bills, make a pot of coffee, and wait for Larry to call. I wanted to do this alone, but the speed needed between the spells to keep the chance of discovery to a minimum dictated at least three magick specialists working as a team. I'd talked to a couple of the magick professionals at the police station, and had asked Fawn if it was all right to hire them for the job. I'd seen the police magickers work, and had been impressed with how they handled the spells on the books. Fawn assured me that, if they decided to work with me, they'd get paid leave to do so. I offered them each three-month's salary to work with me. They both agreed, so I had my trio.

Kent Nix was the first one to sign on. He was the oldest wizard employed by the Halifax police, being a nimble sixty-two years old. With a shock of grey hair atop a lanky six-foot frame, he looked the part of a wizard in a business suit. He was a solid, reliable magick slinger from what I'd seen of him. His specialty — if you could call it a specialty — was long-term casting. He was good at working rituals and gathering power for use. The unraveling spell on the books was his work.

His partner was Kevin Love. Kevin was about forty, and had the lean, muscled frame that one gets from regular workouts at the corner gym. A bare wisp of blonde hair ringed his bald head just above his ears. When I'd seen him at the precinct, he'd been wearing a smart button-up short-sleeved shirt with blue jeans, and I almost never saw him without his Fedora. He considered it a good luck charm. Where Kent was solid, Kevin was brilliant. According to Fawn, Love had powered through the magus tests and passed them easily. He could take any spell, break it down, and identify it. His memory was purportedly eidetic and, if that was the case, it made sense that he was able to operate magick so precisely. Together, the two of them were a real asset to the police. I expected they'd be the same for me.

Cobb was still going to be coming along, too, so I sat down and talked with Kent and Kevin at my house before we were to meet him.

"I want you two to know that Cobb is not our friend. He's maneuvered me into this 'service', and has been trying to manipulate how I work and who I work with. He's with us so that I can keep an eye on him. There's another player, too: Judge Kaddus, the fae who ruled in Cobb's favor has some kind of creature he can control. It has attacked me three times now, probably on the Jude's orders, so be on your toes. It produces a tremendous fear as it approaches, so the best guess is that it's a RedCap. If you can beat the fear, you can hurt it; anything solid will work against it, including bullets."

"Now that you warned us, what's this fae supposed to do?" Nix asked.

"His job is to conceal The Way once we have it created. I'm hoping he'll do that. If he doesn't, we can try to do the job, but there's a very big chance that Anolyn will probably sense the barrier being messed with. If he does, he'll come looking for who's breaching it. I don't think any of us want to find out what an angry dragon can do."

Kevin shook his head and chuckled, "Thank you, no. I like my life just fine. No need to complicate it."

Kent murmured an agreement and raised his head, looking towards the door.

"See something?" I said as I turned, curious at what caught Kent's attention.

"No, I was just thinking about what you said about this Cobb fellow. I don't like having an enemy in the camp, to borrow an adage. You're certain he has to come along? That kind of ploy reminds me of your sister."

"Well it was Fawn's suggestion, and I agree with her. I want him where we can see him at all times."

20

AFTER GETTING OUR SUPPLIES AND SOME WEAPONS, in case the creature showed, I drove the PT Cruiser over to pick up Nix and Love. They were waiting at the precinct. I opened the back, and the two men looked at each other. Kevin took a look at the bare floor, and a look at the non-existent back seat, then had me drive to his apartment. He dashed inside, and returned with an old gaming floor chair and set it in the back. Nestled in the rear foot well, and facing backwards, it looked to make a passable seat for the trip.

"Are you ready?" I asked him.

He smiled, and gave a thumbs-up as we drove back to the precinct to pick up Kent. Kent took a look at Kevin's handiwork as we pulled up.

"I'd forgotten about those. That looks like it works pretty well, and there's a little room under it for some small stuff."

We put the equipment on the passenger side so Kevin could stretch his legs out. I kept scanning the sky as we drove. The last thing I wanted was another visit from the RedCap. Paranoia is a good thing for keeping your skin whole. Don't knock it. Happily for the three of us, the trip to the bridge was absolutely uneventful.

Cobb was waiting for us as we pulled into the abandoned visitor center. The place showed all the typical signs of neglect: faded and peeling paint, broken glass windows, empty cans and bottles, and weeds growing up through the asphalt. He approached the car, then looked at the two magick specialists I'd brought along. The two men gave Cobb polite nods, then went back to talking about their latest cases still waiting back at precinct headquarters. It took a few minutes to gather our bags, then we walked out of the parking lot, onto the road, and towards the bridge. The broken end stuck out two hundred meters from shore, and sixty meters above the Nortumberland strait.

The breeze carried the smell of salt and fish. The bright blue of the sky reflected off the low waves that rolled on the surface of the channel, breaking whimsically against the remains of the bridge columns. It looked idyllic and, honestly, I'd have loved just to watch the clouds. I shook my head and focused back on the job. The road led up the rise towards the first column, stopping about ten meters from the broken stump of concrete and steel.

I set my kit down at the broken end of the road. I had to link my spell to the echoes that Kent was going to call up. Kent was tasked with calling the echo of the bridge up, and to activate the bridge echo, so the physical remains could be linked to my spell. Kevin, with his skill at unraveling spells, had the job of creating a hole in the barrier. Without the hole, we wouldn't be able to pass through that curtain of death Anolyn had put around Prince Edward Island, or, what we locals just call "PEI". Mine was to make the echo of the bridge solid. Cobb was supposed to conceal it once we'd finished our parts. What we didn't know was what Anolyn's reaction would be, and how soon we'd see it.

Kent had stayed at the base of the bridge on the last spit of land. Once he had set his septagram, he began the steady work of calling up the echoes of the bridge. I built my seven-pointed star in the sand and used chalk to scratch the symbols for concentrating the magick. When he started chanting, the hairs on my arm stood up as I felt the pull of the spell. Kevin felt it too, and began his part. He worked his septagram alongside mine up at the broken edge of the road. This had been a twelve-kilometer long bridge. We'd be really pushing our limits to get these spells to work.

Once the hole and the echoes were set, I would cast the linking spell, and pour the magick into it, to create a solid echo of the original bridge. My magick would solidify the hole Kevin created, so he wouldn't have to chant all the time to keep it open. Cobb was supposed to create a glamour to hide the echo and obscure any magickal trace. The coordination was a little tricky, but Kevin and Kent had worked together for years, which helped immensely. My job would start when Kevin and Kent finished. Cobb would be last, assuming we all got our parts done and nothing interfered.

I listened to Kevin and Kent's chanting. The low tenor of Kent's measured chant was like a musical heartbeat. Kevin's lower, but more energetic, chanting was like the musical version of a cat high on catnip. His voice sped up, dropped, rose to a low crescendo, and then faded back, wrapping itself around Kent's chant like a ribbon. While they chanted, I scanned the area with binoculars, hoping to see the creature coming before it could attack with that fear aura, while simultaneously hoping that it never showed. A scan of the area over the water, and back landward, showed nothing around us. Similarly, a scan of the sky showed nothing flying around us either.

I reached over to my emergency bag and got out my father's old Thompson/Center Contender. It's a little bolt action pistol that came in many calibers; my dad liked the heavier ones for target shooting. With a scope on, it was close to a rifle in accuracy. I gathered up four bullets, put the first of the 7.62mm NATO rounds into the chamber, and closed the action. I set the other three about an arm's reach from my knee and upright, so they would be easy to spot and pick up. I may not like guns, but I grew up around them and know how to use them, as did a lot of kids after the magick came back, and society was forced to rediscover some old skills in order to survive. In Halifax, you'd be hard put to find someone who hadn't seen any practice with a rifle or shotgun.

There was a sudden flapping, and a dark blur skimmed past me and dropped on Kevin. He grunted under the impact. Kevin and the creature rolled wildly downslope in the sparse grass and cement debris. I ran until I could see Kevin and the creature. The wild tumble down the road had knocked them apart. Kevin looked frozen as the creature stood up scant meters away from him. I braced against the crumbling cement railing and aimed at the monster.

Cobb came running, sword in hand. He leapt to Kevin's aid. Fear suddenly rolled out of the creature, and Kevin wailed like a lost soul. I saw Cobb stagger back as the raw essence of fear washed over him. He then leaned towards the creature, trying to move closer. He screamed words that made the fear ease just a little. Kevin, curled in a fetal ball, was now barely a meter away from the approaching thing. I grabbed the pistol more firmly and then shifted my grip, my missing little finger made the gun feel off balance, and lined up on the creature, looking for an open shot.

Kevin was still screaming, and I pulled the trigger to scare the thing off him. The bullet hit a concrete boulder near it, spewing cement chips into the air, peppering the creature. That surprised it, causing it to fly up and look my direction. I flipped the bolt up and racked it back, the empty casing flipping over my shoulder as I grabbed the closest cartridge and dropped it in the pistol. The bolt slammed home as the creature flew under the bridge, appearing suddenly up over the ragged, broken lip, and arrowed straight for me. There was no time to aim.

The roar of the pistol was almost drowned out by the scream of the creature as the bullet plowed through it. It lurched drunkenly in the air and then smashed into me. I tried to relax and roll with the impact. Fat lot of good that did. It was like being hit by a truck. I was smashed flat, the wind knocked out of me. A bright flash filled my head as it slammed on the cement. The pressure vanished as the RedCap's own momentum carried it away, rolling back down the angled road towards Kevin and Cobb. Blood, and something that looked like yellowish mucus, splattered the ground near the broken edge of the bridge. The road wobbled crazily in my vision as I tried to get up. I fell over, my head landing next to the two remaining shells. By a bit of luck, they were untouched and still upright. It was an effort to move. I knocked one over grabbing at it.

Terrified the creature was going to be on me at any moment, I managed to grab the remaining upright shell. Working the bolt action with my wrist, I flipped the spent casing over my knuckles to land on the ground with a musical *clink*. I dropped the round into the pistol, slammed the bolt home, and slapped it down as I brought the weapon up and took wobbly aim at the creature. It was ten meters past me, its blood leaking downhill as it slowly pushed itself upright.

I didn't care where I hit the thing, so long as I hurt it. Aiming at the center of the rising creature, I pulled the trigger. The recoil brought the gun up in front of my face. The thing screeched as the slug hit it, bleeding heavily. I managed to grab the last cartridge, and got up slowly as I worked the bolt action.

"Stop!" rang out from down by the car. Cobb ran towards me, the creature turning its head at the sound of his voice. "Stop!"

"Why?" I yelled back at him.

The creature lurched into motion, a soft, agonized whine coming from its throat as it began to stagger towards Cobb. Cobb yelled again as I aimed at the center of mass and shot it in the back. The creature tried to scream, but only a wet gurgle came out, and it collapsed in a wet, mucusy heap.

Cobb ran to the creature. He looked at me. I could see the cold anger underneath the calm face as he straightened up.

"You bloody-minded mortal excrement," Cobb said through gritted teeth. "That was our best chance to find out what was happening here."

"I think keeping myself in one piece is more important! You don't like it? Tough. You got me for this service, so you're stuck with me!" I shot back. I was mad and still frightened. The adrenaline had me as twitchy as a rabbit surrounded by weasels.

If he was wanting a confrontation, I was more than ready. I held the empty pistol in my right hand. At this close range, if he tried any magick, I'd crack him over the skull before he even had the spell started. He stared at me as if trying to force me to wilt; I just glared back at him. From downslope of us, Kent yelled up.

"Hey, Fernie, can you get the first aid kit in the trunk? Kevin's got a slash along his arm, and I'd like to clean it and get it bandaged if you two are through yelling at each other."

"Okay, I'll be right down," I shouted back.

I walked past Cobb and went to the car. The kit was in the back. When I'd gotten it, I trotted back down to Kent. When I got to the two men, Kent had a blood-soaked shirt wrapped around Kevin's arm. Kevin was bare-chested, his whole body a pale, pale pink. His head wavered a few times. He was fighting shock. I was probably pale, too. My head had settled into a dull, throbbing ache. I didn't notice any blurred vision, so I guessed I hadn't gotten a concussion. Something like what just happened tends to do that to a person.

I set the first aid kit next to Kent and watched as he pulled Kevin's shirt away from the wound. He rotated Kevin's arm gently so he could see the damage, then slathered on an antibiotic. Next, Kent ran tape across the wound to close it. Kevin hissed, teeth clenched as Kent worked, using up the last of the gauze bandage to wrap the wound, and carefully tape it down.

"I don't think we're going to throw spells today, Fern. He needs a doctor to look at that arm."

I ground my teeth and, although I wanted to finish this, he was right.

"Okay," I told the two men. "Let's go over to Pictou and get this looked at."

Kevin was able to get up and walk to the car, which was good, as it meant he'd not gone into shock from the attack. He didn't complain of any burning or itching, so I didn't think there was any poison in him. Cobb did not come down to join us for the trip, and I wasn't going to wait for him.

It was a short drive, but it felt like hours. We pulled into the local clinic, where the staff quickly looked Kevin over and then prepped him for surgery. He'd had a number of larger blood vessels cut, along with nerve damage. There was a staff magick specialist on duty. His job was to assist the doctor in binding the wound, then to encourage healing. Magick is great, but major changes in a target, such as changing a chair to a living dog, or calling up a storm, take major amounts. Closing a bone-deep gash in a forearm from wrist to elbow is not as trivial as it might sound.

Kent came over to me while we were waiting for Kevin to get out of surgery.

"You want to get Cobb, or should I?" he asked as he sat down and stretched out.

"I'll go," I told Kent. "I asked him along, and no telling what's gone on since we left him there. I'll pick him up, and get us a room for the evening. No sense in driving home today."

"You mean he's going to stay with us?" Kent looked at me and his eyes asked the question, *Are you sure that's a good idea?*

"He's part of this now, and I still want him where I can watch him. Now more than ever."

I drove back out to the bridge, and arrived at near sundown. Cobb was waiting for me at the spot where Kent and Kevin had set up their septagrams. He had obliterated each one. That was a good idea, actually, as they had been casting when interrupted, which could be bad. Magick might dissipate quietly if a spell's interrupted, and it might not. No one has really discovered why one blows up and another just fades. The current best guess is that urgency creates the impetus, but, like I said, no one knows for sure. Cobb didn't move as I pulled up. Only after I had stopped the car did he rise and approach.

"Come to retrieve your precious things, Fatelli?" He asked with a slight sneer to his voice.

"Actually, yes, though seeing you again made me wonder why I didn't wait until tomorrow."

He glared venomously at me for a moment, then strode angrily to the car. He used a wadded cloth to touch the door handle, then slid onto the passenger seat. He said nothing as I put the car in gear and drove back towards Pictou. He just stared straight ahead as if he was a statue. I think it was his way of trying to make me nervous, but in truth, I found it pretty funny, him staring straight ahead like some gargoyle.

We went over to the Northumberland Inn and got four rooms. I paid cash, left Cobb at the motel, and went to pick up Kent and Kevin, who was out of surgery and well-healed, thanks to the doctors' magick. I gave them their room keys and drove them back out to the motel. The night was spectacular with the northern lights in their full glory: a luminous green curtain across the sky that undulated like waves lapping against a shoreline. That's one thing the magick did right. With less light, you could see more stars at night, and I never got tired of them.

As I was standing there, Cobb walked over from the small field behind the motel.

"Having trouble sleeping?" I asked. "Or still upset about us not doing it your way, Cobb? How about you do this? Stay out of the way, and let us do what we're here for, and then you do what you volunteered to do."

He glared at me, but made no comment as he walked over to where I was. He looked up at the sky momentarily, then back over to me.

"Is that all it takes to distract you? No wonder this has been such a tedium. If humans could focus, this would have been over and done days ago."

I lost it. I had almost unwound from the attack, and Cobb's words were like a match to gasoline.

"You are fucking kidding me!" I screamed at him. "Focus? You wouldn't know what the word means, Cobb. You've been waiting for us to finish this. Did you ever bother to think it might be good to help out? No. All I got from you was an attempt to walk in and take the job over when the work was done! What's the matter? No answer for that?" I snarled in his face, and he took an involuntary step back. I followed angrily, and poked a finger in his chest. "You have been trying to get me screwed over ever since you tricked me into this service! Did you ever think to *ask* for help rather than trying to trap me into it? That pretty well guarantees you're not going to get willing support, no matter what now."

I glared at him again, and waited.

Cobb looked at me, and I watched all emotions get dragged away from him until all I saw was a face made of wax.

"You do not understand, and you never will," he said in a flat, unemotional voice. "You do not have the intellect, nor the maturity."

"Why, you pompous, idiotic cretin of a fae!" I clamped my mouth shut.

He was goading me into this argument. Why? The easy answer was he was trying to get me to say something in the heat of the moment that he could leverage me with. I'd had enough. I turned and stalked angrily back towards the motel parking lot. I heard Cobb say something, but I was focusing only on getting to my room without going back and trying to rip him apart verbally.

The slamming door was like an opening bell in a boxing match, and I beat on the bed and the pillows for I don't know how long, cursing and snarling. I finally collapsed onto the bed. My anger still burned, but it was more a smolder than a forest fire. I had no clue why Cobb wanted to work me up so badly, but I was certain it had to do with the service. He was hiding something. He was manipulating every step we took. I wanted to know why.

21

THE NEXT MORNING, I put my pack in the car and knocked on Kevin's door. He answered sleepily, and opened it as far as the security chain would allow. His hair was a short, wild mane, with random tufts standing up on his scalp, making him look like a gerbil that had stuck its head in a light socket.

"Fern, what's up?"

"How's your arm, Kevin?"

He disappeared behind the door for a moment, and I heard him tear velcro off the temporary sling. "Huh," I heard, and he reappeared in the chained doorway. "It's sealed over and there's no pain. Doc did a good job." He closed the door, and I heard some things being moved around. "I think I'm ready to go, Fern. Let's hit it after breakfast."

"Okay, see you then."

I stepped a few paces to my right and started to knock on Kent's door when it pulled open and Kent was there, dressed and ready to go. His three-piece suit gleamed like it had been just pressed, and a faint scent of spiced rum wafted from him. I think I must have stared blankly at him as he smirked and stepped past me.

"I'll just throw this in the trunk then, and we'll be off to breakfast," he said with a smile. He carried his duffel over to the car, waited for me to open the trunk, and flipped it in just beside mine. "You think they have espresso out here?"

I shuddered theatrically. "Ugh, barbarian, you're trying to eat your stomach away?"

He chuckled and said, smiling, "I'll have you know that espresso is the ultimate civilized drink. All the caffeine that you'll need for a day in one four-ounce cup. Saves time and water."

"I stick with my beliefs. You won't see me touch that vile concoction."

As I finished closing the trunk, Kevin appeared, lugging his duffel towards us. He had on a pair of old blue jeans, and a black t-shirt with a khaki photographer's vest over it. I reopened the trunk, Kevin threw his duffel in, then slammed the trunk closed.

"I'm ready, let's get chow," he said, as he hopped in the passenger seat.

We drove a short way over to Keneally's, a nice little hole-in-the-wall diner that has some of the best sausage and gravy that I've had in a long time. We all tucked in and soon finished. Kevin eyed me as I grabbed the check.

"Is Cobb going to be there today?" he asked me in a carefully neutral voice.

"Probably, though I'm not certain. He volunteered for this, and since he wants this done, I'd expect him to show," I replied, equally neutral. "Is there a problem with him and you that I don't know about?"

He shrugged slightly, and then shook his head.

"I just don't know for certain." He shrugged again.

I got the feeling whatever he was going to talk about had given him troubles for a while.

"The Doc said that my wound was from a large rock chip, not claws. I think I got that when you shot the ground near it. When it dropped on me, all I could think of was how you said it was so lethal, and that I was going to die. But all it did was drop on me. It took me all night to think through what bothered me about that fight. It just laid on me." He shrugged yet again and looked first at Kent, then at me.

That was a real surprise. Why didn't it gut him like a fish? It could have, easily. Was that why Cobb was so upset?

"Well, that is very interesting. How much should we tell our associate?" Kent questioned.

I thought about that. What does he stand to gain by coercing me to work for him, then trying to obstruct what he asked me to do?

"Nothing. If he's running some kind of scam or game on us, it is better that he doesn't know we've gotten wind of it. He might try something else. This way we can watch and maybe see what he's trying to hide or keep our attention away from."

Kent had an introspective look on his face.

"You know, Fern, you might be looking at this backwards. He may not have an agenda." He held up his hands in mock surrender when I started choking on my tea. "Hey, I know he's a manipulative son of a bitch, but what I'm saying is maybe you're not looking at things from the proper line." He stopped for a moment to let his words sink in, and then added, "What if that creature had been trying to do something else, like warn us, or protect Kevin from something? Not saying that's what it was doing, just saying what it did do doesn't fit with what I'd expect from a hostile." He shrugged then picked up his fork, tapping it absently on the table as he gathered his thoughts. "I know it's a stretch, but, if it had wanted to kill you, why didn't it follow up when it trashed your car the first time? Why just go for the one shot?"

They had me there. Looking back, I had to agree. Besides creating fear, it never made a threatening move at me, just tried to stagger towards Cobb at the end when I'd shot it. Don't get me wrong: fear is bad. At the right time, it will drive you into a panic or insane. The issue in my head was, "Was the creature truly hostile? Or just acting hostile?" At the time when it appeared, I was so keyed up from the previous attacks that I didn't want to give it another chance at me, or anyone with me. Maybe the creature was not an enemy; maybe it was, just not the way we think. Cobb, no matter how I tried to rationalize it, was an enemy. He just happened to be on our side. But my instinct was fairly screaming that he was an enemy. Until this service I owed was done, I couldn't afford the luxury of thinking he might be something else. This whole thing felt like a scam. Get yours truly to work for him, then create obstructions, delays, and detours.

We got up from the table and I left a ten-dollar tip, to ease my troubled mind a bit. Once out to the car, Kent grabbed the front seat and Kevin sat in his floor seat. We headed out to the bridge.

Cobb was waiting for us there, near where Kent had set his septagram the previous day. The wind was blowing fiercely. Whitecaps danced in the strait. The wet wind cut through my clothes and chilled me almost as soon as I was out of the car. Kent flipped up the collar of his suit. Turning his back to the wind, he watched Kevin get out of the back, acting like it was a warm summer day. Kent smiled sourly, then turned his head to look at me.

"So we gonna do this, Fern?" asked Kent.

I looked out again at the strait. Staying out in the open was going to chill us all pretty thoroughly, but if we got the casting done, we wouldn't have to come back again.

"Yeah, we're going to do it." I glared at Cobb, who was happy to glare back at me. "Faster started, faster done with this bloody thing."

Kent and Kevin went back out to the spit of land and used some brushes to clean the spot and ready the ground for the new wards. I hiked back up to the broken end of the bridge, and used a steel welding brush to clear away the old septagram and ready the ground for the new one. Cobb just watched the preparations. He saw me watching him, gave me an insolent grin, and then turned slightly to look out over the strait. I sat down to wait my start, which would coincide with Kevin opening a quiet hole in the barrier. I couldn't figure, in all this time, why someone hadn't tried to do this before. It seemed that someone would have thought of it long ago. But then again, we were trying to go to the island, not come from it, and it had been a long time since anyone had tried to breach the barrier with magick. Angry dragons tend to discourage that.

Kevin and Kent began their chanting. It would be a couple of hours before my part was due. Mine was going to need the most power to set its effect, so I sat back, relaxed, and watched the waters of the strait while I gathered my strength for the casting. This was by far the biggest thing I'd ever "volunteered" to do. Ritual magick is great for slow projects that are intricate; you can coax power to do your desire and, given time, you can build really powerful spells. That was what I was doing while the others built their parts. I would be the one working the most power into the spell to anchor it, and create permanency where there was just the barest existence remaining. It wasn't delicate or difficult; just a lot of time and power needed.

The sun was just barely up. Its reddish glow gave the waters the appearance of liquid fire dancing to the flow of the wind. The barrier hung midway into the strait: a grey, reddish-sparkling sheet that looked like fog, but, at the same time, had a harder, almost crystalline glint in the early morning sun.

It looked magickal — a hard, harsh kind of magick. There were few birds here, and most of the fish and other water creatures had died when they came in contact with the barrier. The first few years the barrier was up, the whole strait supposedly reeked of the dead and decaying animals it had killed. Now it looked placid and beautiful, but that placidity disguised the sterility of the waters and the surrounding skies. That became more apparent when you tried to listen for birdsong: there was none.

I wasn't at all certain what might have survived on the island, with all things dying around it. Prince Edward Island is small — as provinces go, it's the smallest one in Canada. It made up for that in the past with scenic beauty, and a smart local government that looked forward, balancing the past with the needs of the present, and an eye on the future. All that was long dead since the barrier went up. That people had survived the return of magick was one of the things that kept reminding me how tenacious we are as a species, and how adaptable.

I began my chant after both Kent and Kevin adjusted their cadence. I joined in, my alto shifting to match the cadence of my two partners. I could feel Cobb in the background, his magick aching a bit like a pebble in a shoe. We were drawing power from pretty much the same source and area, which could have been problematic, but since the three of us overlapped in intended use, we actually were able to coax and stabilize the power more easily together than we would if separate. It was one of the side effects of group ritual magick. You felt the others, and were comforted by them in a way I have yet to be able to hear explained in any way close to the true sensation. It was glorious.

Cobb had remained by the car since we had arrived and set up, conspicuously staying away from us "murderous" humans. Truthfully, I was glad for the reprieve. He'd worn out his welcome, and the only reason now to have him here was his concealment spell, and the trip back and forth across the Way to prove it was open.

Kevin and Kent's chanting filled my ears, and I watched as the echo of the bridge began to take shape, reaching out across the strait towards Prince Edward Island. The echo started from the edge of the bridge where I stood and formed like mist outwards towards the barrier. The barrier sat out there: a hard, reddish-grey shimmer. The echo reached the barrier and continued through it. The spell was nearing the other end of the bridge. Kevin now increased the pace of his chant, and I felt a pressure build.

Cobb was suddenly beside me; I could see his shoes just at the edge of my peripheral vision. I was focusing outward and didn't have the time to be distracted. Kevin's chant raised to a quiet climax as a spark flashed against the barrier. The flash pierced the barrier, and magick pressure flowed away from us. The barrier seemed to vibrate: a low throbbing pulse against my skin. We watched a hole form and dilate like an iris. The circular opening grew rapidly in size until the echo was able to continue through. I heard Kevin slow the chant and hold it at its present size, which was just enough for the superstructure to slip through to the next load-supporting pier. Kent continued to pour power into the chant, and the echo grew and extended to the limits that I could discern.

"It's almost to shore," Cobb said loudly, and I think that was the first thing he'd actually done to help us.

The end of the echo was way beyond our vision, but because the spell was part of the caster, the spell dimensions could be felt. Kent's slight change in cadence gave a clue that the far shore had been reached. His cadence felt less of water and more of earth. He felt the connection to the other side. Both the echo of the bridge, and the opening in the veil, were holding. It was up to me to pour power into the echo and the hole to solidify them both, then there would be locking the spell and concealing it.

I had to hurry, relative to the others, though. They both had their spells up, but those would only last as long as they chanted. It put pressure on me to be fast, and finish before they collapsed from exhaustion, so I took a few shortcuts and pulled along with the coaxed power. It was easier to do once Kent and Kevin finished the building of their spells and just maintained them. I focused, envisioning myself reaching deep into the ley line that ran through this area, and pulled a thread from the line to me. This shortcut could kill, if not carefully handled. The thread from the line would continually feed me magick, allowing me to rapidly build up a store for use. The downside was it would keep feeding into me, whether I wanted it to or not. If I didn't cut the link after a certain point, the link would grow too strong to cut, and it would feed so much into me that I'd burn up like paper in a flame.

I kept the chant up to bleed some magick off, and to prime the echo for the power I was going to feed into it. The magick kept increasing its flow. The power started to raise the hairs on my arms and neck, and skittered along my arm like a live electric current. I looked out at the echo of the bridge and started feeding the power into it. The slight yellowish vapor that made the echo began to solidify, turning an opaque grey-white as the power rebuilt the bridge bit by bit, and soon the first section extended beyond where I sat out into the strait. The filling-in and solidifying accelerated, and continued as the spell poured more power into the echo, and, in minutes, the bridge solidified up to the barrier.

The bridge continued to settle and become more solid. I felt the link thicken and strengthen as I pulled from the ley line. I wanted to finish soon, as the line was now bleeding a slight amount of power into me from the spell, and that signaled I was at the limit of my ability to fully control it. From now on, I'd be absorbing more power as the link strengthened. The bridge built quickly past the barrier, but it was another ten minutes before I could feel the end step back to land from the sea. I'd finished the echo; now it was time to finish the opening.

The ley line flow strengthened, pouring more power into me as I worked the second spell. I started to push my will around the link to choke the ley line, but choking the line *and* finishing the spell was beyond my skill. I began to feel the first stirrings of panic as it resisted me closing it off.

I was at a point where there were two choices to be had. One, I could forget about keeping the barrier open and focus on choking the link. If I did that, the barrier would close on the echo, destroying it and putting us back to square one. The big problem would be that Anolyn would know what we were doing. Two, I could use the power to finish locking the opening in the barrier, and then fight the link. If Kevin and Kent were still in the spell with me, they would be able to sense the problem, and maybe help to a small extent, but for the most part it would be me against the link. Every moment pushed the odds closer to me burning to a crisp.

Call it stubbornness, but I went with choice two. The power surged into the opening Kevin had crafted and reinforced the hole. I felt Kevin break his link and leave the spell to me. The whole barrier tried to snap down on my opening. I aimed the wild torrent of power into the barrier, reinforcing the gap. The veil bucked and ground at the gap, but Kevin's spell held, and the ley line's power locked the opening in place. It solidified and held. Now I could work on saving me. I cut the power to the echo and the gap. The two spells remained rock-steady. The ley line, now with no spell to flow into, chose the next best thing: me.

I tried to choke off the power, but only barely slowed the flow down. I could feel the electric itching increase to painful levels, and I tried to scream as the power held me rigid. The magick had filled me, and I could feel myself start to expand like a balloon. The pain was like being electrocuted: you knew what was happening, but the current locked every muscle in place, rendering you helpless to stop it. As my body twitched from the power overload, I reached the bursting point. I thought I was dead, when the power suddenly vented somewhere. The pressure fell away, but I was still helpless, with the ley line power roaring through me into wherever.

Cobb stepped in front of me and murmured something. He pulled his sword and looked at me, then raised it to strike. There was no way I could dodge, or even use some of this massive power, to protect myself. My hands felt molten as the ley line continued to pour power through me and into elsewhere. Cobb was shouting now, and I felt dim vibrations through the ground. He looked back at me, stepped to the side, lowering himself to one knee, and then thrust the sword right through my hands.

The cold pain of the silver blade cutting through my hands was minor compared to the hot blast of power from the line when Cobb severed it. My hands and arms blistered from the heated backlash. My whole body went violently rigid as the power blew out from me. I don't remember passing out.

I awoke to feeling a pressure working its way around my hand. When I could get my eyes to focus, I could see Kent wrapping my left hand in gauze. The right had been wrapped to the elbow, and I could fuzzily make out the same on the hand Kent was wrapping.

"Hey, welcome back to the Great White North, kiddo," Kevin said cheerily. "Next time you want to do something like that, please let us kick your butt around the block first. I do not like thinking about what Fawn would do to us if you were to die on our watch."

He looked over at Kent, who was putting the first bit of tape on to hold the bandage in place.

"What part of cop Siberia would she put us in, d'you think?"

Kent looked at Kevin, and gave a slight smile.

"Parking meters," he said. "That, or cleaning the K-9 kennels."

Kevin thought about the choices, theatrically shuddered, and then said, "Oh my god, I forgot about the kennels. A fate worse than eternal traffic tickets."

I managed a woozy, pained smile.

"Gee, your thoughts for my safety have me so underwhelmed, I just don't know what to s—ow!" I yelped as Kent stabbed me with a dull needle and gave me a shot of Darvon to ease the pain.

The world went pleasantly fuzzy for the next few hours as we went back to the local clinic. The doctor on duty was the same one that worked on Kevin the night before. I wish I could have made out what he said, as I heard both Kent and Kevin laugh, but I was too mushy from the Darvon to do anything but nod and smile along. Better living through chemistry.

22

KENT SAID I WAS FIVE HOURS IN THE EMERGENCY SURGERY and magickal healing, due to the massive nerve damage to my hands from the sword, and the backlash from the ley line. I woke back at the Northumberland Inn, lying on the bed, with Kent and Kevin playing whist at a small table nearby.

"Hey, Kent, look! It lives," Kevin said, with a smile on his face and in his voice. They had spent all their time here making sure I was all right.

"How are you feeling now?" Kent asked me, as I slowly propped myself up.

"Lousy," I told him, and my head throbbed. "No talky," I whispered to them.

They both looked over at me, stood up, gave me a thumbs-up, and left the room quietly. They knew how to make an exit, and I passed blissfully out and slept until eight the next morning.

I awoke to the door rattling as Kevin knocked energetically on it.

"Fern, wake up! Time to get food and head out!" he said loudly through the door.

I winced, expecting to feel like nails were driven into my skull. When it didn't happen, the lack of pain made me a touch slow, mentally. It took me a few more pounds on the door to finally register that it was time to wake up. I grumbled to myself and sat up.

"All right, I hear you! Stop the noise, and I'll be right out after a shower!"

"Okay, Kent and I'll head out then. What should we bring you back?"

"Sausage and toast and some coffee," I shouted through the door.

"Got it, see you when we get back." I could hear them laugh as they headed out.

I unwrapped my arms and saw loose skin peeling off. The skin had been regrown by the doctor. Now the blistered and burned parts were sloughing off. I scrubbed vigorously in the shower, and got most of the itchy dead skin to loosen and drop away. I'd finished and just gotten dressed when Kevin was pounding on the door again. Doesn't anyone just knock?

A short stalk to the door, and a quick open to the end of the safety chain startled both men, who quickly recovered and held out a cardboard box that smelled like heaven would, if heaven were made of sausage.

"Here's breakfast," Kevin said.

It was hard to get the chain off, I was so hungry. The door seemed to take a perverse glee in obstructing the way, until I finally broke the chain in frustration and opened the door. Kent reacted with a soft chuckle as I snatched the box from his hands. I carried the food over to the postage stamp-sized table and tucked in while Kent and Kevin walked my pack and gear out to the PT Cruiser, putting the bags in the back. They waited politely while I savaged my breakfast, then closed the door behind me as I walked to the car. I'd get a bill for the chain, certainly, but that venison sausage with real maple syrup was worth the expense.

I handed Kent the keys, and he drove us back out to the site. The wind was brisk, creating rolling whitecaps in the Northumberland Strait. The soft sound of the waves against the shore almost covered up the lack of animal and insect noise. As before, Cobb was on site waiting for us to show. He stalked over to the car as we started to get out.

"You three, I have words for you!" he said loudly, as he approached the car.

I stood my ground, and saw Kent and Kevin ease to the sides and unobtrusively ready themselves for trouble. Cobb sounded majorly agitated. I really didn't want to fight with him. I looked him in the eye as he approached and he slowed to a stop about ten feet from us.

"Good morning to you, Cobb. Now what's the problem?" I said acerbically. "The bridge up in the wrong place?"

He watched us for a moment and relaxed slightly.

"No, I finished the concealment after you three left for Pictou, and stayed on watch here through the night to see if Anolyn would show. He has not, and that worries me." He looked at the three of us again, and then said, in a faltering voice loaded with emotion, "I ... also wanted ... to thank you for your work in this. In truth, I had not ... expected that Fern could have done this. So I apologize for my ill manners and the trials I have put you through to date."

"Well, a late apology is better than none," Kent said. "But we're not done yet, I do believe. I seem to remember that we must cross to the island, and re-cross back to here to finish the service."

Cobb quirked a smile.

"Yes, that is part of the terms of the service. But I do recommend caution. I would have preferred Anolyn to show rather than not. At least then we would know that he had sensed and decided to investigate. His not showing makes me think that a trap is being set." Cobb sounded strained. I don't know if elves sleep, but he sounded like a punch-drunk conspiracy theorist — too many caffeine shots and just *knowing* the bad stuff's coming. I think most of us prefer to see and know the enemy, rather than not see him and scare ourselves half-witless with possibilities.

"Well, it's going to be a twelve-kilometer walk, which is about three hours there and three hours back, given a leisurely pace since we're carrying packs. I'd like to get back before it gets dark," I said.

"I'd love to use the car," Kent sighed wistfully. "But that much moving metal is too easy to spot, and Cobb's glamour might not be able to take its touch."

Damn, I hadn't thought of that. It meant, before we could go across, we had to shuck any cold iron we had, or the glamour might go poof. I really didn't want to try the bridge in the open. Part of me realized, too, that we were tired, and that could lead to little mistakes now. A more rational part of me was hinting another night's sleep would be a very good idea; the stubborn side argued to get it done now before something else happened. Stubborn won.

"Okay, let's go to the opening and remove anything metal there. I want to get this done."

Guess who was nervous? Absolutely, I was. About the only thing I'd have for protection would be my feet, and a few quick-and-dirty spells to blind or confuse aim, and they might not affect a dragon.

Cobb asked if we could wait a moment. He went over to his pack that he had lugged around since we got here, pulled a longbow and a quiver of silver arrows out, and laid them on the ground. He also produced a sword and two daggers from the sack, and a small silver shield the size of a dinner plate.

"It is not much, but each of you may use what is here. I will carry the shield and sword. My accuracy with this," he motioned to the bow, "is at best poor. So if any of you can draw the bow, please carry it."

"But won't this amount of metal be just as bad as the car?" Kent asked.

"No, the silver will not disrupt the glamour on the bridge, and we shall be able to cross without endangering any of the spells," Cobb replied evenly.

"Well, then, can we get going, please? I really don't like the idea of crossing this thing at night," said Kevin irritably.

After dropping Kent and Kevin's service ten-millimeter, and my T/C Contender, plus my metal thermos and Kent's steel canteen, we gathered up the remaining spell equipment. Of the gear he brought, Cobb took the sword and the shield. I took a dagger, and felt ridiculously like I was in a fantasy movie doing so. Kent grabbed the other dagger, leaving Kevin the bow, which he picked up reluctantly. He looked at all of us, then picked up the quiver.

"Before you ask: yes, I can shoot. I might hit the broad side of a barn, if I was shooting on the inside, so don't expect miracles."

That got a chuckle out of Kent. Cobb just scowled, and I hid my nervous smirking giggle behind a hand. So equipped, our "party" gathered up our backpacks of camping gear (just in case the unthinkable happened and we got stuck on the island), magick accoutrements, and snack food, and we ventured out onto the bridge and towards the barrier.

The trip was uneventful, and almost pleasant, listening to the waves roll underneath us as we traversed the one hundred meters to the echo bridge. The waves did nothing to relax any of us, though, and, when we reached the barrier, we all stopped just short and listened, trying to hear any sound from the other side of the opening. Nothing, except for the rolling of the waves, was heard by anyone.

"Want to do the honors, Fern?" asked Kent.

I took a deep breath, but Cobb stepped in front of me. Then Kent stepped past the barrier, while we all looked at him in surprise. He grinned.

"I'm too old to run away fast. This way I get my choice of how I go." Definitely a morbid sense of humor there.

We crossed the barrier, and nothing really changed, except the knowledge that we were on the opposite side of a barrier that no one had penetrated for sixty-odd years. It made me really wonder why we were able to do so, when so many others, who were probably as good or better, did not. I put it down to looking at the obvious, and not trying to go head-on, which a lot of wizards seem to want to do. You may win big going head-to-head with a spell, a summoning, or another practitioner, but you also tend to lose very big if you fail. Quite often, it is the permanent, fatal kind of loss.

23

S O MAYBE WE WERE THE FIRST to apply a sneaky or sideways thought to the problem, but I doubted that. There was an answer to why, and it bugged me that I couldn't quite figure it out. We stopped about a hundred meters past the barrier and looked down. Forty meters down, the waves still rolled, but the wind died at the barrier. The noise of waves striking the columns sounded the same, but the noise felt more sterile, less alive.

There was a sense of decay, one that niggled at the edge of my memory. One place I didn't want to remember, and yet the sense of rot was like six months ago, when we went back to the old cabin where my parents had tried to use magick to kill Fawn and I, and to save us. The wind itself hadn't changed, but it felt greasy as it slid over my clothes and ruffled my hair. There was an unwholesomeness that permeated everything around us. We hurried our pace slightly and, after two hours of walking, got to the shore of Prince Edward Island. Back at ground level, we stopped to look around and record in our minds the place all our efforts had led to.

To give you a little idea about Prince Edward Island: it's exactly that, a not quite so small island off of the borders of New Brunswick and Nova Scotia. It's roughly one-hundred-sixty kilometers long, around thirty to forty kilometers wide, and looks like a slightly bent bone. Both the eastern and western ends are slightly wider than the center third. Most of the central portion, where we were, was cultivated fields with small copses of trees scattered about. The western side had a fair bit of dense pine forest and undergrowth, while the east side had more cultivated ground. That was before Anolyn made it his home. Now, it's all just dead.

In a very real — and very eerie — sense of *deja vu*, the PEI reminded me of Ahiah's vale, where my parents and uncle had died, where we'd managed to break that glass bottle that Ahiah had used to inflict such horror on people. Everything had the same feel: yellowish-gray, dusty, lifeless remains of buildings, and vegetation that had been sucked dry of its essence by some unclean thing. Again, I was struck by the absence of birdsong, and what we'd come to think of as "normal" background noise: frogs, crickets, bugs. The grass was a sickly yellow-green, as were the pines. The color was brittle in appearance — like paint that had been weathered too long.

It was more than a little disquieting, like the silence in a horror movie just before the ominous music cued a hideous death. The Welcome Center didn't look welcoming at all. Two hundred meters from the shoreline, "Welcome to PEI, your adventure begins here." in English, then in French underneath, was spelled out in white on a faded blue sign. The building was barely standing. Untouched for fifty-odd years, decay had had its way with the building. The glass was still in the windows, but faded and peeling white paint hung off the dry wood underneath it. This was the only building still standing near this end of the bridge.

Where the small town of Port Borden used to be was a blackened patch of ground. Aside from the Welcome Center, a few charred and partly melted brick buildings were all that poked above the devastated earth.

"So, we're here. Now all we have to do is get back, and this service of yours is done, Fern," said Kevin, looking over at Cobb, who had picked up a handful of dirt and was letting it sift through his other hand.

It hardly looked like normal dirt. It had that brittle texture, and sickening yellowish cast to it, as well. It bothered me to see that stuff disturbed. It felt like he was disturbing a grave. I shook off the feeling as best I could, and looked around. We were at the base of a low hill that rose going inland. Cobb was sifting more energetically now through the dusty earth, as if he was searching for something and, as we approached to get him to start back with us, he pulled a lump of metal from the earth. He looked at it for a moment and then looked to the three of us.

"Are any of you psychometric, or able to build a spell of psychometry? I am unable to do such things."

"If we can, do we have to stay here to do it?" Kent asked him, with a very quiet and direct tone to his voice.

I agreed with him. I didn't want to stay on this ground any more than I had to. There was something very inimical to us, and it was raising the hairs on my neck.

"Let's take it with us," I said to the others. "We can do the past-reading when we get back to the car. This place is beginning to creep me out big-time."

Kent was already stepping back towards the bridge, when Cobb said suddenly, "Wait!"

"Wait?" argued Kevin. "Why? I agree with Fern. This place has got a bad vibe to it. I don't like it. It's creeping Fern out, to quote her, and you want to wait? What the hell for?"

"Because," said Cobb with a weird, intense tremor to his voice. "Psychometry is best done where an object is collected from. Those impressions or echoes are strongest and easiest to read at the location where you find an object. We go back and we lose detail that might be important."

Kent had stopped by the road that linked to the bridge.

"What are you waiting for? We made it here, and now we go back. Get a move on, you youngsters." He sounded impatient, and I was getting that way too.

Cobb was suddenly wanting to do a past-life spell on a piece of metal? I got that manipulated feeling again. Cobb had played — or was playing — us right now, and I had had enough.

I stalked over to him, and stretched out my hand, palm up. "May I see what you have there?"

He looked at me curiously for a moment, then handed the lump to me. I turned and threw it as far as I could into the thickest dead bunch of brittle-looking brush I could see.

Cobb looked at me, his jaw muscles twitching. I was ready for a shouting match. Instead, he turned his back to us, took a deep breath, then a second one. He then said, to no one in particular, "I suppose it is good that there is one less piece. There are so many in the ground, they would be a hazard if more were exposed."

With that, I looked hard around the area, expecting to see little things here and there poking through the soil that we had missed when we looked the area over earlier. Nothing of the sort could be seen. Cobb kneeled down and dug about a finger's length into the dry soil and pulled up a lump of something, which looked crisped and charred. Kent and Kevin walked over to Cobb to take a quick look.

"What do you think this is, gentlemen?" Cobb asked them, as I fumed a short distance away.

I was about ready to head back on my own and to blazes with them. This place was making my skin crawl, and Cobb pulling those pieces out of the ground didn't do anything to settle my nerves down.

"Looks like a piece of safety glass. Here, see this? You can see the layer of plastic between the two glass layers."

I walked over to the three of them and slapped the thing out of Cobb's hands. "Can. We. Go. Now?" I said through gritted teeth.

"Uh, yeah, she's right. Let's get outta here," said Kent.

Cobb looked at the two of them and ignored me.

"How long does it take for a human practitioner to do psychometry on an object? This is the event site. I'm certain the safety glass has been untouched since the event. That would surely make things easier, wouldn't it?" he asked in an eager voice.

Kent and Kevin started to get up and check their packs, pulling a few pieces of their magick equipment out. The items Cobb had picked up were laid in the parking lot. I really didn't want to touch anything. The sense of death in the still air felt like a warning that we were desecrating a graveyard.

"Takes about an hour, regardless," replied Kevin. "All the site does for psychometry is give the caster a more intensely intimate connection to the past events."

"Can we try it here?" asked Cobb very intently. "There is something that is very important to me here. A reading would be a start to unraveling a mystery that has been hidden since the veil was created."

There was a long moment of silence as the two humans stared at the elf. Slowly, they began shrugging their packs back off. Fear and fury rolled through me to see them give in to Cobb. I stomped three steps to Kevin and Kent, the movement catching their attention. Cobb glared at the intrusion. I mentally flipped him the finger and crossed my arms over my chest.

"I can tell you what happened, you idiot. A dragon happened. Most of the stuff around here that you'd find would be pieces of cars and trucks. Dragons breathe fire, or did you forget that? They tend to like things extra-crispy, and I have no intention of sticking around to see how well-done my tan could get when he finds us."

I was starting to really get a bad vibe. I was close to freaking out, and angry that we weren't moving away.

"Why aren't you guys feeling any …?"

I stopped talking. Pieces clicked together as I put Kent and Kevin's reactions with Cobb. I gazed at both men, who seemed singularly unimpressed with the argument in front of them. Being the paranoid person I am, I opened my mage sight. The background was so hideous I don't remember falling on my knees. The next minute was spent puking my breakfast out on the dead earth.

Mage sight gives you more than just what you normally see: you can see the spirit, or balance — or whatever you want to call it — of what you're looking at as well. It also shows how it's been warped and polluted by forces that have affected it. This place had been blasted not only with fire, but death magick. I could see the echo of the magick, and the hate that made up the spell. It was a miasma that clung to the remains of buildings, machines, and bodies.

I spent a few moments concentrating on my hands and knees, feeling the ground under them. The vertigo faded as more of my focus went to my sense of touch, and I was able to stand up. As I slowly straightened, I gazed over to Kent and Kevin, and noticed faint violet lines that encircled both men's heads. The lines appeared to run around and through their heads, with the ends of the tendrils leading back to Cobb. He'd cast a spell, one that looked like it messed with their mind or perception. Maybe both. This was a deliberate manipulation of people I knew. My anger went cold.

"Cobb," I said very quietly. Cobb looked at me, then stiffened, reading the outrage in my features. "Take the glamour off them. Now. This is over."

Cobb looked at me, his own features showing desperation and anger.

"I need to find out what is here!" he said in a quiet voice. I could hear the desperate frustration in him. Whatever he was after here, to him it was worth gambling his life for.

To me, nothing other than family and friends were worth my life. I had to get control of this, or we'd be fighting Cobb. I took a deep breath, trying to stay calm when my instincts were screaming at me to run away right now. The stub of my missing finger throbbed. It felt like it was being dipped in acid. Enough was enough.

"No, you don't. We need to get back across the bridge, now. It's going to be dark soon. I do *not* want to be over here when it gets dark," I said, glaring back at him. "We are leaving now, and if you want to come back tomorrow, go right ahead."

Kent reached languidly to his throat, and wrapped his fingers around his small cross. Cobb jumped as he did, then his eyes narrowed venomously. Kent smiled, then placed a hand on Kevin, who blinked as if coming out of a daze. Both men turned to me, then back to Cobb.

"Nice catch on that glamour," said Kent, who continued to stare at Cobb.

The elf returned the stare, straightening his back as if expecting a confrontation. I'd had enough of mysterious manipulations, damn services that screwed up lives, and mind-altering glamours. It was time to go home and call the service done.

24

W HEN WE STARTED UP THE BRIDGE ONCE MORE, Cobb lost it. "We can't leave! Not yet! We have to ..." Cobb snarled.

When we refused to stop, he started intoning some kind of spell. I listened and caught the gist of the spell.

"Oh, hell, not good!"

Any time a caster starts a spell, another caster can sense the intent of the spell. It's how the magick resonates in the caster. It takes a while to listen as you're learning how, but, like anything, you practice long enough, and you start to catch on to the ripples in the magick, how the caster is weaving tone, emotion, and will into the spell.

"Ms. Fatelli, officers, please do not force me to do this."

He held the unmaking. We were on the echo. If we called Cobb's bluff, we had two choices: run for the New Brunswick shore twelve kilometers away before Cobb could unravel the echo's anchor, or run back ninety meters to PEI before the spell collapsed. I was mad enough, and terrified enough of the island, to be stupid and try for the continental end.

What was so weird was that it just didn't feel real. Cobb's actions were so outrageous, that the word was insufficient to describe them.

Kevin had no problem finding words. "What kind of bug-nuts, dumb-ass desperate-attitude dope-head crap is this?"

Kent laid a hand on Kevin's shoulder as the younger man took a step towards Cobb, fists clenched. Cobb had retreated into that haughty attitude I'd seen before when he'd pushed his agenda in Underhill, and when he'd laid the legal trap that forced me to do this miserable, terrifying job. He was certain, I realized, that he had the upper hand completely. If he wanted us to stay here, all he'd have to do was just unravel the echo, and we were trapped here. Of course, that would be the case if he was still alive to do so, and the way we three humans were feeling at the moment, Cobb just might have made a very serious miscalculation about his situation. Me, I was tempted to suggest we dump him off the echo.

"Just what is it you expect to accomplish by marooning yourself and us here on a dead island that has a dragon somewhere on it? What is so important that you risk all of our lives for?" Kent asked him in a reasonable voice.

I could see his hand clenched tight on Kevin's shoulder, hard enough to make the younger man wince. Cobb just stared quietly at us.

"This won't get any of us to do anything for you. No one likes being forced into a situation."

For a moment, I couldn't figure who was speaking, then I realized it was me. My hands were clenched like Kent's, only I had the dagger Cobb had lent me in my hand. I was gripping the weapon so hard my hand was trembling. I was terrified. I knew … I knew somewhere deep in the old instincts, when humans were food for bigger predators, that something bad was here. Something that hated and hungered. I'd seen its hate with my mage sight. Everyone can feel; it's our own minds second-guessing ourselves that causes the truth to get lost. That's when you get killed.

"I hate him, too, but that isn't going to get us out of here." Kent's voice broke the silence that had built up. Kent took a breath and slowly took his hand off of Kevin's shoulder.

"We're over a barrel right now. Our, host," Kent gritted his teeth around that word, "is being very insistent that we stay."

That was the absolute truth, and I hated every word of it. Cobb had his power in the echo. If he wanted to, he could maroon all of us here.

I looked up at the sky. The shimmering dome of force gave the blue a sickly yellow-green color, matching that of the ground and vegetation. It was all the silence that I found unnerving. It was exactly like being back at the cabin, back where my parents had tried to cast that spell which had done something to me and Fawn. We still weren't sure what, but things kept happening around us.

Uncle Todd had told us, and we were both convinced by his argument, that it was magick trying to balance things out. As we'd gotten older, little things grew into bigger things — like me choosing to go look for trouble, first as a skip-tracer, then as a troubleshooter-slash-girl-of-fortune. I did the things others didn't, and got paid really well. I also took some pretty nasty risks for the money. Not bad, though. Uncle Todd was convinced that both our jobs put us where magick wanted us. I'm a little, no, very skeptical on that, but Fawn agrees with what Uncle Todd said.

"Please understand," Cobb said with an icy calm. "I would not have resorted to this if there had been an agreement to search the island. There is something here I need, and am willing to fight for. All of you have things you would go to extremes to protect, or find, if they — or it — was lost. How is my desperation any different from yours?"

"Explain why it's important," Kent said firmly.

"I need to know something about the attack here. It's important to me."

Kent sighed, lowering his gaze, then bringing it back up to Cobb. "At this moment, it's important for us to know why. Fern has completed her end of the bargain, and now you're forcing her to do something else. You owe her an explanation as to why she's being held here, and you owe us the same. We're Halifax Police, and this, under any law, is kidnapping, and highly illegal."

Cobb allowed himself a ghost of a smile.

"It won't matter, if you can't get off the island. Those who care can't reach you here. No one can. You, your partner, and Ms. Fatelli will just become another missing-persons case." Cobb eyes glittered, like a snake that was ready to strike. "However, if you do two certain services for me, I will not unravel the echo, and you all may return home. And we will consider all things equalized."

I watched Kevin and Kent. They'd walked away from me to confer and, from Kevin's animated gestures, he really did not want any of what Cobb was offering. Kent stayed calm, like he always seemed to. Finally, they seemed to come to an accord, and waved me over.

"We've a choice, and it involves you as well as us. So to be fair, you need to know so you can make your own choice."

Kent closed his eyes, then gestured. A bluish screen sprang into being around us. I could faintly hear what sounded like a distorted guitar riff take off, rising a little on each note, then taking off in a fast boogie shuffle. It took me a moment to identify an old American staple, Southern Fried Rock. The strains were muffled inside the dome, but Cobb's obvious distaste indicated he heard every note loud and clear.

"Huddle up, people," Kent told us. "Just because he can't hear what we say now doesn't mean he can't read lips."

We lowered our heads together as Kent laid out the situation. "He has us by the short hairs. We know he's willing to go to the extreme to get what he wants. The only clue we have right now is the psychometry request. If there's more, and I'm certain there is, he's playing it very close to the chest."

I didn't need this. They didn't need this. I know I should have asked how Kent knew all this, but I wasn't in an asking mood. I was too self-absorbed with being upset and trapped in this dead place.

"How about we just do it and get it over with?" Kent said with a resigned smile that didn't reach his eyes. "The sooner it's done, the sooner we can get out of here."

We all nodded. Unfortunately, "getting it over with" suddenly became a much different statement as the echo started to shimmer.

"Cobb! What have you done?!" Kent shouted angrily.

"It is not my magick!" Cobb shouted back. "Someone's unraveling it from the other end! I can't hold the echo!"

Fear spiked through me as I felt the continental end begin to fray. If we had time, we could counter the unraveling, but we didn't have any. Who — or what — was doing this had caught us totally flat-footed. I sensed the unraveling. It was part of me in the casting, so anything that affected the echo, I also got a twinge from. Cobb's magick I'd felt through his casting the veil to obscure the echo. This was like his, but it wasn't him.

"RUN!" Kevin screamed, as he and Cobb were already scrambling down the echo towards PEI.

I followed suit as fast as my legs would carry me. I could feel how fast the spell was breaking down. Whoever was at the other end was powerful, and smart. The unknown caster blew Cobb's obscurement spell away like dust, and the echo was unraveling exactly as I'd built it. There was a *pop* behind my eyes as the anchor was dispelled. The destruction roared along the echo at a speed that had me wobble badly as I tried to steer towards land. I put everything into a panicked burst of speed, and my feet hit solid ground just as the echo collapsed with a bright flash behind me.

25

KENT STOOD BACK AS KEVIN RANTED WILDLY at the end of the bridge. Cops hear a lot in their lives, and I think Kevin paid homage to everything twice, just to be thorough. I just stayed quiet, and tried not to run in circles screaming, because we were trapped on this dead island with a live dragon. We hadn't seen it, but we'd certainly seen its handiwork. You could feel the hate even without opening mage sight. All the remains emanated it like a faint heat from a fire.

It took us humans a while to calm down after being so dramatically stranded on PEI. Kevin finally screamed himself out, and I eventually quit shaking like a leaf in a hurricane. Cobb waited with martyred patience, then led us back down the ramp to the remains of Port Borden.

The fine dust on the ground rose up from our tracks and hovered over the dead earth like the smudge of a distant forest fire over the trees. The wind had become dead still once the echo unraveled. I don't know if the completed barrier did something to the breeze, or if the wind simply had died over the island naturally. Regardless of the circumstance, the place was like being in an open coffin, which really pushed my dragon paranoia to new heights.

The three of us followed Cobb as he walked over to what might once have been a parking lot near the Welcome Center. The parking lot was scorched, broken asphalt, and covered with the sickly yellow-brown dust. The Welcome Center building was a charred rubble of broken sheetrock, carbonized wood, shattered glass, and crushed cinder blocks. No insects buzzed. No birds sang. Nothing made a sound, except for the scrape of our shoes on the asphalt.

Cobb walked over to a large melted former police car, and pulled a piece of glass from its shattered and partly melted windshield. The safety glass had broken into small pieces, with the plastic sandwich holding them into a semblance of a whole. He walked over to Kevin, and held out the hand-sized piece of glass. "Test this."

Kevin looked at the shard like it was a live, angry snapping turtle. He delicately plucked the glass from Cobb's outstretched hand, then looked about him for a place to draw the spell. Walking to a flat piece of ground, he grabbed a small stick and scratched out a trefoil of overlapping circles, with one point facing directly west, one point northeast, and the last point southeast. There was a small area in the center where all three circles overlapped, and this is where Kevin sat. He faced the western circle, placing the glass outside in the west circle. He put his shoes in the northeast circle, and left the southeast empty.

He sat, legs crossed, back straight, and began chanting. Kent motioned to me, then stepped over to Cobb. I followed, curious at what Kent was doing.

"What are you expecting to find?" Kent whispered to Cobb, who never took his attention from Kevin as he replied in a low voice.

"Evidence."

Kent opened his mouth to ask something, which is when Kevin screamed. His voice was raw and wounded. He shuddered, then fell over, still screaming like a damned soul, pulled into a fetal position, rigid with terror. He tried for one last wail of horror, but his throat was so raw by then, it came out as a rasping croak. He shuddered once more, then lay completely still. I started forward, but Kent's outstretched arm held me back.

"Let me. I've worked with him. He knows me better than he does you."

I nodded and stepped back, biting my lower lip. We couldn't afford to have him hurt.

Kent approached the circles, smudging a break in each one before stepping into the center where Kevin lay. He knelt by Kevin, and solemnly intoned, "Twas brillig, and the slithy toves did gyre and gimble in the wabe; all mimsy were the borogoves, and the mome raths outgrabe."

Kevin started twitching by the second line, then a weak chuckle came as he turned his head towards Kent.

"That's a hell of a wakeup call, Nix."

"You like reading the classics. What's more classic than Lewis Carroll?"

"Nothing much," Kevin, replied, then stiffened, eyes widened in panic. He sat still and shivered for a moment, before whispering hoarsely, "Still flashing back. I don't ever want to do that here again. It … I don't have words."

Kent reached out a hand, which Kevin gratefully clasped. Kent helped him up, and the two men walked slowly back over to Cobb and me. Cobb went right for the jugular.

"Explain it all, in detail. It's important."

Kevin glared at him, then moved to a twisted and scorched bit of sidewalk and sat down.

"It's not something I'll be able to forget. Being burned alive and seeing the dragon. The people in that car had lost their home, and two of their three children, to Anolyn when he first appeared. They found the police car abandoned and piled in. They sprinted for the ferry, but it had been sunk. They tried for the bridge. Everyone else had the same idea. It was FUBAR. They got hit by a guy in a big SUV, who tried to tear the father out of the car, so he could take theirs. Anolyn made a pass right over them and breathed. They died screaming. I felt everything. I heard Anolyn say something, but they were too terrified, and in too much pain dying, to remember any of it."

He rubbed his temples as he gathered his thoughts. I was glad it was him and not me. That kind of terror I'd been through once back at the cabin. I never wanted to repeat it.

Kevin took a deep, calming breath, and then continued. "I think Anolyn said, 'Worthless! Useless!' Something like that."

Cobb had been paying rapt attention as Kevin recited his vision. "Was there anything else? Any activity in your vision other than the people?" Cobb asked, a strange hunger in his voice.

Kevin shook his head. "I don't remember seeing any. Everything was panic and confusion, especially after the crash. They were just yelling at each other and trying to get up the bridge and across it."

Cobb nodded, and seemed to be considering another question, when Kent spoke up.

"Kevin, they were going up the bridge, and got caught in a jam at the base?"

Kevin nodded. "There were automobiles all over the place. I don't remember noticing any moving. I think that's why they were so panicky. But I didn't see anyone leaving the cars and try to run across the bridge. That's what I'd do if I was that scared."

Kent nodded and glanced over at Cobb, who continued staring at Kevin with an intense gaze. "That is quite interesting," Kent murmured quietly.

"How is it interesting?" Kevin asked. "They were panicked right at the front of the bridge, cars all over, and no way to get across."

Kent pointed back towards the bridge.

"If that was the case, why aren't there burned vehicles on the bridge and jammed up here next to the Welcome Center?"

I looked in the direction he pointed. There was nothing in the lot. Not one burned out hulk; no crushed metal.

"There's nothing," he continued. "Nothing at all, except buried junk. Now why would he bury it, I wonder?"

Cobb looked over to the bridge, then back to where the scorched and burned windshield had been. "That is a very interesting question," he said absently.

"Interesting or not, what's next?" I grumbled.

I hated waiting here and feeling useless. Cobb had talked to the two men a lot, and it felt like he was avoiding me, or didn't think I was worth talking to. Either way, the information spooked me a little. Why would a dragon take the trouble to bury all the cars? Cobb turned north, and started walking, not appearing to care if we followed him or not.

"Your other service is this way," he said without looking over his shoulder.

I really didn't want to go further inland. That meant further away from the bridge, and from home. We hesitated, then hurried to catch up.

"Where are we going, Cobb?" I asked him. My jaw ached from gritting my teeth and holding my tongue. Being scared makes me mouthy. I get real sarcastic and vicious with my words. Right then, I was too scared to dial the attitude up. "What kind of drugs are you using? This isn't the smart thing to do."

Cobb never turned around. "Shut. Up."

I took a breath as a hand fell on my left shoulder. I turned to glare at the owner. Kent was there, a tight frown on his face. He shook his head "no" ever so slightly as our eyes met. I reluctantly shut my mouth. While Cobb's attitude really rankled, I kept quiet and continued walking.

We'd gotten a kilometer or two down the road. The numerous small tourist buildings lined up along the road gave way to open fields. The land around here had been cultivated. The road was slightly above the surrounding ground, which indicated the earth had been tilled for years. There were also remains of old fences out in the fields, and areas of thicker brush between flat areas. The thick areas were probably property lines. The houses that weren't burned down were broken, scattered pieces on the ground. Here and there, charred bones lay in black, bare earth: dragon fire and its victims.

The most heartbreaking sight was of two small skeletons lying on the ground, with a charred animal on top, as if trying to protect them. These were in front of the blackened remains of a small house. The scene was repeated all along the route Cobb took us. The dead lay in ashes; the houses burned or destroyed. Animals charred beyond any easy recognition. Over it all was the silence. Not a sound. It was a walk through a gigantic cemetery.

Cobb led us north. He used the remains of the highways, as those were mostly clear of debris. The raised, and only occasionally bubbled, asphalt made walking much easier. We went along Route 10, meandering north until it became too dark to continue. We'd made it to a small crossroads called Searletown: a tiny seven-house place, which, like all the other buildings we'd seen, had been leveled and burned.

We stopped for the night and set up camp. We set up on the south side of the remains of a trailer home, such as it was. With the dragon still very mysteriously unaccounted for, we opted for a cold camp. Kent and Kevin put together a lean-to of scavenged wood, and covered it with brush to hide us if the dragon flew by in the evening. Cobb added his own illusionary magick to the shelter to hide our heat and obscure our smell. The lack of wind kept the cold night air from digging into our poorly protected bodies. The silence felt doubly ominous at night. "Quiet as the grave" became real, rather than just a metaphor. Nothing made noise: no insects, no animal calls — nothing to relieve the dark silence.

With the sky overcast, it was impossible to see our hands in front of our faces after sunset. The air carried the faint stench of dry rot and dust. Because of how long the dust stayed in the air, we tore up Kevin's spare shirt, and made some makeshift cloth masks to cover our mouths and noses, so that we could try to sleep without coughing.

There was no food, except for a few snacks that Kent had brought along. Each of us had a bottle or a canteen of water, but we had brought enough for one meal, not one whole day. If whoever had unraveled the echo refused to let it be rebuilt, we'd die here either of dehydration, or, if we were lucky enough to find drinkable water, starvation. That is, if the dragon didn't find us before that. None of which was something any of us wanted to experience first-hand.

We stayed in touching range of each other. This dark, it was too easy to wander off and get lost. I think the inside of a cave might have been brighter. We huddled through the night, the massive, ominous silence keeping all of us quiet. Noise seemed an intruder here.

"We should get wherever we're going tomorrow. The island to our north is about only another thirty to forty kilometers long at the most. We can do that in a day," Kevin said, in what I thought was a way too optimistic voice.

We'd made good travel on the road, but there was no guarantee that Cobb would stay on the road.

The rest of that black night had us resting in fits and starts. Anyone shifting in their sleep sounded like a loud rumble to the rest of us, and we bolted awake, trying to sense what had just moved. I don't think we actually slept, just dozed.

When dawn finally arrived, Cobb got up, looked over at us, then said in a flat, cold voice, "Get up. We leave in five minutes."

Kent shook Kevin awake as I got my few remaining belongings, and the silver knife Cobb had supplied me with. I visualized for a moment how he'd look with it hilt deep between his shoulder blades, then sighed, and started packing Kevin's things into his day pack, while Kent worked on his. We were a minute late moving off. Cobb had started down the road without us, forcing us to hurry to catch up.

"What's got the stick shoved up his ass this morning?" Kevin grumbled sourly. His gaze was on Cobb's back as if he could bore a hole in him with sheer willpower.

Kent just shrugged and chuckled, actually making Cobb half-turn at the incongruous sound. "I am reminded of Groucho Marx, who seemed to have a saying perfect for today." He raised his right hand to his lips and mimed shaking a cigar. "I, not events, have the power to make me happy or unhappy today. I can choose what it'll be. I just think about what would make me happy." He then gave a meaningful look at Cobb, who returned the stare, then turned his back on us and continued walking.

"So what'd you think about, Nix?" Kevin theatrically whispered in Kent's ear.

Kent smiled then shook his head, which caused Kevin to chuckle.

"Humans," Cobb said with a voice dripping with contempt. "Silence is a wise decision, being out in the open with a dragon somewhere on the island."

That shut us all up, and brought home the fact that, for all our joking, we were still on the island and trapped with a creature that nightmares had nightmares about. It made being paranoid very easy.

We kept to the roads, and Cobb kept up a fast walk. We were all breathing hard when he finally called a stop about an hour or so before dusk. We'd stopped by what looked like the charred hulk of a gas station. A partly burned and melted "eads Corner Es" sign was on the ground next to a burned-out car.

The leaden grey skies blocked out everything. We could make out where the sun was on occasion. The clouds would thin for a little while, and we could make out the sun as a white ball hanging in the grey sky. As before, there was no wind at all. I looked back down the road we'd been walking. The dust hung like grey-brown smog behind us. It stayed in the air for the fifteen minutes we took to build a makeshift shelter out of a couple tree trunks and some dead brush, just across the road from the station. After the shelter was set, we shared the last of our water, and lay down, trying to ignore the chorus of growls and murmurs in our stomachs. The last I saw of Cobb that evening was him looking north. It was an uncomfortable night, and a more uncomfortable morning.

Stomach cramps had set in overnight. It was difficult to stand and go through the motions of breaking camp. We picked up our meager equipment, used dead branches to obscure our footprints, and scattering the materials. Hopefully the dragon, if he chanced upon the location, would have as difficult a time as possible tracking us down. Kent nodded at me, then at Kevin, and motioned for us to walk with him.

We walked over to a small mud-covered pond. Kent walked to the edge of the water, then fished out something from his inner suit pocket. It was about five inches long, and looked like one of those pipes you see a Hindu *fakir* play to charm snakes, only with the bulbous portion just below the top end of the straw.

Kent kneeled down, swept aside some of the mud scum to reveal the water, then lowered the narrow end into the water. He put his lips to the top of the pipe and drank. He took four large swallows, then handed the straw to Kevin. "This will work for one thousand liters of pond water, so we won't die of thirst right away. The problem is, I've never heard of one being tested in a situation like this. To be safe, I'd say we've got maybe ten days of drinking four liters of water apiece before it might clog." Kent chuckled as he caught the look from Kevin.

"There are three things I always carry," Kent intoned solemnly. "First is a Leatherman all-in-one tool." His face soured. "Which, unfortunately, I had to leave behind at the opening. Next is a Mylar emergency blanket, and last, is this," he held up the straw. "I might have to dump my pack to escape a bear or other hungry predator. So, if I keep these on my person, then I at least have some items to get by on." Kent looked back towards where Cobb was finishing his obscurement spell. "Why don't you two get a fast drink? We don't know how long we're going to be here, so staying hydrated is going to be important."

Kevin and I nodded, then took our turns using Kent's survival straw, then we went back to the camp to rejoin Cobb.

When we'd finished the hopeful exercise of throwing the dragon off our trail, we followed Cobb towards an unknown destination, for an unknown reason. Elves, just like people, have secrets, and both humans and elves — or any race for that matter

— have a lot of trouble sharing with others outside their own kind. What that means is: We wouldn't know when we got there, until Cobb said we were there. Isn't being in the dark wonderful?

26

KENT WAS A REAL VETERAN. I mean that in the purest sense. I hadn't known, and he hadn't told anyone, but he was actually around seventy-five years old, and had lived through the change. He'd lied on his application to the police. He'd been afraid that they wouldn't give him a job if they'd known his true age. How he managed to be so spry at his age was something I'd like to do — if I am able to live that long.

"I was going to hold out a little longer before I used the filter, but," he shrugged, "it seemed like now was a good time."

We continued in silence, except for the soft scuff of our shoes on the grit-covered asphalt of the 10.

"Why this way?" Kent asked me.

Kevin snorted, then replied, "That's easy. He wants you, me and Fern for something specific."

Kent smiled tiredly. "That was supposed to be a rhetorical question, Love." Kevin continued on as if he'd never heard Kent's comment.

"Think about the negotiations," Kevin continued in all seriousness. "Mr. Cobb seemed awful willing to finish them fast. It's like he's trying to make sure we don't think too much about our options, whatever they are."

I think both Kent and I straightened at the same time. In retrospect, we should have noticed that. Thinking back to that tense discussion back at the bridge, I didn't see that Cobb had been overly eager to get us to agree. At the same time, he didn't let any of us stop and think about what we were agreeing to either.

The job seemed straightforward, and that may have been the trap. He got us to agree to something without counting those things that we might have to do to get there, or complete whatever he really wants. My mind flashed back to Cobb's first appearance in my office, with the plea for immediate action. This felt the same.

What was the same, too, was the sense of lifelessness. Just like the casting my parents did behind the cabin. The life was torn from all the creatures and the earth itself. Here, the dragon destroyed it all. The thing that nagged at me was why. I mean, seriously: the dragon puts a barrier around an island, then reduces it to a total "dead zone", with nothing to eat? Get serious. Nothing in the world wants to destroy its own place. Scratch that, nothing but man is willing to burn their own home down and dance in the ashes. Just look at history, if you want proof. So, why would a dragon resort to this kind of total destruction of its own territory? I had no clue.

"What would make anything do this to its own home?" Kevin muttered.

"I've read in history that some political groups did this to their own countries, to mold it into their own vision. Or, in the case of the Nazi regime, it was done because their leader decreed that, if there was no victory, then there would be nothing left." Kent replied softly.

Both of them looked like they were on sensory overload with all the "nothing alive anywhere" vibe. This was like walking through one huge continuous cemetery or, if you wanted to be a little more dramatic than morbid, a battlefield.

I really haven't mentioned all that we saw, because I really, really don't want to think about it. I still have nightmares of that place. Everywhere we walked, there were burnt or smashed vehicles on the road — in the ditches, some in fields — the old tracks of their crazy route trying to avoid death still showing the violent shifts of direction as the driver tried to live, to beat the death that was hunting him down.

Looking at the burned hulk in the dead field, my mind wandered again to the Welcome Center, and why we didn't see a whole slew of cars there. With the ferry sunk, according to Kent's vision, the bridge was the only way off, and he saw a number of vehicles in his psychometric vision. The only thing that made sense — well, made sense to me — was that most of the vehicles tried to escape back inland when the bridge was attacked. The families may have tried to find a hiding place where the dragon couldn't find them. The trouble with that idea was we hadn't, to this point, found any evidence that anyone survived on the PEI long enough to leave anything behind. If that was true, my internal logic was telling me there should have been a lot more cars near the bridge, and burying them all seemed pretty far-fetched to me. Why go through all that trouble? Why not just leave the cars?

The other part was out here in the countryside: we kept seeing bones here and there. Back at the bridge, there hadn't been any bodies. Pieces of a car, yes. A whole car, no. The whole thing had me in a mental loop looking for the *why*. It just didn't make any sense at all. We crossed a scorched bridge, which had a pair of bent metal posts with the sign missing. On the left of the road, a small concrete welcome sign said: "Summerside est 1877". Ahead were a cluster of cars that stretched across a road that went roughly southwest towards the center of town. The remains of a gas station bore a burned sign that proclaimed it to be "ead's corner Esso".

We'd gone through all the snacks we'd brought along, and now our only water came through Kent's purification straw. The ground remained cheerless, sickly yellow-brown and dead, for as far as the eye could see. We broke into the Esso station, hoping to find something that might be edible. Kevin kicked in a window, which shattered with a dull crack, sounding more like an egg breaking than glass. Kevin and I found a pair of brooms, swept the glass behind the counter, and used a dustbin to throw it in the dust-coated trash can. Yes, it's probably crazy to do that in a place where no one was around to care, but we did it anyway. It felt like the right thing to do. The snack food still on the shelves was fifty years out of date, and so stale that all of the bags were swollen like blood-gorged ticks, or burst open. Food had rotted in the large freezers and, though there was no smell any more, the sight was bad enough to make my stomach think seriously about turning over. Going back outside into the sick, yellow-green sunlight wasn't much better. The sense of stillness and rot assailed me as I walked into the sickly light.

There were a number of vehicles near the gas station. They were arranged in an arc across the road that led into Summerside. The placement was too deliberate to be anything but some kind of emergency barricade against something. It was too unusual to pass up. Kent, Kevin, and I walked over to the barrier, intent on looking this unusual evidence over thoroughly. As we moved closer, we caught glimpses of charred bones in and behind the vehicles. A pistol and a rifle lay by the last car on the north end of the arc.

At first glance, the wreckage looked a little like the other vehicles we'd passed by: scorched and twisted. A second, closer, look told a different story. The cars were in an arc, nose-to-tail: twelve of them. The major damage was on the sides of the cars facing away from town. On the inner side there were holes, but more like a bullet had punched its way through the metal. The difference was that the hole was perfect and flat; nothing like torn or stretched metal where an object had pushed its way through. Just a perfect hole. Each car had numerous holes, making them look somewhat like a metal version of Swiss cheese.

"What are you doing?" Cobb growled irritably. "We are not here to sight see. We have a destination that we need to get to as fast as we can."

"Stuff it, Lord Elf," Kent said very politely, and with a slight bow to Cobb. "This is the first bit of evidence that people actually survived long enough to leave something behind. I, for one, am very curious how they managed it. Perhaps we might learn something that could be useful later."

It may have sounded polite, but there was steel in Kent's voice that I hadn't really heard before. Cobb certainly hadn't. He went from being arrogant to uncertain, then to a kind of petulant irritation. He stayed on the road while we checked out the vehicles.

"Offensive magick, Nix. Look at the holes, like they were just made. Rifles and handguns against spellcasters."

Kent rubbed a scorch mark, then lifted his blackened fingers close to his nose, and inhaled slowly, his eyes closing in concentration.

"Or one big spellcaster," Kent said, as he slowly exhaled. "Look at what got put around this island. Anolyn probably decided to have a little fun with these folks." He finally opened his eyes and looked over to Kevin. "I'm not sure what kind of spell it might have been. It's probably been way too long to hold any trace. My guess would be like that 'magick bullet' taught back at the academy. That would explain the holes."

Kevin sighed, and shook his head. "Those are so slow, they're hardly used, and only when you can't incapacitate the perp with anything else. I'm one of the fastest in the station, and it takes me ten seconds to fire the thing off. Anyone with a firearm — or a knife, or a bow and arrow — would take me out in that amount of time. It's a last-ditch spell when nothing else works. Even then, it's dubious."

I looked again at the cars, and all the holes in them. "If it's so slow, why use it at all? This looks like a hundred mages throwing the spell."

Kevin held up a hand. He started to say something, but closed his mouth as he gazed past me. I turned and watched Cobb as he walked towards us. He was not in a good mood. His Elven features were drawn down in a scowl so deep that I wondered if his face would sink into itself.

"We have wasted enough time here. We must be moving on, unless you want the dragon to find you out in the open."

We all straightened and turned to face Cobb. Being reminded of the monster that lived here was like being splashed with ice water.

"I think we'll stay a little longer," Kent said firmly, the hard, steel edge back in his voice again. "This situation is, to trot out a dictionary word, 'anomalous' to everything we've seen so far. I think it's worth the risk to check it out."

Cobb stared at him, angry and uncertain. "The contract —" he began, and Kent cut him off, politely, and firmly.

"We never agreed upon a time, merely that we would do your request. There was nothing in the wording that said we had to hurry."

Cobb's face shaded towards purple. His cheek muscles bulged as he gritted his teeth so ferociously I thought they might break. He bent down, picking up an arm bone. He held it a moment, staring at it like it was a live viper. Then his lips curled in distaste and he flipped it towards Kent.

"If you want to find out, do psychometry on this. I'm certain you will get your answers."

He turned as the bone arced lazily towards Kent, not the least bit concerned that his throw wasn't perfect. It was. Kent simply raised his hand to head-high, and caught the bone. He gave Cobb's receding back a long stare before walking over to the dusty asphalt road.

Kevin joined him and stage whispered loudly, "You are so hot when you go all alpha male, Nix."

Kent snorted derisively. "Keep saying sexy things like that, and people are going to start talking."

He raised his head, and Kevin and I followed suit to stare out at Cobb, who was crossing over the road and into a field on the opposite side. Beyond Cobb was the burned and smashed hulks of a mercantile store and agriculture combine repair barn.

I watched Cobb a moment longer, then turned my attention back to Kent and Kevin. "So another trip into the past?"

"I'd really rather not," Kent replied shakily. He took a breath to calm himself. "But, if we want answers about this, then the psychometry is the surest way to get it." He looked over at Kevin, who was just outside the trefoil. "My turn since you got to do the first one."

Kevin nodded, his eyes concerned. "If you're sure. That wasn't pleasant in the slightest. If anything, the emotions were so raw. It was too real."

"Duly noted," Kent replied.

He used the bone to scribe a trefoil of circles as Kevin had at the bridge. The top of his trefoil was aimed roughly at the cars;

he put the humerus in that circle. His shoes went in the southwest circle closest to town, and a bullet casing he'd picked up in the southeast, away and towards where we believed the dragon had been.

Kent stood in the center, and took a deep breath. He looked over at Kevin and I, and said, "Go time."

Unlike Kevin, who'd sat quietly, Kent chanted in a soft, melodic voice. It took me a moment to realize he was actually singing. I didn't recognize the song, but it was slow, and filled with loss and longing. That seemed about right for this place, with death all around us.

Kent's chant shifted. I could feel the shift in power flowing to his design. He'd pulled power, now he sang a different song to focus it. His way was much slower than Kevin's, but there was also a solidity to it that Kevin's lacked. I could feel the stability, like walking on solid ground versus mucking about in a swamp. His voice and cadence were steady. Kevin shifted restlessly as he stood next to me.

"He's got a three-step approach: set the base; set the 'level', as he puts it; and start the recall. The level is how clearly he wants to experience the happenings his psychometry pulls up. Keeping it a little blurry or obscure to stop something from really affecting you intensely."

That was something I hadn't thought of before. It made sense, but sounded really tricky to pull off. Kent's voice shifted, and sounded strained. He was singing, but singing what he experienced from the psychometric vision. His voice rose and fell in terror and uncertainty, singing every stanza with a pure emotion that transcended the words, and brought them alive in full, awful glory.

"I am standing, with my friends, behind all the cars,
watching the dragon come.

His bulk is great, his power huge, glows start forming,
     like stars over the field.
Each is a lance, a shaft of light, they pour at us,
     in an infinite rain.
I fire a shot, that bounces off, his red-gold hide,
     and he fires again,
destroying us men, like mowing down wheat,
     blood throws about, limbs spin away.
He never uses his fire, just bright light power,
     into our ranks, never a chance to live,
     to see my home, once more.
He leaps away, and burns the ground,
     destroying the field after we're down.
It grows dark, I grow cold."

Kent bent over, hands on knees, as he gasped for breath. He stretched his foot out to scuff a break in the circle, releasing the remaining magick back to where he'd called it from. Kevin was at his side the moment the magick dispersed.

"Easy, old man. That sounded pretty intense. Where'd the haunting melody come from by the by? I've never heard it before."

Kent coughed, and replied with a hoarse voice, dry from all the singing. "A show a long time ago in my very early years. I'm not certain a copy of that particular anime survived the changing. I think it was called *A Beats.*"

"Never heard of it." Kevin said.

"Before your time, obviously." Kent replied hoarsely. He shivered, and looked over at Kevin. "Did you hear everything? I get locked into the chant, and can't recall what I sing. That's a side effect I can't seem to circumvent."

Kevin nodded. He repeated it word-for-word, and with every inflection, as far as I could recall. When Kevin finished, Kent nodded and looked out towards Cobb, who was still standing on the road, staring back at us.

"That sounds about like what we saw of the cars. He basically called up hundreds of light attacks and shot-gunned everyone with them. That's way scary: a dragon that can call up a cluster of individual spells to create one huge casting. But why bother, when you can flambé everything in one pass?" Kent said contemplatively. "There's usually a reason for everything; I wonder what the reason is for this."

"You know," Kevin said. "We might be pushing our luck, but if that field's over there, we could take a quick look before pressing on."

Kent nodded. I didn't want to stick around here after the casting. I'm not one for pushing anything that involves luck or dragons or both. Heck, just being on PEI smacked of dragon-assisted suicide just waiting to happen. Kent and Kevin, though, were determined to explore this mystery further, much to both my and Cobb's consternation.

Our protests fell prey to selective hearing. Kent and Kevin walked out into the field, with Kent occasionally looking behind him towards me and the cars. There was a distinct burn crater in the field. Because of the terrain, it wasn't visible from the road, but once into the field, you could see it. The area was about twenty meters across, and about thirty long, in an oval. Scattered throughout the oval were carbonized lumps. A quick search produced no weapons, and no indication of any clothing or protective gear.

"What do you think, Love? A bunch of nude ninjas going all beat-down on a dragon?" Kevin smiled, but there was no humor in his eyes.

"It looks like this spot got so hot that everything just vaporized. But if that's the case, why here in the middle of an empty field?"

Kevin straightened up and did a slow circle. They were both in 'detective' mode, and my best option was to stay on alert for anything moving. Cobb scanned the skies constantly as the two of them tried to make sense of what they were looking at.

"They will get us all killed, if we stay in this place too long. Have you noticed how easy it is to feel when spells are cast? If we can feel them, then others can feel them also," Cobb said in a quiet, intense voice.

The implication was very, very clear: the dragon. If Anolyn felt the "vibration" of magick, he'd come and check us out — permanently. What was bothering me about all of this was: where was the dragon? We cast that huge echo spell, punched a hole in the veil of death, cast not one, but two, psychometric spells, all in Anolyn's front yard, and he'd never shown as yet.

I glanced over at the two detectives. Kent was looking at the ground, seemingly deep in thought. Kevin was making "come here" motions with his hands. I moved back into the field and, surprisingly, Cobb followed.

Once we were together, Kevin declared, "I'm not so certain we have to worry about the dragon."

Cobb exploded. He turned in a flash, stepping right up and pushing his face so close to Kevin's I had the crazy thought Cobb was going to kiss him. Instead, he began screaming so loudly that I covered my ears. I moved a good ten or so paces away, and his voice still cut at my hearing like a knife.

"What do you mean!?" Cobb's face turned a bright crimson as he continued screaming. "That dragon destroyed this place! Look around you! Desolation! Death! Even magick is gone from this place! There is nothing! Nothing! And you want to invite that creature here to kill us all!? No! We will move on, now! We will not wait for death to come find us! We will —!"

Kevin's angry punch knocked Cobb to his knees.

"Get a grip! Have you even checked the skies? I've been doing it since we got here! There's nothing! Zip! Nada! If that dragon was here, we'd have seen him at least ten minutes before he got to us. Something that big in the air, and the only thing in the air, would be noticeable kilometers away! This island is only about a one–hundred-fifty kilometers by forty! If a helicopter was flying a search grid, this place would have been covered within twenty-four hours. We've been here at least that long, and haven't seen one scale, or smelled anything close to lizard! Look around, Cobb! It *is* all dead! What's he going to eat? There isn't anything here *to* eat!"

Kevin kept glaring at Cobb, his fists clenched, openly daring the elf to stand up and try something.

Cobb slowly straightened, and fixed Kevin with a venomous glare right back. "We will save this, dispute," Cobb said slowly, and oh-so-very-clearly, "until after your service is completed."

He straightened his clothing, then turned slowly, and the arrogance of the movement had Kent grabbing Kevin's shoulder when he started to take a step after the elf.

"No. Calm down. He's got a point, Love. We don't know squat about dragons, excepting the notes Fern collected. They didn't have anything to say about food, excepting dragons like sentient prey. For all we know, it might be hibernating until food appears on the island. Food like us."

Kevin shut up. He didn't want to; I could see that in his eyes. His gaze was like a pair of hot coals. The heat of his anger radiated from them. The old adage "if looks could kill" was so appropriate.

Kevin took a deep breath, let it out slowly, then took another, releasing it equally slowly before he answered Kent.

"You're right, old man. You're right. The thing is," Kevin paused, then took another slow deep breath and released it. "Something feels off to me."

Kent shrugged elegantly, then adjusted his jacket. It had gone blue-brown from all the dust, which billowed out around him like a brown miasma. Kevin and I coughed and backed up, shuffling up more dust from the dead ground.

I looked back towards the road. Cobb was a good hundred meters away, traveling northeast. Kent finished with the failed attempt at sprucing up, then turned to walk in the direction Cobb was going. Kevin frowned as he watched Kent follow after Cobb, then turned to look over at me.

"I know Kent's right, but that arrogant elf bastard really irritates me with his whiny, 'We have to move', every time Kent or I get curious about something." He scuffed at the dusty ground with his right foot, then began walking after Cobb and Nix. "Guess we ought to catch up. There's not much else here anyway."

I moved beside him and we started after the others.

Cobb kept going until dusk. We continued walking generally west by northwest. The terrain slowly changed from open fields and low hills to dense dead brush and a sickly, brown-coated marshy water. As dusk spread its blanket of darkness across the landscape, Cobb kept moving. He didn't want to slow down, and didn't apparently feel the need to rest. Us humans, however, were totally exhausted. It was past time to stop and sleep, in our collective human opinion. Another kilometer brought us to a crossroads, which had a partly burned building with the sign "uck's Din" on its northwest corner.

Kevin picked up a large rock and walked up the rickety, scorched wooden porch to the door. He raised the rock overhead and heaved it against the door. Rather than crashing through the glass, the large rock rebounded back at him, nearly landing on his foot. Kevin swore irritably, and picked up the rock again.

"Uh, Love?"

Kevin stopped as he raised the rock overhead. He turned to look at the speaker.

"What, Nix?"

Kent shrugged, and said quietly, "Is the door unlocked?"

Kevin let the rock drop, which landed with a *thud* next to him. He stared hard at the door, then walked up to it. He grasped the handle and pulled. The door swung open with a rusty screech. He turned to stare at Kent, who shrugged once more.

"It seemed like a reasonable idea to me," Kent said blithely, as he picked up the large rock while Kevin held the door. He walked over and placed it against the door, propping it open to let the fifty years of mustiness out of the building.

We sat outside while the building aired out. The veil could be seen clearly arcing up and fading in intensity as it reached its apex above us. The night was overcast, so the only light was the sickly green-yellow of the veil. Kevin was seated just to my left, leaning against the wall of the station as he looked up at the veil. Kent was just to his left. Cobb, being the anti-social sort, had stomped off into the dead woods to the north. What he was doing, I didn't have a clue, nor was it something worth moving to go find out. We'd drunk our fill of water using Kent's filter. A second day without food had my stomach feeling like it wanted to crawl up my throat and eat my tongue. Kent's chose that moment to growl loudly.

Kevin laughed. "Instead of crickets and frogs, we get Sonata de belly in E-sharp."

Kent chuckled quietly. I just enjoyed listening. We'd not talked much during the walk. Hunger and exhaustion will do that to you. So, it was nice to hear them banter a little as we waited for the mustiness to fade. Don't get me wrong. I'm sure we could have slept outdoors with no problem, since everything here was dead. But that was why I didn't like sleeping outdoors at all here. Everything was dead. Just like at the cabin. The parallels creeped me out. I half-expected Ahiah to rise out of the dead ground and tear us all apart. I shook my head to clear it of that ugly thought.

Head in the game, girl! If I don't focus, I won't see trouble coming until it's too late!

Kent looked over. "You know, I don't think any of us know why Mr. Cobb is so adamant about getting to this mysterious destination."

Kevin nodded as he listened to Kent.

"I'd like to know what's got him so obsessed, but I really want to know who collapsed the echo behind us. That is the real big question to me." He sat up, and ran a hand over his face. "We're stuck in this dead zone without a clue who stranded us here. We can get back, sure. We made the echo, built the hole, we can do that again. But," Kevin held up a finger, "the truth is we're totally in the dark about who, what, and why."

27

T HE NEXT DAY STARTED LIKE THE LAST ONE: dry, hot, and very dusty. Our feet kicked up clouds of dust that hung in the still air for what seemed like hours. It got into everything: shoes, clothing, what have you. The fields were worse than the roads, as the stubble that remained in the fields also had its own dust to spread when jostled. We'd turned north and, for a good part of the day, the road went straight for kilometers. Twelve hours later, dusk caught us still traversing northeast along Route Two, near what used to be Profits Corner. Food was getting to be a real problem.

My stomach was protesting the lack loudly, as were both Kent and Kevin's. Cobb did not seem to have the same problem. In fact, he didn't seem fatigued at all. He seemed tireless — an automaton that needed neither food nor water. In fact, he'd never taken water with us, and I know he didn't have any food. Whatever kept him going, I wish I had some of it. We found another small bit of open water. Kent shared his filter, and we three drank our fill. Water helped barely, but another couple days of walking would have us stumbling over our own feet.

If you haven't heard the old adage of survival, I'll give it to you here: a person can go three weeks without food, but only three days without water. The straw wouldn't last that long with all of us using it, but it would help us last longer, hopefully long enough to figure out how to get off this deathtrap of an island. Right now, it wasn't looking wholly optimistic. Someone on the continental shore unraveled the echo and, for all we knew, might be waiting to hit us with magick if we tried to rebuild it. That was a worry for later, when we got back to the bridge.

With it getting dark, we decided to stop and rest for the night. A long cluster of charred and wrecked houses, and a few gutted stores, were roadside. Up ahead was a small house away from the road. It sat amongst some pine, and that may have been the reason it wasn't burnt or battered like the other buildings here.

With no food, we were all pretty tired and hungry. The night was absolutely still. Our own breathing sounded harsh and unwelcome to my ears. It took a long time to relax enough to slumber. We'd set watches, but I don't think any of us remembered to wake up. I know when I awoke, I was the only one not asleep. Once I'd roused the others awake, we went to the nearest pond. Kent brushed the mud away from the water, and used the straw to get a deep drink. Kevin and I did the same.

Cobb refused Kent's offer, and impatiently waited for us to finish waking up. I hadn't had food in two and a half days, and the previous day we'd walked steadily for thirteen hours, by my watch. My whole body ached. It was a chore to simply get up, pick up the little possibles bag, and drink. My body wanted to lie down and rest, and, very preferably, eat a whole moose. However, what my body wanted, and what my mind wanted, were two very different things. My mind wanted off this island. Cobb would help, if we did this job for him. After two days, I was thinking that this "service" Kent had brokered was turning into a royal pain in my ass.

The land might have been part of my sour mood. When all you can see is dead things, it's hard to remain optimistic. We had been looking at nothing else since we got here. The smell was indescribable. It wasn't overpowering; but it never faded. It was a constant scent, and sense, of decay. We weren't welcome here. Nothing living was.

Kent adjusted his jacket again, leaving a cloud of yellow-brown dust in the air. Kevin settled for simply stretching, as he readied himself for more walking. Cobb watched us with barely checked impatience. Out of sheer spite, I gave him my best winsome smile, and walked out of the parking lot onto the road. I could feel Cobb's glare between my shoulder blades: the old "if looks could kill". I'm sure I'd have been blasted to pieces. But I wasn't, and I dropped in behind Cobb as he quickly moved in front of me, and began moving at a near trot, forcing us to match him or be left behind as we continued north on Route Two.

I'm not certain why Cobb kept to the roads, but he never deviated from them, even to relieve himself. He insisted that we keep walking down the road, while he took care of "business". I sure didn't look back; I thought he was bugnuts for wanting to come here in the first place. If he wanted to piss in the open, then let him. I liked privacy, and so did Kent and Kevin. Anyway, we continued northward for another four hours, reaching a small crossroads called Tignish Corner around nine in the morning. Why there are so many crossroads called "corners", I have no clue. It's just the way it is.

The land had a low, ankle-high fog that was thick enough that I had trouble seeing the tops of my shoes. It was like one of those old Hollywood horror films from way back when, that are shown sometimes late at night, when you're in a civilized place with a television and some warm pizza to snack on. Dead grass poked above the fog like little stick fingers trying to claw themselves out of the shroud of white that covered everything.

You might think it kind of whiny to complain of an empty stomach. All I can say is: you really don't know what it's like until you've experienced it. The knot my stomach was tying itself into as we got back on the road was an aching hole. Each step seemed to tighten the knot to the point that I couldn't breathe without doubling over to loosen up enough to draw a breath. None of us, excepting Kent, had any idea what it was like to go without. Experience is a hard teacher.

We stopped and drank our fill of water from another small brown sludge-covered pond. As much as I wanted to feel the warmth of the sun hanging overhead, the light was cold and sterile, like the inside of a morgue back at a Dayning Police station.

Having nothing to eat, we sat for a half-hour before turning onto a gravel road off Route 2. The sign at the crossroad said "Ascension", which seemed to me to be absurdly funny, despite my insides trying to eat my outsides. It became less funny after only a half-kilometer hike. The fog had gone to thigh-high as we continued Northwest. Even as high as the fog was now, it couldn't hide the devastation here. The ground was ripped into scorched piles. Nearly all the forest had been blasted flat with fire. The few trees still upright had holes as large as my head through them, making them look like they'd been attacked by monster woodpeckers. The earth was churned and torn. Piles of earth rose above the fog. Cobb slowed down, drawing his sword, and using it to probe for any potholes covered by the clammy, chest-high fog. Everything was off as we moved slowly forward. The only thing I could hear was my own breath, so thoroughly did the fog smother everything. The wet ground was like trying to walk on an ice rink. We moved forward at a snail's pace. I stopped, and was nearly knocked down when Kent slid into me.

"Fern, say something a step or two ahead of time, please? It's hard enough staying upright as is."

His voice hit me sharp and loud after being used to silence. Kent's suit hung loosely on him. While we had been without food for three days, and hadn't lost a lot of weight yet, both Kent and I were feeling the change. I'd had to punch a new hole in my belt to keep my blue jeans from sliding down my hips. Kent, a slender man normally, had a gaunt cast to his features. His cheekbones stood out like knife edges against the hollowness of his cheeks. Kevin hadn't lost enough weight to affect how his clothes draped, and Cobb didn't appear to have changed at all. I got so lost in these thoughts after looking at Kent, I'd nearly forgotten why I'd stopped in the first place.

"Kent, I'm going to see if I can call up a wind to disperse this fog."

Kent nodded slowly.

"Not sure it'll work, Fernie. Have you taken a look at all of this yet?"

Kent's question had me facepalm. "Gah! You'd think I'd remember something so basic."

Kent chuckled softly as Kevin walked up to the two of us.

"What's wrong? Why'd you stop?"

Kent turned to face Kevin, and straightened his soggy mud-caked suit. "Fern decided she wants to try a casting," Kent replied.

Kevin stared at me for a moment, then made a sour face. "You know, if I was as smart as everyone says I am, I'd have thought of something like that." He waved his hand about him.

"Fog, no wind, really creepy cliché type place. Why not try and shake things up?"

My stomach, and Kevin's, chose that moment to rumble. The cramps had me nearly bending double until they ceased a few seconds later.

"What are you doing?" came Cobb's irritating voice as he stalked ill-temperedly to us. "Why did you stop? We're almost there!"

Kevin's face started to go red as he whirled to face Cobb. His mouth opened, then shut again with an audible click of teeth when Kent's hand landed on his shoulder.

"Don't, Love. This isn't a time for it." Kent spoke with quiet authority.

His words got through to Kevin, who took a deep breath and let it out slowly. "Fine. You're right. We all need each other, for now." He looked like he was going to say more, but Kent's hand clenched on his shoulder. Kevin winced and remained quiet, very reluctantly.

Cobb ignored the tension, then shrugged elegantly. "If you have decided upon trying your luck with a, spell, I'll not disagree, considering how you are a determined hu—" He paused, then continued as if nothing happened, "… sort."

The hunger made us all short-tempered. I didn't say anything, but I wanted to. Oh, I wanted to tear his skin off and pour salt in the wounds. I wanted to scream at him until his eardrums burst. I couldn't do it, but oh, how I wanted to!

"Well, then," Kent said with irritable good cheer. His hand was still on Kevin's shoulder. I could see the muscles standing out as he squeezed it, holding Kevin from jumping Cobb, "Let's get to it."

"Yeah, let's." Kevin grimaced as Kent put a little more squeeze into his grip.

The ground was higher here, and fortuitously level, which goes back to that old adage that magick makes the time and place for itself. Yeah, I thought it was a little more than coincidence too.

We kneeled down to draw the circle. Between us, we had a full kit for spells, plus more. But that was about all we had. Everything else, except our clothes and a few personal items — like a silver earring in Kevin's place, Kent's bronze cigarette lighter, and a few silver coins in my pack — had been cached to avoid carrying extra weight. We still had the weapons Cobb "gifted" us with, but none of us really wanted to use them. Paranoia runs deep when it's encouraged, like Cobb had done over the last three days.

I used a pencil to scratch the circle into the soft earth. I wasn't large, being only about a half a meter in diameter. It took about twenty minutes to complete. Unlike most spells we'd done to this point, our circle had no items to help focus the intent. This time, Kent drew in the symbols for the four winds at the ordinal points on the circle: north, south, east, west. Kevin drew out two larger circles around us, and filled the space between them with a written ward that was intended to slow anything down to walking speed if it crossed the outer ring.

I thought Kevin was being a little melodramatic with the protective ward, but it's true I'd hadn't tried a spell like this in a while. If I screwed up royally, we could easily get a tornado visiting us — or really, really dangerous winds filled with large debris picked up by the howling air. So, thinking about it, he was probably smart to set up some protection like that. The upside, if being on a dead island was an upside, was that we were *on* a dead island. The only ones we'd possibly hurt would be ourselves if the spell broke away from our control. Once the circles were done, we sat near the small circle.

Kent sat on my right; Kevin on my left. Both men quietly murmured the spell to raise the protection, which popped into a hemisphere of power anchored on the inner line of the protection circle. My job was to raise the wind. This would be a tougher spell than the protection. It would need a hefty bit of power. I volunteered, since I seemed to be in better shape than Kevin or Kent. Maybe it's because I'm a lot smaller, so I don't use as much energy. Or I just had more magickal power to draw on. Either way, I volunteered, so it was show time. I started the casting with a spell to feel the wind, building on that to influence it to strengthen and move away from me.

It was a lot harder than I expected it to be — and I'd been expecting difficult. Hey, you would too, if you stumbled into an area where the fog never seemed to move. The only thing that can do that is magick. So I had to influence the air to move, then sense the resistance in the magick holding the fog in place, and influence that to weaken. Or, if not influence, overcome with expertise or brute force. I'm not an expert caster, so it'd have to be the kick-it-until-it-crumbles style. I hoped not, as my stomach was currently trying to gnaw its way out of me after three days without food. The hunger made it harder than usual to concentrate.

The air stirred, like the soft breath of a lover blowing softly on my cheek. The fog stirred, rippling as the air began to move. It clung to the ground, faint translucent claws reluctant to release their grip on the ground claimed as its own. Finally, though, the fog shredded reluctantly in the wind. The spell holding it in place was old, and had a strange spruce and lavender wildness. I'd never had a sense touch my magick like that before. Not scent. Sense. It's like a smell, but not. The sense was more like what I remembered as a "texture", a memory that rippled against my senses as the spell operated. All my natural senses went into overload. Light flashed like a lightning strike. My ears heard the grinding of the earth as the fog slowly was pushed away by the growing wind, which smelled so rotten that my throat gagged. My skin was a magnet. Anything in the air clung to me like a wet, slimy cloak that kept increasing in weight as it turned to acid, burning my nerves. The spell I was casting started to falter as my concentration weakened. The respite from sensation let me recover my focus.

I fed power into the spell more slowly. It was a feedback loop: the more I pushed at the spell, the more it unraveled, but, at the same time, that unraveling created static that affected all my senses. So a slower spell lessened the feedback. I took a few deep breaths, and slowed the flow of magick into the air. The fog struggled to remain, but could not. The air around us cleared as the strengthening breeze lifted the fog and carried it away from us. The land — slimy, brown, and dead — slowly revealed itself.

The ground we could see, which was about four meters around us, had been torn up violently. Two parallel furrows sprinkled with the shattered wood of uprooted pine went to either side of the spell circle. Of the few trees standing in the widening hole in the fog, most had the same kind of holes we'd seen in the cars back at Read's Corner. As the fog continued to recede, other things became visible. The first was a huge dead oak with an iron band as tall as a man locked around its trunk. On this band was a mounting ring as thick as my thigh. On the ring was a link of a huge chain that stretched back into the fog.

"Is that a chain?" Kevin's voice came out as an incredulous squeak.

Both Kent and I would have probably sounded the same, if we could have uttered a word. The link connected to a second, and to a third, each held taut by something still covered in the fog. Each link seemed to take forever to appear as the fog reluctantly gave way. The links kept appearing, and kept receding into the distance. A huge mound of white revealed itself as the fourth link appeared. The mound seemed to curve up and back until it got a few meters off the ground, then continued. It looked a little like a fishing boat turned upside down. Partway back was a huge hole on the right side, the left showing a near-identical hole a moment later. The bottom of the boat appeared to be torn, with small, triangular gaps shown along the edge. It was only when the end of the boat started arcing upward again, and the two eye sockets slowly appeared in the thinning fog, that we realized what it was we were looking at.

"That's a skull! A freaking dragon skull!" Kevin exclaimed.

Kent and I just looked as the spell lifted the fog away, slowly revealing the extent of the massive skeleton in front of us.

Kent smiled grimly. "And a full skeleton attached to it. I believe we've found the reason Anolyn didn't greet us."

The chain stretched across massive neck bones, attached to a spike the size of a telephone pole. Other spikes and chains appeared as the fog thinned, overlaying the emerging skeleton in a chaotic crisscrossing of the body: over wing bones, the body, limbs, and the tail. The flat, unnatural black of the links seemed to hold down more than the skeleton. An agony permeated the air. It was as if the bones cried out in pain from the touch of the massive pieces of iron.

Cobb stoically watched as the skeleton was revealed. Whatever thoughts he had were kept behind an exterior of absolute neutrality. I kept sneaking glances at Kent and Kevin, who were both awestruck and, like me, more than a little uneasy at being so close to the remains of such a monstrous being, and Cobb, who looked like he was watching a boring speech. His eyes were half-closed, and a "seen it before, and it was boring then, too" frown marred his sharp, elven features. Something about Cobb's attitude made me wonder if he had seen this before. He said he had family here. Did that mean he lived here before Anolyn set the veil up?

Kent seemed to read my mind. "Cobb, you said you had family here. How long did you live here?"

The direct question surprised Cobb. He opened his mouth and started to answer, then shut it, his teeth clicking audibly. "It is of no concern at this moment, human. My familial history is not a topic I intend to discuss."

Just like that, the emotional stone wall dropped between us once more. He would not talk about anything other than his demands. Kevin looked like he wanted to argue or, more likely, punch the arrogant elf in the teeth, but a little good sense, and a lot of self-control, kept him from following through with that thought. I kept the chant going, and the fog continued to reluctantly release its hold on the ground.

The complete dragon skeleton was finally exposed, being easily as long as a football field. The wing bones were weighted down like the rest of the body with the huge chains, and looked like their span would be twice the length of the exposed body. Once I felt the magick that the fog was held by finally break, I dropped the chant. It wasn't a hard spell, just long because of the tenaciousness of the fog. It was like running a mile, when you're not used to running. I was physically exhausted. Kent and Kevin were not much better.

The ground, now fully exposed, looked like a vision from a battlefield. Trees still stood upright, but many more had been knocked down by the titanic struggle that had occurred here. Deep furrows and scorched areas dotted throughout our field of view. The skeleton lay upon ground that had been furrowed violently by the dragon's huge claws.

The chains looked like they were meant to anchor a battleship. One looped around a wing, the huge links clamping it closed and anchored with a spike that looked over a half-meter in diameter. The other wing lay on the ground, its bones broken. Each chain, of which there were seven that undulated across the dragon bones, was anchored by an oak at one end, and by a spike at the other. All the chains looped back and forth across the tortured skeleton.

"Cobb gave us silver weapons to defend ourselves from that?" Kevin said, in a soft, awestruck voice.

28

"I BELIEVE THE SILVER WEAPONS AGAINST ANOLYN was his idea of humor," Kent replied dryly, as he gazed at the skeleton.

Cobb didn't bother to respond. He was slowly turning in place, scanning the area around us. He stopped, then strode back up the path we'd made. I looked back, and spotted a small flash of green, barely visible amidst the slimy mud and shattered wood. I began walking carefully after Cobb.

"Is that alive?" I called to Cobb's back.

He stopped, giving me a sour look. Kent and Kevin tore themselves away from gazing at the dragon skeleton to stand next to me. Kevin saw it immediately.

"It's magick. The green glow is a magick ward on that tree."

Kent thought about what Kevin said, his left hand cupping his right elbow, and the right hand cupping his narrow chin as a long finger tapped his cheek.

"Why would there be a warding spell on a tree so far from the dragon?" Kent mumbled more to himself than any of us. "Is it protecting something? Is it just a random remainder of another spell cast?"

Kevin shrugged. "Any of the above at the moment. I think we should join our elven frenemy and get a better look at it." He was already heading towards Cobb as he spoke, making both Kevin and I hurry to catch up.

Cobb was standing some three meters away from the greenish glow. The glow was on part of a dead branch that had fallen onto the muddy ground. I was at a loss to understand why a spell would be placed on a piece of apparently discarded wood.

"Is it some kind of warning?" I asked Kevin.

He thought about it for a moment, then shook his head. "It doesn't feel like a warning, but I can't be sure without opening my sight, which I really don't want to do in here. There's something off about the chains and the dragon. I've never seen a spell like that."

Kent looked back towards the skeleton. "What's your opinion on doing a psychometric reading on that skeleton, Love?"

Kevin looked at the dragon, then at the greenish glow that Cobb had now reached. "I think that to do so here would be really unhealthy, like leaking my brains out my ears unhealthy."

Kent nodded quietly, then straightened his wet, mud-spattered suit jacket. He looked mournfully at the ruined jacket and pants. "I think my first visit back home will be the tailor's. This suit will need some taking in and proper dry cleaning."

Kevin crossed his arms and attempted a scowl, aiming it at Kent, who gave Kevin a tired smile. Kevin rolled his eyes as he exhaled sharply, trying to stifle the laugh that bubbled from his lips.

"That has got to be the largest understatement, ever — or the most calculated one-liner I've heard in a long time, Nix." Kent chuckled softly as he laboriously straightened his cuffs. "Humor is better than despair." He looked back towards the skeleton. "I think humor's what's really needed at the moment. Otherwise I think I might just break down."

That remark really caught me. I hadn't felt right since getting onto the island, and my unease had spiked just before casting the spell. It may have compelled me to do the casting.

Whatever the reason, it felt like I was being pushed somehow and, since I'd used magick, my own paranoia had me considering the possibility that magick was using in its own agenda. The stump of my finger ached. I rubbed it absently with my thumb as I watched Kent and Kevin walk over to where Cobb was standing. Cobb had stepped off the trail to stand next to the glowing branch. It lay on the ground, broken in a "V", with the point aimed at a rotted, torn stump. The open end faced back up the trail towards the skeleton. The ground here was torn, with one large scorch mark that started some twelve meters away, then widened as it approached the stump, where it simply cut off, making it look like half of a circle.

It was odd for a scorch mark to stop like that in the middle of open ground. I knelt at the flat edge, taking a closer look. It was six meters long, and perfectly straight. The scorch mark just stopped. There was no indentation that indicated a shield, or some kind of obstruction.

"Hey, you two, take a look at this."

Kent and Kevin ambled over.

"What'cha got, Fern?" Kevin asked as he reached the edge of the scorch mark.

"This appears to be a conundrum worth investigating," Kent interjected as he walked up.

Kevin nodded, adding, "There's no way I'm doing psychometry on this. After what I saw at the welcome center, I don't want to experience that again. This looks worse … if that's possible?"

That piqued my curiosity. "How do you figure it could be worse?"

Kevin shrugged. "It's all in the picture." He pointed at the scorched half-circle. "What do you think caused this?"

"The obvious answer is magick. There's no evidence of a physical barrier. A full scorch mark, from a dragon, overhead, would be a circle, or an elongated oval. This pattern is cut off, like it hit a barrier."

Kevin nodded. "Exactly. Someone threw up a barrier, probably at least a couple of someones, if it was to survive a dragon attack." He looked at the ground, then at the surrounding vegetation. "There's no splash to the surrounding brush if the fire had hit a solid wall and spattered. That means the attack was absorbed."

That was kind of disturbing. Absorption is a way to do two things at once. One, it literally absorbs an attack, and then turns it into spell energy. That spell energy can be used in nearly any kind of action you can dream up. You can use the spell power to attack your attacker, use it to strengthen the spell the absorption's attached to, or use it personally to augment your own physical attributes. Each of these takes time, and absorption is finicky. You want to know the attack you're going to be facing, or the absorption won't work. It's a difficult spell to get right, and time-consuming to cast. But when you have the right circumstances, it is tremendously powerful. Against a dragon, it could be powerful enough to wound it. That the scorch mark was close to the skeleton had me considering the two might be related.

Kevin echoed that thought a moment later. "Think this and the skeleton make two?"

Kent nodded, saying, "One skeleton, and one potential absorption spell, are more than coincidental in my estimation."

When Kevin looked over at me, I nodded, "I think it's more than coincidence too."

Kevin smiled grimly. "How's that for a consensus?"

Kent tapped his chin as he turned to look back at the dragon. "Our elvish host seems to be very unsurprised by the events here. I'm wondering how much knowledge he has of this situation."

At the mention of Cobb, Kevin looked up and towards Cobb, who appeared to gesturing at the greenish glow.

"You note how that green, the scorch mark, and the skeleton lineup?" Kevin asked me. "You're thinking that the spell, if it was an absorption type, was used to down the dragon and protect that green gl—", then something clicked. "That's a camouflaged entrance. There's a spell on the place. The green glow is the lock."

Kent tapped his chin as his fingers covered a thoughtful smile. "That would explain our host's interest, and the fact he isn't pushing us to move rather than observe."

Kevin chimed in. "So this is where he wanted to get to so passionately." His smile took a malicious edge. "And, observing his intense concentration, and apparent ritualized hand gestures, it would appear he doesn't know how to get in."

The laugh bubbled out of me before I could control it. "Oh that is rich!" I howled. "To come all this way only to find the door's locked!"

Cobb glowered at me as he continued attempting to open the hidden doorway. I call it a doorway, as it's the first thing I think of that you'd hide with a glamour. That made me wonder if it was hidden when the dragon attacked. The only one likely to know that was Cobb, but the possibility of him sharing information like that was very unlikely in my mind. It was probably elven magick, which means it wasn't for humans to know about. His attitude had long since worn my nerves raw, and hunger exacerbated it. That was why it struck me as so vindictively funny. A elven spell, refusing to work for an elf.

Cobb continued his fruitless attempts. His whole body radiated frustration as he tried variations on the hand gestures.

Kent, ever the diplomat, walked over next to Cobb. "Is there a difficulty, Lord elf, that might be surmounted with offered assistance?"

Cobb's scowl deepened, if that was possible. It had to grate on his pride: that a human would offer to help him. I wondered if he'd be smart enough to welcome the help, or if he would reject it, like he'd done with every previous attempt at interaction.

To my, and Kevin's, shock, Cobb replied in an equally formal manner to Kent, "A request to assist is a gesture to be honored, Lord man. Two may find a solution that one stumbles against."

Just like that. Yeah, I didn't believe he'd changed for a second.

Cobb talked with Kent for a few minutes explaining what he understood of the situation. Kent listened intently, as did Kevin and I. I'm certain Cobb noticed, but he gave no indication that he did. My paranoia kept whispering it was his way of catching all of us up, getting us invested in finding the solution, and making us do all the work. Hey, I'm nothing if not cynical. In the end, we found that it took two people repeating the same gestures to open the doorway.

A green disc flowed from the piece of glowing wood, which then seemed to spin and iris open like some science fiction doorway. The glamour disguising the tree fell with a soft pop. Darkness and stale air wafted from the opening, and we stayed outside for ten minutes to let the stale air mix with the fresh.

Cobb led us into the darkness. Once his foot hit ground, a pale, blue-green glow flickered to life, illuminating a large, roughly circular room that seemed to be carved out of solid wood. The wood was a deep red-brown, with lighter wood accenting the nine archways spaced evenly along the perimeter of the room. Each archway was dark, nothing within any of them could be seen — probably like the main room, simply waiting for someone to enter before illuminating. The main room we'd entered was bare of any furniture, being simply an open area that was roughly ten meters in diameter.

The faint aroma of cedar permeated the air. Underlying the cedar was the smell of rotten flesh. Kent was moving slowly counter-clockwise in the room. The way his head was tilted made me think of a dog on the scent. Kevin had begun moving clockwise, doing the same thing. Cobb simply stood to the left of the entryway, silently observing the room. He took a step further into the bare room, then closed his eyes. He raised his left hand, palm facing outward, and began a slow clockwise turn. I heard him begin a low chant, and he suddenly smelled of focus. He wanted something so badly that the need assaulted my nose like being blasted in the face by a skunk at point-blank range.

I lost my balance, and fell back on my butt. The noise startled Kent and Kevin, who turned in unison from opposite sides of the room. They seemed to catch the same sense I did, and both looked sharply to Cobb, who seemed to realize what was happening. He opened his eyes, and lowered his hand, and disappeared from my senses as fast as a snap of the fingers. He was completely blank. Kevin snarled, and took four quick steps towards Cobb.

"What is so freaking important!? You push us like crazy to get here, then you give off a … vibe, like hunger, that's so intense it hurts! Now you pointy-eared asshat, you explain what's going on or so —"

Cobb didn't give him a chance to finish. His sword was in his hand. Kevin's eyes widened and he stepped backwards to avoid the sword, eyes wide with surprise and fear. Kent stepped closer to me. I had the long knife Cobb had given me. I followed what Fawn had taught, blade down, and angled back along my left forearm. I crouched, bringing the right at chest level to block or trap an attack. Cobb took a step back from us. He held his blade low and to the side. It did not threaten anyone, but could be brought quickly to his defense if one or more of us attacked him.

"Detective Love! Cease and desist!" Kent's voice cracked like a whip in the air.

Kevin had started to crouch, freezing in place. He stayed that way as Kent slowly pulled the silver dagger from his belt, carefully placed it on the ground by his feet, and straightened.

"Cobb, as a show of good faith, I ask you to place your blade on the ground beside you. No one wants to hurt anyone. Let's all take a deep breath and relax."

We all remained still as Cobb thought the situation over. He nodded his head.

"I agree to your suggestion." He lowered the blade to the ground, laid it by his feet, and straightened, holding his hands out to show they were empty. Kevin still had an angry snarl on his features, but stood up slowly, holding his hands open, mimicking Cobb to show he had no weapons. I put my blade back in my belt, slid it to the small of my back, and then followed Cobb and Kevin's example with my hands out and open. My heart was racing, and I hoped that we all didn't explode again.

"Lord elf, as a show of good faith, could you please explain what your vested interest in this place is, so that we can more fully understand the situation."

Kent was in full-on diplomatic mode. Everything he did was to show respect and ease tension. Despite his effort, Cobb wouldn't bend.

"I cannot discuss it. It is not something to be shared with humans. It is a trust that I will not break." His face was completely unreadable. Every emotion had been completely suppressed in his voice, and his body. He stared at Kevin, but his words were for all three of us. "You must leave. You are not welcome."

Kevin growled, "If you're not going to share, then screw diplomacy."

Cobb tensed as Kevin bent his knees. I whispered a fast spell of wind, ready to release it should anyone move. Cobb moved. It's inadequate, but it's the only word that works. One instant he was standing, relaxed, and the next he'd snatched up his silver blade, and had closed with Kevin in an eye blink. Kent shouted and started, way too slowly, to rush to Kevin's aide. I let the spell fly at the two. Cobb dodged the air jet. Kevin didn't. The burst skidded Kevin across the floor, ricocheting him off an arch and into the second arch on the right.

Cobb turned on Kent, and slashed at the older detective, who fell backwards as he tried to avoid the attack. The sword cut his suit open, slashing the shirt, and scoring a long cut across Kent's chest. Kent fell back, clutching at the wound, screaming in pain. The light flickered in the room that Kevin had slid into. The blue-green light snapped on, drawing my attention for an instant. It was almost my last.

My eyes flickered away from Cobb, who saw my shift in attention. He charged, moving like liquid light. The sword descended, and I froze. It arced murderously down, then angled away at the last moment, cutting a deep furrow in the wood floor. I didn't question my good fortune, but ran for one of the dark arches. I may know a little about self-defense, but I am not a fighter. So I did the sensible thing, and ran. If I could get time to re-cast the wind spell, I could use it to knock Cobb down, and hopefully keep him from running me through.

As I reached the archway, I dropped and slid into the room, trying to be as small a target as possible. Kent was moaning in pain, and I wasn't certain of Kevin. Cobb spat something out in Elven. I changed tactics, quietly chanting a flash spell. If I could blind Cobb, we might be able to escape. As I was focusing on my spell, Kevin beat me, and Cobb, to the punch. As Cobb readied his casting, wood at the archway exploded, filling the air around Cobb with shards and splinters. A wheezing shout emanated from the room. A pulse of heat that scorched wood blasted over the staggering elf, burning his clothes to ash. Cobb screamed in agony, then darted into a darkened room to my left.

Kevin staggered from the room he'd been blown into.

"Freaking bugnuts elf." His voice strained from the casting of the heat spell.

He leaned against the charred archway, gasping for breath. Spells take energy, and the three of us were seriously depleted without food. Kevin looked like death warmed over. Kent groaned in pain as he dragged himself slowly towards his partner, leaving a glistening trail of blood behind him on the floor. Kevin pushed away from the archway, staggered towards Kent, and the whole room jumped. Kevin fell face-first. The floor jumped again. I scrabbled for a handhold, trying to stand up as everything in this wooden cave flew into the air. I was hit from behind as a greenish-yellow light flared in the room.

The room Cobb had retreated into lit up with a similar pale, yellow-green light. Glass rods, as thick as my thumb, and as long as I was tall, bounced crazily past me as the tree continued to shake like a rat in a terrier's mouth. Bones of various sizes bounced off of me and followed the rods into the central room. A skull ricocheted off my foot. The shuddering stopped. Dust floated in the air, burning my eyes and lungs. Kevin rolled Kent

242

onto his back. He pulled his shirt off and pressed it against Kent's chest, attempting to staunch the wound.

Cobb stalked out of the room he'd retreated into, his naked body blistered and burned from the heat Kevin had cast. He was carrying what looked like a black chain with a ring on one end, and a spike on the other. Two other chains were over his left shoulder. He whispered a quick chant in a liquid series of syllables.

I started my own wind spell, but I wasn't as fast as Cobb. He finished the chant, tossing the chain at me. The spike drove into the wood at my feet, the chain wrapping around me, then enlarging. The weight of the chain forced me to the floor, and the ring end anchored itself by clamping on the archway.

He started the chant a second time. Kevin began his own, but Cobb took a quick pair of strides forward, kicking Kevin in the chest, interrupting the chant. Cobb finished his, tossing the chain at Kevin, who became entangled like I was. The weight of the chain bore him to the floor. I started a chant to bring wind, but the chain shifted, then a pulse of power tore into me. It was like being hit in the chest by a chainsaw. The sensation of my chest being torn open had me screaming in agony. A moment later, I heard Kevin begin screaming too. The chain shifted like a snake, coiled tight and heavy around me.

Kent was pale, the third chain wound tight around him. I turned my head to see Kevin glaring at Cobb. Cobb returned the glare, then gestured. The chain around Kevin tightened, and literally melted the skin it lay against. The scream Kevin gave off sounded like a metal tearing. It was raw agony given voice. Cobb, as if to prove a point, gestured twice more, each time drawing a new level of screams from Kevin.

I wanted to do something, but the chain seemed to sense my intent and coiled tighter. I quit moving; I was terrified of the pain. I lay there as Cobb tortured Kevin. Kevin whimpered in agony; the raw, acidic-looking wounds looked to go right to the bone. What was liquefied flesh dripped off the chain around Kevin, and I thought I saw the bluish white of actual bone underneath the links. Cobb dismissed Kevin and Kent, like one would insects. He turned towards me, his eyes boring into me like white hot iron.

"Ms. Fatelli, you have no idea what is at stake."

He was talking to me? The absurdity of the statement had me speechless, which was probably a good thing. My usual reaction to fear was sarcasm and very cynical statements. I was terrified. If I opened my mouth, he'd have the chains do to me what he'd had them do to Kevin. I stayed still and quiet, which seemed to encourage Cobb to continue talking. Why someone feels they have to explain why they're doing something is beyond me. I didn't question it. As long as he was talking, he wasn't making the chains do anything. You have to be thankful for small favors, or long-winded talkers.

"This world is dying. What your species did to it was a brutal rape. Open wounds that were never treated; plastic trash poisons the oceans. Humans overpopulating their home, devouring the resources without counting the cost or consequence."

I couldn't help myself. He was crazy calm and rational.

"Am I supposed to be awestruck at your brilliant master plan?" I knew it was a bad idea before I opened my mouth. Fear had me opening it anyway.

Cobb reacted about as you might expect. He made a quiet chant and gestured. The chains writhed, tightening and burning. I screamed myself raw and don't remember passing out.

29

T HE AGONIZED CROAKS OF PAIN finally penetrated my brain, dragging me reluctantly back to consciousness. I opened my eyes, and saw nothing but a blurry gray. It took a few moments for my eyes to adjust. Slowly, the room came into focus. The room, as best I can call it, was circular. Thick slats of wood grew from the floor to the ceiling, three meters overhead. The slats were in an arc about three meters from the wall all away around the room. Vertical roots were growing between the slats and the walls at roughly every two meters, creating a series of wooden cells. Kent was in the cell closest to the door, I was in the one immediately to his left. The hoarse, croaking gasps of pain I was hearing I guessed were Kevin's.

There was a soft murmur, then Kevin tried to scream again, and again he was only able to produce a weak, gasping croak. I sat up from the floor and immediately regretted it. A sharp, tearing pain made me gasp. Raw, burned flesh bled freely. The wounds had scabbed over. I'd torn them open sitting up. I glanced down at my arm. The wounds wound from just behind the back of my hand, around my forearm, and disappeared under my t-shirt. The shirt had perfect, link-shaped holes in it where the chain had wound about my body. How the shirt managed to stay in one piece, instead of falling off, was a minor mystery. I lay slowly back down, trying to avoid tearing the scabbed wounds open further.

Kevin tried to scream again, his voice slightly distorted by the echoes of the large central room. Kent lay on the wooden floor, still and pale. I thought I saw his chest rising and falling, but his breathing was so shallow that I was afraid I was fooling myself. The thought of being alone here, under Cobb's power, had me nauseous with terror. There was a moment, listening to Kevin's raw gasps of pain, where I was ready to do anything to avoid that agony. I was ready to sell out to survive.

Kent's soft cough brought me back from my frantic imagination. Him being alive gave me something to focus on beyond the possibility of torture. I watched Kent as he slowly rolled onto his side.

"Kent?"

He barely moved his head, but the soft reply he gave me restored some of my courage. I suppose most of us react that way; we're social animals after all. Concern for another helps cover up your own weaknesses. I know it did for me.

"Ms, Fatelli, you are alright?" Kent coughed, curling around the slash on his chest, whimpering quietly.

The pain of the scabs tearing as I sat up again were less important now that I knew Kent was alive. I could ignore the discomfort, at least partially.

"I'm sore, and the chains did something to me, but other than pain, I'm okay."

"That is better than alternatives." Kent tried to chuckle, but wheezed painfully. His body stiffened at another groan of pain from Kevin's raw throat. "Is that Mr. Cobb causing Detective Love's agony?"

"I'm not sure. I woke up in here, with Kevin screaming somewhere out of sight. I haven't heard Cobb's voice, or seen him, but I'd bet money he's the cause. The chains were sure his doing."

Now that we were talking, I had enough presence to look at the room again. As from my previous glance, it was circular, with the various cells going around the outside edge, and seemingly grown in place from the wood of the tree. The doors themselves were a slatted growth like the walls. I couldn't see any hinge, and my fingers couldn't feel any on the other side of the door, so I considered it a wall until I learned something more. Hopefully, Cobb would bring back Kevin alive. If he did that, then I'd see how the doors worked, which might give us something to work with.

Kent lay on the floor in the cell to my right. He was still pale. The shirt Kevin used had been replaced with what looked like vines around his chest. I could see the inflamed edges of the wound, swollen and red. It'd gotten infected. Kevin's gasping moan of pain was much softer, and more desperate. It sounded to me like he was dying, and my anxiety spiked. If he killed Kevin, we were certainly next, if only to get rid of witnesses. I prayed that my imagination was running crazy and he wasn't dying. My gut had the opposite opinion. It was certain Kevin was dying. No one sounded that lost when they had a chance at life.

"What … is that …" Kent gasped as he struggled for words, "hateful creature … doing … to Detective Love?"

I think Kent knew too, what was happening. Like me, he didn't want to believe it, but his face told the same story my gut did. Kevin was dying, and we were going to be next if we didn't figure out a way to get out of these cells and beat Cobb.

Kevin's next scream was pure agony. The sound was ripped out of a throat that could not hold it anymore. It went on without pause for a good minute, slowing only to pull in a breath to scream again. I've never heard anything like that pure pain and despair before. It was like someone's soul being filleted like a fish.

The screams of pain faded away to a dead silence. Both Kent and I stared at the archway. We heard soft footsteps get slowly louder.

"Kevin ...?" Kent queried, concern coloring every word.

Cobb strode through the arch, and the room seemed colder. He didn't look at either Kevin or me, but moved with an icy, dispassionate deliberation to Kent's cell.

Kent, wide-eyed at Cobb's approach, tried to push himself to the back of the cell, but only shifted a few inches before Cobb gestured. The front slats sank into the wood, and Cobb stepped to Kent, then reached down to grab both ankles. Kent gasped, and tried to kick loose, but it was like a mouse trying to kick free of a cat's jaws.

"Why, when you declared that you would remember courtesies?" Kent was half pleading, like a cop trying to connect with a would-be suicide.

"I didn't mention they were other elves." Cobb yanked hard on Kent's legs, twisting as he did and throwing Kent across the room.

Kent hit the floor after two meters, then rolled another two. I could see the pain of his wounds, the hunger of not eating for days, and this sudden change by Cobb. I could smell it all, feel it all. Kent lay like a broken doll against the back of the cell.

Cobb remained a non-entity to my senses. No scent, or sensation, emanated from him. Kent looked at me, but didn't seem to see me. His hopeless, lifeless eyes froze me in place as Cobb walked over to him. He leaned over again, grabbing the old detective by the lapels of his jacket, heaving Kent up over his shoulder like a sack of flour, and strode mechanically out of the room.

Kent kept looking at me. It was a haunted, terrified, and resigned gaze. One that said he knew he was going to die. He opened his mouth, and I heard a soft, helpless "Why?"

Cobb stopped, partway through the door, Kent dangling helplessly over his shoulder. "Your pain will make a cure. Your death will bring a rejuvenation." Then they were through the arch, around the corner, and out of sight. Cobb's footsteps receded, then stopped. The nub of my finger ached. I heard a sodden thud, then some gasps. A second softer thud, then Kent screamed. The agony ripped a moan of fear from me.

My stomach clenched along with my jaw. Killing to cure. That's what my parents had tried to do to me and Fawn. That was the frozen ritual that Ahiah had tried to finish. Cobb was trying to do the same thing, only on a larger scale. It didn't make sense, but nightmares don't have to make sense to terrify you. I was back in the same nightmare, only with Cobb taking the role of Ahiah.

Here's where you're thinking that a tough-as-nails trapper and skip-tracer like myself would swallow that fear and figure out a smart way to turn the tables. That only happens in movies and good detective novels, not so much in real life. The truth is, it — the whole place — was like despair made physical. The weight of hopelessness sagged down on me, and I couldn't see any way to escape. I'd failed my friends, whom I talked into joining me. They trusted me, and I'd put my trust in an elf that only saw us as tools, and victims.

Kent screamed again, his voice raw with despair and terror. I moaned and tried to huddle in the furthest corner, hands wrapped over my head. I fell into a fetal position, and shut the world out.

30

A SOUNDLESS ROAR FILLED MY HEAD. The pain fought with my own despair, rage versus hopelessness. I tried to tighten up, and force the ... whatever it was out of my mind. I didn't want to deal with the world; I wanted to hide and make it all go away. The voiceless rage wouldn't let me. It had a foothold, and wedged itself deeper into my psyche. The pain tore a furrow of agony behind my eyes, and my head felt like it swelled like a balloon. Bones seemed to shift, each pop and crack sending new misery spiking through my mind. Screaming didn't help, but I couldn't do anything else; the pressure shut down my eyes, and my ears. I could feel my throat going raw from screaming, and my chest hurt from all the abuse.

There was the sense of another in my mind with me — something so immense, that it was threatening to blot me out entirely. It was hard to think. The immense pressure kept me feeling like my head was going to crack open like an egg.

????

The soundless roar filled my mind. I think I was on my side in the cell. Everything was so disoriented from the pressure in my head, like a horrible case of vertigo. No physical sense, well … made sense. What I saw smelled like hot ash, burning my eyes and ears. The scream of rage rippled my skin, expanding me like a balloon. I couldn't think; everything was so claustrophobic. I was me, but crowded into a small corner somewhere inside.

????

"HELP ME?"

I vaguely felt the screaming from the other room stop. The footsteps coming back towards me tasted like dust and blood, as if I'd bitten my tongue. I felt larger than the cage, larger than the room, and larger than the immense tree itself. I felt, more than saw, Cobb enter the room.

"What have you done, human?"

I looked at, and down, at him. He was a mite before me … and an elf who was capable of tearing my throat before I could blink. His wild, desperate look tasted foul, like burned grease and hair. The tree shuddered like before, only the lurch tasted strong. The floor rippled, the movement rolled along my skin like electricity. Cobb moved back a step. He pronounced the syllables to lower the slats at the front of the cell.

!!!!!

I curled up, the pressure nearly making me black out. I could feel myself and the other in my mind.

Stop this! You're killing me!

I screamed it mentally as, at the same time, I tried to shrink away from this overwhelming presence in my head.

!!! FIGHT.

What? I can't hear you.

The noise made my teeth itch. It felt like they grew. I caught a glimpse in my mind of Cobb stepping into the cell, blade in hand and raised, as he snarled syllables of a spell.

FIGHT. OR DIE.

The sudden, imperious order had me uncoiling as Cobb advanced. I raised a hand and started to draw wind like before. Cobb was too close. I knew he'd kill me before I got the spell off. I knew I was going to die. I dropped the spell, and raised a hand to try and fend away the coming blow. I screamed in fear, and the scream was a key.

Something snapped deep inside me. POWER — a veritable tidal wave of it — powered into me. It rolled out into the scream like a runaway train.

That power roared against Cobb, blasting him backwards a good three meters before he hit the ground and rolled into an open cell across the room. I didn't look a gift horse in the mouth. I ran for the door. The Other had other ideas, and fought me for control. My sprint slowed to a drunken walk as I desperately tried to keep running. My body faltered, then turned to face Cobb, who was back on his feet, holding the sword towards me. He smelled of shock, and anger.

"You're supposed to be dead!" Cobb was screaming. "How is it you …" His voice dropped as he thought about something. "The chains. They're keeping you here!"

There was a flash of a phantom pain. My nub ached abominably for a moment, then faded. The Other howled in rage. I tasted its anger like ashes in my throat. I reeled sideways, the intensity of the emotions surging through me. Stumbling against the side of the cage, I crashed through the thick wooden slats like they were cardboard tubes. My momentum carried me into the adjoining cell. I could sense the broken wood like sharp flashes of light behind my eyes.

Cobb started mumbling something; his words smelled like cinnamon. The Other took over, lurching my body forward, crashing it through the cell front like a charging bull. I/it stumbled at Cobb, who sidestepped, and slashed at my side. There was a searing pain and the other roared, driving me back into a mental corner.

FIGHT WITH ME. OR DIE WITH ME.

The command went against every instinct I had. No one likes to be ordered and, some like me, make a living out of going against the grain. But the imperative behind the thought had me obeying blindly for the first few moments. I/we roared again, the noise hammering at Cobb, driving him back against the cell once again, and holding him there. The power that had begun to fill me flowed through my veins, setting them afire with magick. The sensation lit up every sense I had. Taste shivered with touch, vibrating with sight and sound into a complete whole of feeling. I don't have words to describe the transcendent awe of the experience. I wasn't me anymore. I *was* the magick. I could feel every tug at my being, spells being cast, what kind were being cast, and the intent in each one. The Other with me roared in agony and joy. We looked at Cobb, actually looking down at him as if from a great height.

Cobb looked at us, mumbling a spell that I simply swatted into nothingness with a flick of a claw. The spell shattered into motes of light that danced in the air like fireflies. Cobb barely dodged the motes as they streamed towards him. They impacted the back of the cell, flaring into an intense blaze that ate hungrily at the wood. The crackling sound of dry wood burning and the smoke soothed my skin as I and the Other focused our attention on Cobb.

"Anolyn!" Cobb screamed in frustrated rage, "Why can't you just die?!"

The Other seemed to preen itself as his name was spoken. The fire started spreading further around the room, aided by the floating motes. Everywhere one landed, a fire flashed to life. Cobb shifted to the doorway, standing between the main room and us.

"Open the Ways, and your little puppet will be saved."

He meant me. I was Anolyn's puppet. Somehow, I didn't mind that nearly as much as I should have. There was a comfort in the sensation, which was at odds with what I thought, barely being able to move my own body. I fought to pull control back, and the entity stepped aside, retreating into the back recesses of my mind. I started coughing immediately. The smoke was thickening, and now the heat was burning my skin.

Cobb was still standing, apparently unaffected by the heat and smoke. The magick still surged in my veins. I thought of the pain, and the magick answered, dulling the heat. That was nice. I didn't have to use my hands.

"Open the Ways, Anolyn. Otherwise I'll kill your puppet, and open them myself."

The rumbling growl smelled like a laugh. I couldn't tell, as our minds weren't in synch with each other like in your typical movie possession. I was there, and mostly in charge. Anolyn still could exert control. I could fight him on it, but we both seemed to see Cobb as a mutual enemy, so "enemy of my enemy", and all that. I could fight him later if need be. At least, that's what I told myself. Amazing how we can rationalize nearly anything if we don't want to confront it.

Cobb was a flicker of movement. I was caught flat-footed. I couldn't bring my hands up as *he* was on top of me, sword pulled back to stab. I wanted him away from me — and he was launched away like a leaf in a hurricane, ricocheting off the edge of the archway, and out into the central chamber. I followed at a leisurely walk as Cobb staggered upright.

"What have you done to her?" His eyes were wide, his pale skin bruised from the impact with the archway.

Behind me, the flames crackled loudly and continued to spread. The smoke was filling the central chamber rapidly. The first tongues of flame had started to lap at the archway, threatening to invade our location at any moment. Cobb watched the flames dance, then stared at me/us for a moment, torn between two desires.

I could taste his desperation. It was like a thin, watery honey on my tongue. The taste crystallized into a bitter, salty one as he threw his sword at me/us and ran for the second doorway to my left. I/we followed, again at a walking pace. It wouldn't do to rush into an ambush. Besides, Cobb couldn't go anywhere. We were between him and the only way out of this growing conflagration.

It grew hotter by the second as the fire spread. When I/we got to the door of the room, I saw Cobb trying to pack up metallic glass bottles, just like the one Ahiah, the Nephilim, had used. Yeah, it was messed up. Ahiah tried to finish it, but some luck kept him from completing the spell. He was banished back to wherever he'd come from, and I hoped that I'd never see another bottle like that again. Now, I was looking at four — four that Cobb was placing in a wooden box lined with a soft-looking cloth.

A soft moan of pain drew my eyes away from the bottles, to a limp body that twitched as its owner hacked a weak cough. His stomach had been sliced open, and his insides were outside, hanging from skin and ligaments. The body was shackled to an adjustable table that was set vertically, with Kent hanging in wrist cuffs a quarter meter off the floor. The horror of it was he was still alive. A tray of knives, clamps, saws, and other tools more fit for a garage than an operating room, was next to the table. To Kent's left hung Kevin's remains from another vertical table. Every organ — lungs, eyes, intestines, etc. — had been removed, but not cut away. They hung outside his body. He, like Kent, had been vivisected.

I don't know who reacted first, but Anolyn and I both screamed. Me, in fear; Anolyn in outraged fury. Cobb tried to hold onto the wooden box, but he was blasted backwards by the magick, and lost his grip as he slammed into the back wall. Anolyn walked over to the box, crushing it underfoot as Cobb dazedly tried to push himself up from the floor. Smoke wafted in, thick and choking. I stepped over to Kent and, after a moment found the lock holding the table upright. I slowly lowered it to level, as Kent coughed up blood.

Kent looked at me, determination in his eyes. "Made, bottles, from," he coughed more blood, then forced himself to continue. "us, pain."

He tried to say more, but he couldn't draw breath to do it. He died, his body spasming trying to get one more breath.

Cobb was frantically digging through the wooden splinters that were all that was left of the box. His voice gave way to a panicked whine as he found broken glass instead of whole bottles.

He stared, wild-eyed, at me/us, and I/Anolyn growled. Cobb shrank back, then took a rapid step to the surgical tray, grabbing what looked like a filleting knife off of it and brandished it at me/us.

"You've ruined everything again! Why didn't they kill you!? You should be dead!"

Anolyn showed me what had happened. All of it. No words: just images, smells, and sounds. He'd been trapped by the elves when they'd thrown the shield up. They'd taken to hunting all humans, orcs, trolls, etc. to make more of those cursed bottles. Anolyn had attacked the tree where they'd started to make more of them, and killed all the captured peoples, and every elf he could, before they'd trapped him in the chains. He'd killed most of the elves, because he'd been aimed, by some bit of luck, at the tree.

The few that survived his rage had been killed by other survivors, or starved to death over time, as Anolyn had woven death into the elven veil. Nothing could enter, or through the Ways of Underhill. A few survivors had actually made the stone boat and floated through the veil, just like the legend. The elves embellished the truth with hints and exaggeration, which turned into the tale I'd heard from Zhirk.

In that moment of disorientation, Cobb struck out. I/we twisted as he thrust, and the blade stabbed through my side, cutting muscle, but missing the body cavity. Anolyn/I back-handed the elf, which sent him crashing into the wall again. A loud *whoof* announced that the fire had spread through the tree.

Cobb lay against the wall. I/we fled down the burning corridor out into the fading sunlight of dusk. The tree glowed red from the fires eating it from the inside out.

Once outside, I felt Anolyn leave. The bones of the dragon crumbled to dust as the fire burst through the bark and began consuming the tree from the outside and the inside. It collapsed in sparks and embers when the burning trunk could no longer hold itself together. I watched it burn, half hoping to see Kent or Kevin pull themselves from the fire, but knew that couldn't happen. Part of me wanted Cobb to appear, so I could have a target for all the rage and anguish in me. I just sat down, and watched the tree burn until the next morning. The smoke angled up into the sky as a breeze greeted me for the first time in days.

What I didn't realize, until the helicopter began working its way towards the smoke, was that the veil had gone down. I think it happened when Anolyn finally passed. He'd modified the veil, trapping the elves, so none could escape him. And when he'd finally died, the power to the veil died too.

After the helicopter airlifted me back to Halifax, the doctors checked me over and told me I had lost twelve pounds. The hospital kept me overnight and brought some simple food so my stomach wouldn't rebel too much. I savaged the grilled cheese sandwich, attacking it like a starving — well, starved — human.

I talked to Judge Kaddus after I'd recovered. He admitted sending the beast to keep me from going to the island. He didn't apologize for the attempts at frightening me off, but at the same time, he seemed relieved that Cobb was gone. What his and Cobb's feud was about, I never really learned. Elves are close-mouthed about elvish things.

As for what happened back on the island, it's all just speculation on my part. The final result is that the veil was gone. Prince Edward Island is unbound, though I have no clue what will happen there. With everything dead, it could stay that way, or life could start reclaiming it almost immediately. Time will tell us, eventually.

Fawn is definitely showing. She'll be on maternity leave soon. I think Larry's more frazzled by the upcoming birth than Fawn. He's gone overboard with solicitous. Half of the stuff Fawn wants is just something to get him out from underfoot. Despite the over-the-top attention by Larry, they're both doing great. Kent and Kevin were both honored a week later with a joint funeral. Two empty caskets. I had nightmares for the next two weeks: of their bodies, organs pulsing, pleading and begging not to be left behind. It took time to fade, but over the next month the horror finally dulled enough to let me sleep through the night.

I never generated any pay from all this, so I'm back at work, which should be in the next ten minutes, and the place could use some sprucing up before the client shows.

ABOUT THE AUTHOR

J Dark is a latecomer to the writing profession, but enjoying every moment that life will allow. "The best thing to me is writing a story that someone enjoys. If I've made something fun and entertaining for people, it's a win-win."

J Dark lives with a house full of dreams, three cats, and various friends who occasionally drop by and stay for a while. J Dark lives in Kansas, where the winds blow all the time, and, if you blink your eyes, the weather changes.

You can find out more about the works and world of J Dark at *The Pandemonium* (thepandemonium.net).

YOU MIGHT ALSO ENJOY

Best Intentions
Book One of the Glass Bottles Series

by J Dark

When your past is left undone, it will come find you.

GRIMAULKIN

by L. A. Jacob

Treading the straight and narrow is not natural to one who summons demons.

HOMECOMING
A War Mage Novel

by Jake Logan

Even wizards in the U.S. armed forces have to go home some time.

Available from Paper Angel Press in
hardcover, trade paperback, and ebook editions.
paperangelpress.com